# BUTTER ROAD

# BUTTER

# ROAD

A NOVEL

JACLYN
GILBERT

ACRE
CINCINNATI 2026

Acre Books is made possible by the support of the Robert and Adele Schiff Foundation and the Department of English at the University of Cincinnati.


Printed in the United States of America

Designed by Barbara Neely
Cover art: Cornfield #4, lumen print by Sarah Crofts, reproduced with permission of the artist.

Epigraph from *I Walk Around Gathering Up My Garden for the Night* by Marie Lundquist. Translated from the Swedish by Kristina Andersson Bicher. Copyright © 2020 by Kristina Andersson Bicher. Reprinted by permission of The Bitter Oleander Press.

ISBN-13 (pbk): 978-1-968209-06-3
ISBN-13 (ebook): 978-1-968209-07-0



The press is based at the University of Cincinnati, Department of English and Comparative Literature, A&S Hall, Room 248, 2700 Campus Drive, PO Box 210069, Cincinnati, OH, 45221–0069.
www.acre-books.com

Acre Books titles may be purchased at a discount for educational use. For information please email business@acre-books.com.

*For Leland*

ALSO BY JACLYN GILBERT

*Late Air* (novel)

Two women watch over your grave.
Me and the person I could have been.

—MARIE LUNDQUIST

I would like more sisters, that the taking out
of one, might not leave such stillness.

—EMILY DICKINSON

# AUTHOR'S NOTE

*Butter Road* is a work of fiction, but it was born out of the real grief of the West Nickel Mines schoolhouse shooting. I did not set out to retell what happened on October 2, 2006, nor could I. That story belongs to the families who suffered the tragedy, and to a community whose traditions of privacy and humility I have tried to honor throughout my writing. The characters in these pages—their voices and inner lives—are imagined.

This said, *Butter Road* would not exist if not for the generosity of many who trusted me with their memories. I am indebted to the friends and family members of survivors who spoke with me, sometimes over the course of years, and who corrected my inaccuracies. I owe particular thanks to a local doctor called upon in the aftermath to help identify the children; I am indebted to his willingness to share with me his medical notes, his writings, and his deep understanding of a people he has devoted his life to serving.

Where I have taken liberties—with geography, chronology, medical detail, and the texture of Amish life—I have done so in service of the novel's emotional truth, with no intention of my story supplanting factual accounts or the lived experiences of the survivors.

Readers should know that the book contains descriptions of gun violence against children, grief, and trauma, though I have tried to write those moments with restraint out of respect for those who still remember.

This novel is offered in the spirit of the word *Gelassenheit*—a yielding, a letting be—that I encountered so often in my research. I hope it honors, in some small measure, our shared humanity, our larger quest for forgiveness.

# BUTTER ROAD

## OCTOBER 2, 2006

DUTCH MEADOWS was the name on the milk truck he drove through Amish country. Chilled, cream-topped bottles clacking like muffled bells as he turned onto the access road. It was morning, October, sweat under his gloves as he knocked on the door of the one-room schoolhouse, and when the teacher, mull-capped, in her dress of plain violet, opened the door, he asked if a clevis pin went missing, if it had been stolen. This teacher said, "No, I don't know what you mean," and then he covered her pale lips with his glove and ordered the girls inside not to move. He took the boys to collect lumber, rope, wires, chains, eye hooks, nails, clothespins, toilet paper, candles, and plastic ties from his truck. In the time they were away, the teacher escaped out the back door. He heard her screaming for someone to call for help. Waving his Springfield, he sent one of the boys to catch her, and he lined ten girls along the chalkboard, shouting for each to kneel, and he pressed the nose of his gun to the temple of one, sighting through the eight heads he had chosen, sparing some to bear witness to their wounds. Not a desk or chair or wall untouched by blood, bullet, glass.

# EMMA WALSH

## SPRING 2018

Twelve years after the shooting, I started this, my diary, on the backs of old feed calendars. Now there seems no end to my words. Stacks of pages bound together with string.

Each time I write, I hear the voices of that morning. Feel the warm sunlight on my face. Hear Teacher Martha ringing the bell after recess. See my bare legs dangling under my cape dress.

I can't tell anyone because we aren't allowed to keep diaries. Hochmut, Mother would say. Pride under the Ordnung.

Mother says I am to forgive the man. She says remembering lets the evil live on. That we should turn our questions to the Lord Father.

I want to tell Mother I am trying. Want to ask her if Beth still haunts her dreams. Does she see my sister in everything like I do? In my hairpins and dolls. My bare feet in the grass. Hear her laugh in the mornings before school? Smell her in the spring peonies and summer bee balm.

But Mother wasn't there that day. To hear the whisper of Beth's voice, *Take me first*, her head covering in line with the man's heavy gun, black and shining while she knelt.

Mother insists on *Martyrs Mirror* in times of doubt. Stories of the Holy ones who sacrificed themselves for Christ. Andrew the Apostle crucified at Patras. Geleyn the Shoemaker tortured and burned. Pelagius of Córdova whose limbs were severed. Dirk Willems burned at the stake after saving his captor from drowning.

We must think no evil of the man who took Beth away. As long as we are humble before God, Mother says, we are saved. She reminds me of Corinthians. *Remember, any woman who prays or prophesies with her hair uncovered dishonors her head. The head of every man is Christ; the head of a woman is her husband, and the head of Christ is God.*

Isaac and I are on our Rumspringa year. We can drink and smoke and play rock and roll to try out the English world, but when we marry, we'll be baptized, and there's no going back. Lettie Ames, Isaac's mother, and mine, Ruth, are already busy making quilts and collecting dishware from our families. Father will carve us a wooden clock to keep in our parlor when we start our lives.

Isaac is more interested in English parties than I am. In drinking Yuengling and listening to Creedence Clearwater Revival by the bonfire. I don't know what the point is if it's temporary. Isaac works at an English lumberyard, sawing wood, while I clean and garden for the doctor's wife, Mrs. Caldwell, on Tuesdays. I've been coming since May because I must. My brother Eli has a genetic disease, and Mother and Father need my help to pay for Dr. Caldwell's treatments. Isaac says I should use my money to buy a cell phone. He wants to call me since we are courting. He takes pictures of us kissing by the covered bridge. Selfies for an album on his phone.

When we're young, we're told to fear the camera's flash, the gaze of sinners. When we're young and at the market selling our baked goods, our embroidery and quilts, we cross our wrists, covering our faces before the lens. Yet we depend on the English money for our goods. We need English money to live.

Today is Tuesday, and I'm wearing my new orthopedic shoes. I dressed plain, because I prefer it this way—my cape dress with an extra layer of fabric over the bust, my hair covering a half-inch thick, pinned tight, my stockings thirty deniers like Mother wears even in the summer. Mother says we must be witnesses wherever we go, so when people look at us they see God.

But some girls on Rumspringa, like Rachel Yoder and Esther Zimmerman, won't comply. They hem their dresses above their knees, show extra straps because they can. The only thing I could do without is the shoes. They're sturdy enough for walking two miles from our farm to the Caldwells' house on Butter Road, but they're bulky and warm.

Mrs. Caldwell thinks the distance is too great after a long day, that I must be tired. I don't tell her I'd prefer to tend her house barefoot, nor that, even with the shoes, walking clears my head.

*I'll drive you home*, she frequently offers, tapping the forecast on the narrow rectangle of her phone. Once I agreed because it was raining, but otherwise I prefer to walk.

Three weeks already that I've been housekeeping for Mrs. Caldwell. She can't be much older than Mother, her hair long and silken down her back. She wears a sun hat in her garden, and through the window, I see the light catching on the straw the way it used to with Beth's braids in an open field. Thoughts I'm not to think. I turn my attention to the rhythms of work to empty my mind. Never miss a crumb in the kitchen. No smudges on the chinaware. No film on the windows.

In the living room, I dust a black television screen. When I catch my reflection, my eyes look like a stain.

I never mean to see myself, but it happens sometimes. I beg God for pardon. Same as I do for reading Mrs. Caldwell's books of poems when she isn't looking.

One is *We Women* by Edith Södergran. Poems about joy and longing, about loneliness. *A silence rests. . . . a whispering lying in wait.* I murmur the words aloud, wishing they were my own.

This Tuesday, after my work is finished, Mrs. Caldwell brings out a turntable and lifts the clear top. Its pointed spindle shines as she lowers a disc in place. I set down my lemon spray, my handsewn cloths.

"Heard one of these?" she asks. A thin crackle, then slowly, soft music fills the room. "Verdi's Requiem," she says.

The music is hushed, sung in a language I've never heard. Sweet and full as a winter slumber.

"I have other records too." She pulls out a handful of thin squares from the cabinet, lying them flat on the floor.

"The dust sleeve," she says, slipping out the disc. Tissue crinkles. "Each track of the album starts on a groove. You count the grooves to know which track you're on."

When she hands the cover to me, she points to number two. Eleanor Rigby, it reads.

"Count the grooves," she says, and I do. Mrs. Caldwell stops the first record and sets the new one on. "Now you try," she says, looking at the needle.

I freeze—I won't touch anything electric; not a dishwasher or stove or car—and she understands.

"No trouble," she says. "The Beatles." She points to the faces on the record cover. "They are the real English." She laughs, but I don't understand the joke.

When the song plays, it's not a woman's voice she hears, but a man's. He sings loudly, his voice low. There is the sound of drums, of popping.

"Stop." I cover my ears. "Stop it!"

"What?" Mrs. Caldwell says. "What's wrong?"

It happens sometimes: the wrong sound or vibration, and I forget where I am. The beat of helicopter blades, the police shouting. The first time, I woke to Mother pressing a cool cloth to my forehead. Eli was still a healthy baby then, swaddled in his blue jumper.

"If you want to, you can tell me," Mrs. Caldwell says. Then she offers to make tea. A little later the room comes back into focus, and when the kettle hisses in the kitchen, Mrs. Caldwell returns with two mugs, steaming with the scent of peppermint. On the sofa, she sips her tea slowly, and I do the same. After a while, she says. "I won't tell anyone. You can talk to me."

*It's like I'm never here*, I want to say. *Like I'm watching myself live instead of living*. Instead, I say, "I miss my sister." This single word, *sister*, and the ripple of feeling expands.

"What's her name?" Mrs. Caldwell's eyes grow soft.

"Beth." I wipe my eyes. But it feels good to have spoken.

Mrs. Caldwell sets down her mug. "Don't worry. We all need to talk to someone. It's how we get better." She pauses. "I should take you home."

"No," I say. "Please, it's still early. Mother will worry I'm short on wages."

"All right then," she says. "I could use some help with the new trellis."

In the garden, we tend to the rosebush. When we finish trimming, I tie the canes along the trellis. Mrs. Caldwell wants to weave the roses through the trellis holes.

"It's best to let them alone," I say.

"You're right. Let nature do her work." Mrs. Caldwell smiles like Mother rarely does, at least not in private. She seems happy.

Dusk is setting in. Reason enough for a ride home. When she parks in our driveway, Mrs. Caldwell reaches into her pocketbook. She hands me the envelope, along with her phone number on a slip.

"If you need anything, please call me. You have a telephone, for emergencies?" Her lipstick is red winterberry. "I won't tell the doctor," she says. "Not if you don't want me to."

"Thank you." I take the note from her. After the milkman, we got a corded telephone in the shanty. Mother doesn't want one inside our home, even to call the doctor, because phones are machines, just as guns are. "See you on Tuesday," I say.

There's a little breeze, and our porch swing rocks in the gray light. Mother has set out new window boxes with yellow geraniums. In the mornings, before school, she prays by them. *May the Lord let his face shine upon you and be gracious to you, may the Lord lift up his countenance upon you and give you peace.*

By the front door, I turn, not wanting to go in right away. Mrs. Caldwell waves before backing out. Mother probably needs more jam, strawberry and rhubarb, Eli's favorite. Out back, I lift the cellar door and go down to collect the jars. I light a candle, take off my shoes, press my bare feet onto the cold concrete floor. The front of the feed calendar has Father's handwriting, numbers for the day of the week, the amount of seed for the chickens in grams. I find an empty space along the back, press my pencil in.

Before the milkman came, Beth and I collected our feed in early October. We knew how to separate the grain from the chaff. How to winnow the sheaves in the barn. We left the doors open so the chaff could blow away in the breeze, leaving behind the grain. We filled the sacks, Beth and I, carried them and emptied them into the elevator with Mother and Father. We listened to the grain fall down the chute, filling the emptiness.

Twelve years ago, I didn't know it would be the last time we would. That I would watch Beth's golden hair in the barn, not knowing it was precious. That I would laugh with her for the last time over the sound of fallen seed.

Now I think of my heart like a grain elevator, my words spilling through the mesh, the wire.

# RUTH WALSH

## SUMMER 2019

Ruth is setting up her dessert booth, like she does every Saturday, in the old English arcade on Prince Street. Cherries are in season, and Ruth has made a half-dozen pies, in addition to cinnamon buns, angel food cake, and sweet molasses cookies. As Ruth places each of her pies on the table, the cherries shine a bright, deep red under the plastic wrapping.

If Emma were here, the work would have taken Ruth half the time. Not to mention pitting the twelve quarts of cherries, making dough and batter from scratch, perfecting the pie crust, and wrapping everything neatly.

At first, Emma had been too young to work outside the home on Ruth's behalf. But when Emma was seventeen, Ruth sent her out to help earn what they needed to pay for Eli's doctor visits. Ruth didn't think it would be different for Emma, cleaning an English home, even if it was for the wife of Eli's doctor. But looking back, Ruth can see subtle differences, how Emma had changed in just a few short months. She'd started reading English books from Sara Caldwell's library, hiding her thoughts from her mother. Ruth is surprised by the resentment that rises at the idea of this—of someone she thought she could trust having sway over her daughter.

Unlike Emma, Ruth had turned a blind eye to the English families whose houses she'd kept in the years prior. First it had been the Wheatleys, and then the McPhersons, the Jasons, the Steins. Each of these families included children, and the children never cleaned up after themselves. But who was Ruth to judge? It wasn't her place. She only ever smiled at them warmly when they were home from school. Ruth dusting, Ruth cleaning the tiles and windows with vinegar spray. The children paid her no mind, eating Lay's sour cream and onion and drinking cherry Pepsi as their mothers reminded them to stay out of Ruth's way, reminded them to go outside to play or upstairs for homework until she was finished.

It had caused Ruth pain at first to see the children's school things, books in piles on the kitchen table. Satchels and lunch pails by the door. There were times she'd catch herself staring out the kitchen window, her mind filled with images of her daughters before the shooting. Ruth would feel her eyes go blank, and then she'd tremble for fear someone might have seen her distraction. But no one ever did. These families usually left her alone to work in peace. All except Mrs. McPherson, who'd occasionally asked her questions.

It had started with simple things. She wanted to know if Ruth was thirsty, or if she needed the air on, or more heat, depending on the season. A few times she asked if Ruth wanted music. It wasn't that Ruth would have minded music in the background—music that Mrs. McPherson herself liked—but she didn't need music for herself. She knew the difference between rock and roll and jazz from her own Rumspringa year, but she didn't care for it compared to gospel music. *I'm fine, Mrs. McPherson*, she used to say. And she was. The rhythm of housework had always soothed her—the steady sound of running water while she cleaned the bathtub, the swish of cloth over floor surfaces and countertops, the spritz of her spray bottle on bathroom and hallway mirrors that she'd never once peered into.

Ruth kept her gaze down, her hand moving in light circular motions, careful never to leave a streak or smudge behind. Mr. Wheatley had cared most about such things. After she finished her cleaning, he'd had Ruth walk with him through every room while he inspected her work, wiping a finger over desks and bureaus. In the kitchen, he looked for stray crumbs or droplets of residue. She would brace herself, fearing the day Mr. Wheatley found a reason to fire her. But that day never came.

Mr. McPherson only ever complimented her. Praised her people for their work, excellent compared to his previous English cleaners who'd charged double the rate. Ruth couldn't fathom this, because Mr. McPherson paid her well, and she always left feeling relieved and happy. Another fifty dollars toward their medical debts, and her savings had accrued enough to buy a booth at the Central Market in downtown Lancaster for selling her pies. Then she'd had two streams of income—the marketplace and, after Emma was old enough to take her place, the cleaning.

"God's way," she whispers to herself. For Emma to work in her place, for the good of Eli. Emma going to work for the doctor's wife. There had been other options Ruth hadn't wanted to consider. Emma might have become a shop girl or waitress. But housecleaning had always paid best—especially because of the reputation Ruth had earned, the referrals between families. Emma had even offered to do the work without Ruth's prompting, hadn't she?

*I'm good at gardening, Mother*, she'd said. *The doctor's wife needs a gardener.*

And Emma had always had a way with flowers, and needlework, an eye for details of the home the English liked. Ruth had agreed it was best, and Abraham, too—that it was only natural for a daughter to follow in her mother's footsteps.

"God's way, the way of the Father," Ruth mutters after her last pie is displayed. It's too loud in the market for anyone to hear her. Men pass her clutching long loaves of bread wrapped in white paper from the French bakery. Women carry vegetables like bouquets. The market smells sweetly of roses and lilies, mixed with oils and cheese and coffee—the Middle Eastern booth with its cheese boats, the Italian stand with its meatball sandwiches and freshly ground pesto. The local café with espresso beans, English cappuccinos, lattes, and mocha drinks Ruth has never tried.

The fresh pies shine even though it's only nine o'clock, the muted light falling softly over Ruth's angel food cakes and cinnamon rolls positioned behind the pies. This morning, she also has some fresh-cut flowers for sale, the zinnias and sunflowers that her cousin Rosalie helped her load into the van. They called in the paratransit every Saturday. The council allowed riding in vans for doctor visits and business dealings because both were essential to the survival of her people. She didn't like the feeling of riding in the van, especially not alone. Usually it was a man driving, and at much faster speeds than Ruth was used to. The milkman's father had been a paratransit driver, and she had begged Abraham for another service—any other service—to take her into town. But Abraham said she must trust in the way of the Lord. And she had.

"The only way is His," Ruth whispers, watching the light gleam over the cherries beneath the clear wrapping she'd secured so carefully to keep her pies fresh.

"I'll take one," an English woman says.

Ruth blinks. How long had the woman been there? She is pointing to a pie in the center, the one with heart-shaped decking.

"All right." Ruth's voice sounds loud to her, despite the marketplace noise. "That will be six fifty."

The woman hands her a ten-dollar bill. "There was another girl here before, no? She used to sell me cinnamon rolls. The grandkids love them. Do you have them?"

"Yes." Ruth reaches for a Styrofoam container. It surprises her that her hands are shaking when she offers the rolls. "Four seventy-five," she says loudly, conveying control. Of what?

"Will she be back?" the woman asks.

Ruth feels a heaviness that goes beyond her ribs—feels it in her feet, her aching limbs. By the time Emma's Rumspringa year was over, she and Isaac had made plans for a home of their own, down the road from the Walsh farm. "She's no longer with us," Ruth says.

"I'm so sorry," the woman says. "I can't imagine."

She wants to correct the woman—*No, you don't understand: My daughter is still alive. I still have one daughter*—but then she would have to explain.

Ruth doesn't feel her own tears, the fact of them, until the woman offers her a napkin from another stand. Suddenly, it seems darker in the market, darker than the day Joseph told her about Beth, about the

Happening. Through a market side-door, a small hole of light expands in her periphery. *Angel of Christ* she thinks but doesn't say. *Angel of God*.

"I'm sorry," the woman says again, clutching her pie. "Are you all right?"

Ruth tries to root her feet in her shoes, come back to herself. "Yes," she says, wiping her eyes. "Thank you." She turns her attention to the table, placing another pie in the empty space. When she looks up, the woman is gone. Mennonites standing across the way fill her view, young girls helping their mother. They're from another borough—Christiana, likely. She can't ignore the girls, giggling over some matter, stacking bags of sweet rolls at the front of their stand. The youngest clutches a cloth doll. One of her sisters probably stitched the eyes, the little x's for the mouth. God's way of reminding Ruth what she's lost? Reminding her how temporary it all is, how precious? Yes, this was God speaking to her.

The morning passes. Finally, there's just an hour left before closing. A short window to sell her remaining goods, but it's something. All but one pie is gone, and most of the cinnamon rolls too. And after the van drops her at home, there will still be time in the day for other chores. She will make more jam after she's cleaned the empty jars.

If it is nice enough outside, she'll sit with Eli on the porch and listen to the birds while she works. Eli loves the sound of the bells as their collies run freely in the lawn. Sometimes he points to the cows eating grass along the hillside, and the horses too. In the early morning, when the rooster crows into the silence, Eli is ecstatic, like God is calling to them, which He is.

On the way home, Ruth looks out the van window. There are fast cars and expensive ones, like Mrs. Caldwell drives. There are work trucks and other vans. It takes twenty minutes, maybe less, to reach the countryside where her farm is. They pass through the covered bridge on Hunsecker Road to get there. Last May, the first time she saw Emma and Isaac by the bridge, the cherry blossoms had been a full, bright pink. Ruth had been in the buggy then, on her way to Dr. Caldwell's. She'd been so happy to see her daughter and Isaac Ames holding hands.

Isaac's mother, Lettie, was practically a sister to her already, and their children were in love. They would start their own family, carry Ruth and Abraham's story into the future, even after everything that had happened. She'd told Lettie this, though Lettie hadn't been so sure. Ruth remembers now, as they pass the Stoltzfus corn cribs and the old barn on Pine Ridge—how at the Sunday picnic, when they were setting out bowls of coleslaw, Lettie had told Ruth she feared Isaac wasn't ready yet.

Ruth thought she meant because of the parties during Rumspringa, the drinking that sometimes got out of hand. But no, Lettie meant the foster home, where Isaac had been during the Happening. Lettie hadn't needed to say anything more. Ruth understood. Lettie and John Ames had lost their youngest daughter to a stroke when Isaac was five. The baby had a bruise on her head, and the English authorities had accused them of harming her, of beating her to death. There was talk of a trial, and their children were taken away. But then Dr. Caldwell had come and proved them innocent. Proved a rare disease had caused the stroke. Dr. Caldwell had saved them, and Isaac and his brothers had come home—reason enough for Ruth to buy an English newspaper from the supermarket and scour it before Abraham could black out the parts she wasn't to read. English newspapers were only good for reports on the weather and predicting demand for their crops. But Ruth had needed to understand what the doctor was capable of. She'd needed proof that he'd been sent by the Lord to help her people.

When Eli first became sick, Ruth had turned to the article for solace. She'd turned to Lettie too. They had kneeled on the front porch and prayed together, and she'd reminded herself that the sufferings of the present were insignificant compared with the glory that would be revealed in them.

Ruth prays again now, in the van, just before it stops and lets her out. She finds strength in her whispered words. The rest she lets go—memories that she cannot alter. Unloading her remaining goods, she tips the driver and collects her bags.

As she feeds Eli his lunch, he slaps at the spoon, spilling the pureed peas. She wipes them away and tries again, then again, until enough food catches between Eli's lips for him to swallow.

When Dr. Caldwell first diagnosed Eli with glutaric acidemia ten years earlier, she'd been ignorant of the conditions and procedures he mentioned. Bone marrow transplant. Genetic drift. Metabolic stroke. Then the doctor had given them pamphlets on the risks that resulted from being a closed community, from marrying amongst themselves. If not for him, Ruth and Abraham might have tried for more children. Might have lost them as Lettie and John had. He'd protected them, cared for them, in accordance with God.

Emma used to help her gather the special foods Eli needed, like bone broth and turmeric, from the English stores. At the beginning of her Rumspringa, Emma even did research, using encyclopedias from the public library. Part of Ruth longs to go there herself—to use their computers without Abraham knowing. If she could figure out how to work them, she could learn more about Eli's needs. Apparently, one could look up anything on the Internet. But the Internet is worse than electric light, worse than using cameras or phones. The Internet sounds like speed to Ruth, like manmade lightning, a threat to God.

After Ruth feeds Eli another spoonful, she wipes his mouth. "Good," she says, "Good boy," and he groans. Eli groans when he is happy, and when he is hungry. With her gone this morning, he has been hungry.

Ruth is not yet forty. Many women still have babies at her age, but she and Abraham stopped after Eli. She was only twenty-four then, with the potential to bring at least five more children into this world, but she'd had to redirect her hopes and prayers. To be thankful that Eli was still alive. *It's a miracle*, Dr. Caldwell had said at Eli's last checkup. *He's a fighter through and through.*

She lets her son sit in the porch chair under the sun. They listen to the birds together. She holds his hand. Eli no longer has seizures, not since his treatments started. She pushes a loose strand of hair from her eyes, adjusting the pin to keep her bonnet secure.

When the light starts to change, the sky to darken, she wheels Eli to the kitchen. She runs the tap, scrubbing at the stubborn red from the previous days' cherry pitting.

Over the years Ruth has made more pies than she can count—why should she worry over the staining now? Still, she holds her hands under the tap, even while she scolds herself for wasting water. She can't help herself. The washing cleanses her of the day. As she dries her hands, she decides she'll deliver the remaining pie to Mrs. Caldwell. She opens a cardboard box, places the fresh pie inside, but before she can close it, her knees weaken. She collapses on the cold floor beside Eli, who says nothing. *May the Lord God let his face shine upon you and be gracious to you, the Lord lift up his countenance upon you and give you peace.*

Shadows collect over the floor, by her hands and feet, while she prays, weeping.

# SARA CALDWELL

## SPRING 2018

Hard to believe it had been over a decade since she and Peter first moved to their brick colonial on Butter Road. Sara still loved the simplicity of the word *butter*—how it made her think of a long yellow strand of ribbon slipping between one's fingers. Had the Amish named the road? But that was counterintuitive. To be Amish was to live namelessly, humbly, among others of your kind.

It hadn't been an easy thing for her to reconcile at first—the idea of Emma Walsh working for them. When Peter had started the clinic on their land ten years earlier, the thought would never have crossed their minds: mixing Peter's research with an Amish family's income. But the more time they spent a few short miles from the heart of Amish farmland, the more the boundaries thinned between their worlds. Even so, Sara was surprised when Peter brought up hiring Emma.

Up until then, her husband had kept his cases confidential, so it was another surprise when he explained the Walshes' troubles making payments for their son's treatments. Sara said she guessed she could use some help cleaning, and in the garden, especially as she was planning to host a garden show for the neighborhood.

That first Tuesday, Emma had arrived at her door clutching a small wicker basket covered with a simple blue towel. Sara had imagined muffins under the cloth, much like the ones her mother used to bake, but as she folded back the towel, she discovered a pie, the word SHOEFLY inscribed on a small sticker over the plastic wrap.

"Thank you," she said. "I can't wait to try it."

Emma was taller than Sara expected. She was a young woman, and yet still a child, with soft brown hair and innocent gray eyes. She didn't avert her gaze like most of them did when they came to Peter's clinic, as if this lack of eye contact made them less culpable in investing in English services outside of the farm. Anything not Amish was English, and it had taken time for Sara to think of herself this way, as a foreigner in the community's eyes.

"Make yourself at home," she said. "I'll give you the tour." Placing the pie on the kitchen counter, she laughed: "This is the kitchen."

Emma only smiled politely, as if she didn't know what could be so funny. Maybe the electric stove came as a shock. Maybe the house was adorned with too many decorations. More than Emma might expect of her brother's doctor, who dressed simply when he treated his patients—almost always in black pants with a plain white t-shirt.

Leading her down the hall, Sara said, "Here's the library. The titles are alphabetical now, but I used to have them organized by the color on the spine. I think that way. In colors." She wanted to ask Emma if she did too—just as something to break the ice—but Emma was worrying the edge of her apron, so Sara showed her where the stepladder was to reach the higher shelves. "I forgot to ask if you have supplies you prefer?"

Emma's eyes widened, as if the word *prefer* had no place in her worldview. "I have lemon spray, and my own cloths, if that's all right."

"Of course," Sara said. There was a pamphlet she had happened upon at a local shop for tourists—*Twenty Commonly Asked Questions about the Amish*, or something like that—and in it was a line about how an Amish woman never learned to form her own opinions. What was it? Yes, an Amish woman was too busy keeping house and caring for her children to bother with self-liberation. The words had made Sara cringe.

She opened the hutch in the dining room. "I don't know the last time I polished our silver."

The girl was silent for a moment, then said, "It's lovely. Your wedding silver."

"Thank you."

Sara showed her the upstairs. All four rooms. There was the master, and then the guest room. Then Peter's office, and the small room she used for practicing morning yoga and meditation. How strange this must seem to Emma, Sara thought—she and Peter not using the extra rooms for children. Should she explain? That Peter was fifty-seven, and she thirty-nine?

"Shall we see the garden?" Sara said instead, flicking off the light in her yoga room. "I thought we could start there today."

Emma nodded.

Outside, Sara brought out the half-dozen flower boxes that needed planting. She told Emma what would go where, and she was surprised by how quickly the girl got to work, how easily she remembered the order Sara had specified.

Weeks into their work together, she was still more impressed by Emma's affinity for growing things. "Do you spend a lot of time in your garden?" she asked one afternoon.

Emma turned to look at her, her gaze locking with Sara's for a moment before veering away, as if she'd been lured by something in the sharp rays of the sun. "Yes," she said. "Mother and I do." Emma crouched closer to the ground, her dress grazing the dirt.

"What do you grow, usually?"

Emma was silent, as though she hadn't heard Sara, but after a few seconds passed, she answered. "Mostly vegetables. We have a section for berries too. And some grapevines, if the deer don't get them."

"Funny," Sara said. "I've never seen deer here."

"It's getting worse," Emma said. "They eat away at our berries."

She was holding a clump of weeds in her hands. Sara thought to offer gardening gloves, but those likely would have felt as strange for her to wear as English sunglasses. She admired how unabashedly Emma let the dirt wedge itself under her fingernails.

"Are you thirsty?" she asked. "For water? Lemonade?"

"I'm fine," Emma said, tugging at more weeds.

Sara went into the garage for her scissors, intending to use them on the side of the house where the ivy was thickening like moss. She thought of asking if Emma had any ideas for taming ivy, but guessed the Amish let their ivy run wild. It was part of nature. She had the idea that her own garden seemed self-conscious in comparison to the Walshes'. She was trying to make it photo-ready for her garden club.

Last fall, it had been all gold and orange tones, but this year she wanted to draw out the pale pink in her magnolia trees, set against the deeper hues of bluestem meadow grass. She wanted those soft shades to bleed into the magenta of the autumn chrysanthemums. She imagined panicle hydrangea, toad lilies and goldenrod, peach-toned dahlias and aster and ironweed and late-season crocus. Emma would help with all this, and with the rows of sumac and bottlebrush buckeye she wanted to plant for winter interest.

"Do you need to see a list?" Sara asked when she was back with the scissors. "I made one this morning." She reached in her pocket for the folded paper.

"I remember." Emma's lips formed a slight smile. "The asters need trimming."

"Right." Sara smiled. "You're a pro," she said, then followed up with "professional" to make sure Emma understood. "I should be asking you all of the questions, shouldn't I?"

Emma looked perplexed, and Sara, not wanting to make her any more uncomfortable, resolved to leave her to work in solitude. She cut away the ivy, then sorted a variety of seed packets on the veranda, but as she planned where each set of seeds would be sown, she couldn't help wondering about the girl. Emma was so close-mouthed. Even after several weeks with her, Sara didn't even know how old she was and whether she was married.

As she watched Emma work on her knees, clipping around an aster as carefully as she might a bonsai, Sara tried to think of other questions she could ask about caring for fruits and vegetables. Or canning. She'd always wanted to learn about that. Something to pass the time. A canning project might make Emma feel more comfortable.

Later, she offered to drive Emma home, but Emma wanted to walk. She knew the Amish could only ride in cars, not drive them, and she hoped she hadn't offended by asking. "Thank you for everything," she said, handing Emma an envelope of cash. "I'll see you next week?"

"Yes." Emma nodded. "See you then."

As the girl walked down the drive, Sara thought there was something familiar about her—something she could see only when Emma stepped away, as if the distance made her image clarify.

Last year's auction, she thought. Yes, that was it, at the farm stand on Hunsecker Road. The one with white pumpkins. Sara had been driving past, on her way home from the nursery in Leola, when she came upon a pair of Amish teenagers, holding hands at the covered bridge. Sara had slowed the car, waiting until the couple passed through to the other side.

The girl was barefoot, but the boy wore a tall black hat, as if he'd just come from church services. When Sara had snapped a photo with her phone, the girl had turned to look at the car, her eyes fearful. It was the worst sin, Sara knew, to be caught in an English camera. But her windows were tinted, and she was sure the girl had no way of knowing she'd taken that picture.

Could it have been Emma? The girl seemed about the same age—of courting age, Sara thought. She might have been on her Rumspringa, too. A time for her to explore the world outside the home and try English things, like shopping at the mall and going to the movies. Wearing lingerie and makeup. Drinking. Sara had heard horror stories of how terribly wrong it could go for some teens. To suddenly have no boundaries when, before, life had been all about them: your way of dress, of speaking, of never tempting any wrongdoing. Any sinful pleasure. Sara had heard stories about how many overdosed, how many crashed their buggies or went to jail for DUIs.

She could hardly imagine Emma testing such waters. How quiet and polite she was. How agreeable. Sara had always been interested in teenagers. She was an only child and had spent her early years longing for a sister, someone with whom she could confide intimacies, and later, someone who was as unsure as she was about all that went into being a woman. In her early adulthood, whenever she thought of having children, she wished they could skip the baby and toddler parts and emerge as teenagers—Amish teenagers at that. She wanted none of that business before they'd learned how to communicate their needs.

Thirteen years earlier, when she and Peter were first married, they'd decided not to have children. On top of being fifty-three, Peter didn't have enough time to devote to being a father, and Sara said that was all right because she didn't want a conventional life. That was a lie. In truth, Sara feared she couldn't conceive, that there was something wrong with her. No doctor had ever confirmed this, but she'd reached sixteen without having a period. Sara's mother thought she should eat more, gain weight in her thighs and hips. She used to bake Sara muffins with an extra stick of butter and brown sugar rolled into the batter. Dutifully, Sara took the warm muffins wrapped in a napkin, but once at school, she threw them away.

Years later she felt guilty about it. The muffins, as well as the problem with her cycle, which she'd thrust out of her mind, perhaps in embarrassment, perhaps in defiance. The guilt had come over her unexpectedly, in grad school—when she was in the middle of leading a workshop for incarcerated teens as part of her master's in social work at Penn.

Every third Monday, she'd brought a stack of loose-leaf paper and miniature pencils into Riverside Correctional Facility, a fifteen-minute drive from campus. She took off her jewelry, except for a watch she used for timing the inmates while they did a silent meditation, then free-wrote for twenty minutes in response to a prompt from a long list of them she'd compiled. Those who wanted to share what they'd written were welcome to.

Sometimes there were snaps or shoulder pats when someone wrote something particularly moving. On a few occasions, when the inmates urged her to, Sara read what she had written. One of those days, she revealed that she hadn't eaten her mother's muffins when she was in high school. A boy of fifteen named Michael opened his eyes wide and said, *You threw them out?* Sara hadn't realized how the admission would sound to a group of teenagers missing out on their futures, who had to eat tasteless cafeteria food, but she guessed part of why she had written it was to feel that shame again, even as she pushed away the larger fear of her infertility. Now of course it was too risky to try for children with a husband nearing sixty. Now she'd never know if it was true that she lacked the ability.

Strange that this was her life now, making a home with Peter in the suburbs. How quickly time had passed since the day they'd met at the correctional facility. Peter had been in the waiting area, getting coffee from the vending machine, when she noticed him there with his gray sideburns, dressed in rust-colored corduroys and a white button-down shirt. His nametag had been pinned to his breast pocket. Sara had always been a shy person, but when he looked up, something about the softness in his eyes filled her with courage.

*Do you work here?* she asked him.

*I don't know if I'd go that far*, he said, tearing open a packet of sugar and pouring it into his coffee. *I'm visiting someone.*

*Oh.* She'd been unsure of what to say next, but then he'd returned the question. She told him about the workshop she was running, and he told her about the medical case he was working on—how an Amish couple, John and Lettie Ames, had been wrongly accused of homicide after their four-month-old daughter, Dorothy, died of a stroke. He explained that Dorothy had suffered from a rare condition specific to the Amish. Now Sara knew it was called GA1, though Peter wouldn't find an official name for it—glutaric acidemia—until after the parents had been exonerated. It had taken him years of research to isolate the gene responsible for the metabolic disorder many had previously assumed was cerebral palsy. And it would take months for Peter to prove that the contusion on Dorothy's head had not been the result of abuse but was rather a subdural hemorrhage caused by a chemical imbalance in her brain.

During that time, Sara and Peter emailed one another updates on their work. Peter used lots of bullet points in his notes, while Sara preferred longer paragraphs for ordering her thoughts. In explaining her ideas to Peter, she found herself exploring more deeply the injustices of the American prison system. She began to see the larger colonial narrative behind juvenile delinquency, to examine the socioeconomic landscape that made the poor, disenfranchised youth more likely to be incarcerated than the teens of wealthy parents, who bailed out their kids time and time again, after they'd committed the same minor felonies the children of less fortunate parents went to jail for.

Over time, Sara and Peter discovered how much they had in common outside of a passion for their own, and one another's, work. They both loved to travel, and when Sara was doing independent work on her thesis, she seized every opportunity to accompany Peter to his conferences across the country. Peter found himself returning to Lancaster County more and more. The Amish had become increasingly receptive to English insights and treatment since the Ames case, and he loved the work, the chance to get away from the clinical hospital setting—and into the weeds with real people with a sacred attachment to their land. The more involved Peter became in applying for grants to fund his research, the clearer his vision became for a private clinic to help those among the Amish suffering from GA1 and other conditions prevalent in that population. And Peter wanted to Sara to join him—not just as his wife, but as a partner equally committed to improving lives. He told her young Amish women especially needed support, mentors they could trust, for navigating the social pressures in their society—to reproduce and preserve domestic order. Most Amish women had between six and ten children before they turned forty, and there was so much that could go wrong. So many pregnancy complications, so many genetic ills that he and Sara could work together to minimize or prevent.

At first, Sara hadn't been keen on the idea, not because she didn't value the work, but because she never saw herself settling down in the suburbs, especially not right after graduate school. But she also couldn't imagine spending her life with anyone else, and when Peter offered to help her start her own practice, she agreed. They'd been on their way to Chicago for another conference, and maybe that had made the idea feel less unsettling, more doable; or maybe it was because the notion of her own clinic, her own wide-open space for working with clients, didn't seem fully possible without Peter. He would know how to get the funding, how to make her services accessible to all.

What Sara didn't expect was to be derailed by the lack of community she felt amid other women upon her arrival in Lancaster County—women far less interested in social justice than in flower gardening, in shopping at the outlets, in sending their kids to lacrosse and tennis camp. Sara didn't have kids to connect with them about, of course, but she did like gardening, which provided her with a circle of sorts. She could talk about how flowers, like children, required certain environmental factors to thrive. She could spend hours online researching seedlings, interviewing botanists, pricing out local strains compared to mail-order stock, crafting her own landscape, and her neighbors wanted to hear about it. She could have lunch with other women and discuss something other than public versus private high school; she could go to yoga class and start the morning sharing her thoughts on spring hyacinth.

In fact, over the years, she'd become so invested in her life as a gardener that she couldn't imagine going back to social work, especially not in an urban setting. She now considered this life among her plants her calling, her vocation, not to mention a happy diversion when Peter needed to stay late at the clinic or go in on weekends. And when Emma came to work for her, it couldn't have been a more perfect marriage of worlds. That she could support Emma emotionally through her transition into adulthood, all while gardening more intuitively, mindful of the Amish way, was an incredibly rewarding prospect.

And yet she had to be careful not to overstep, not to push Emma too hard outside of her comfort zone. Especially after last Tuesday, when she'd put on The Beatles in the living room. Sara had been taken aback by Emma's panic—her posttraumatic state. Yes, that's what it had been. Sara might have grasped it sooner, but she'd been so shocked herself by Emma's reaction. It had taken the time to process, fully, what it meant for Emma to have been one of the survivors of Nickel Mines.

Even now, a week later, she was distracted by the urge to ask Emma about her panic attack. Make sure she was okay. But it didn't seem wise. What would Peter think? *Unprofessional*. So she didn't. When Emma finished in the garden and shifted to housework, Sara drove to the nursery in Leola to pick up the celandine poppies and Siberian irises she'd special ordered last week. This, she decided, would at least give them something neutral to talk about after Emma finished cleaning. Maybe afterward she'd let Sara drive her home.

# EMMA WALSH

## SPRING 2018

"Do you ever wonder about Hell?" Isaac asks me out of the blue. We're on a courting walk, passing Moses Esh's farm along the back road, fields dense with violets and goldenrod.

"No," I lie, but I think he can tell. He stops me in the middle of the road and holds me by the shoulders.

"You don't worry about Satan?" he asks. "If we leave?"

"But we are here," I say. Isaac has never suggested leaving before. On our walks, we usually talk about the others on Rumspringa. Who is dating whom. Weekend bonfires and other parties that he goes to, and I don't—not yet. Isaac wants to bring me to Seth Yoder's on Saturday, but I'm not sure. Part of me wonders what he's like at parties, if he's the same gentle Isaac who holds my hand on walks, or if he's reckless like the other boys.

"We're getting baptized," I hear myself say—out of fear, maybe, that Isaac's doubt is contagious. If he wants to marry me, we will be baptized.

His hazel eyes dart like a small animal's. "What if it's too late," he says.

"Too late?"

"I've done things." His voice trails off. "It's not the first time I've been away." He means the foster home, the English life he knew as a child.

"God forgives you. Whatever it is," I tell him, as Mother would.

"I don't know," he says.

"You were too young to understand," I say.

"I wasn't." He looks away at the open field.

"What did you do?"

"It doesn't matter," he says, letting go of my hand.

In the distance, I see the gray eaves of the Esh house. The chipped white fence around the perimeter, the milk goats.

"Tell me about the home," I say, surprised that I want to hear it. That I'm ready to. Maybe because Mrs. Caldwell has made it feel less impossible to speak about things I shouldn't.

But Isaac looks at me differently then, angrily almost, like I'm prying.

"You don't have to tell if you don't want to."

"That's the problem," he says, raising his voice. "If I don't tell you, I won't be saved. If we stay in the church."

Again I'm alarmed that he sees a life outside our families. Without their blessing. "Tell me, then," I say. "You can tell me anything."

"I stole something." Isaac traces the fold in his straw hat, running his finger back and forth. "A cell phone. I sold it so I could buy food. I was hungry," he says. "I went to a vending machine for a snack. I saved the rest."

I sense there are other things he's not telling me, but I don't say so, just as I don't mention the man at the schoolhouse, because I know it haunts him, too. That he wasn't there to protect me.

"The boy had money," he says. "I don't think he missed it too much."

"Which boy?" I ask.

"The boy I stole from."

I'm stealing, too, aren't I? Pencils from the schoolhouse to write with in the jam cellar? Stealing was the same as turning away from goodness, falling prey to temptation rather than guarding against it.

A dent in the road, lines dribbled with tar. Sometimes there are broken beer bottles that split our horses' hooves, but I try not to think of them as Isaac tells me about the other boy's phone, the contacts and photos he deleted before he sold it.

"I didn't look at the photos," he says.

Before he can say more, I reach for his hand like Mrs. Caldwell did for me on Tuesday, showing me that I wasn't alone. "I forgive you," I say.

His body shivers, his breath slow and shallow at once. Seconds pass, then he takes a step back and wipes tears from his eyes. "How can you marry me, Emma, knowing I am a thief?"

"You were hungry," I reply, though I know what our people would say—that God helps us through our hunger; we need only ask. But what about our invisible wounds? Isn't stealing another way of asking for help? Like crashing a buggy after drinking too much. Like Laura Zimmerman cutting her veins with scissors after learning she was carrying an English man's child. Laura, shunned and sent away to live on food stamps, in a shack in the hills. Once, when she tried to come back, begging forgiveness, we were told not to speak to her, to act like she was dead.

"It's not your fault," I tell Isaac, feeling as though in comforting him I am also comforting myself for what I've been through, what I can't understand, for the questioning Mother cannot tolerate. I think we aren't so different, then, Isaac and I, in what we've had to do to survive. What we've both learned to hide.

"I love you," he says suddenly, and I feel my eyes widen. Is this love, or is it gratitude—or both? When he leans in to kiss me for the first time, his lips are soft. I taste salt, and it mixes with the scent of honeysuckle.

When he pulls back, he is smiling. "Have you thought more about the party next Saturday?"

The warmth of his mouth lingers, and I say, "Yes. I'd like to go."

He lifts my hands and brings them to his lips. "I'll pick you up at seven." He takes off his hat, and his hair looks coppery in the sun. After wiping the sweat from his brow, he settles the hat back in place. "I have to get to work."

"All right," I say. "See you soon."

Clear light hangs over the farmland behind him, and I watch his wide back under his overalls as he walks away.

I feel less afraid than I have in a long while. I feel like writing, just as I did after the record player at Mrs. Caldwell's. On the way back to

Mother and Eli, I look up at the trees and see Beth in the broken parts of them. I resist the impulse to etch these words in the dirt with a stick. I'll wait until I am home again, in the jam cellar. Each time I write, it's like stealing back what I've lost, what I've been told to forgive with silence.

*Do you remember the milkman's theft? When he came to fill his tank from our supply while the others were sleeping? Do you remember watching from the window as he pumped what our cows had provided, a garden hose snaking from his truck, his smeared reflection along the cold aluminum?*

*Why didn't we tell Mother? If we had, would she have told Father, who would have called the English police? Maybe. Or maybe she would have stayed quiet, just as we did that summer.*

# RUTH WALSH

## SUMMER 2019

She wheels Eli into the waiting room of Dr. Caldwell's office. There is a picture on the wall of an uneven red circle on a blue background with a white line and a small black dot. *Flight of the Dragonfly in Front of the Sun* by Joan Miró, it reads, and below that: National Gallery of Art, Washington, DC.

Ruth has never been to the city. Not just Washington, DC, but any city. Did the Caldwells keep other paintings in their house, paintings Emma might have asked about?

But there is no knowing anything, no predicting the future, no changing the past. How can she accuse the doctor's wife of things when she wasn't there? Of course, the doctor was not at fault for his wife's vanity, even if she had filled Emma's mind with the things Ruth imagines—about having a secret talent, about following your dreams.

There are other ways of being talented, Ruth might have explained if Emma had come to her. In sewing dresses and aprons, in darning, in preparing meals. She is still staring at the red circle on the painting, at the bent shape of the dragonfly, when the doctor comes to greet her.

"Good day," she tells him.

"Hello, Ruth," he says. "It's good to see you."

Her hands tighten over the handles of Eli's wheelchair, and she vows silently that all will be well. *I will bring Mrs. Caldwell the pie, after the appointment ends,* she tells herself

"Hello, Eli," Dr. Caldwell says. "How are we today?"

Eli grunts, flails his arms a little, and she says, "It's the doctor, Eli. Say hello to the doctor."

Dr. Caldwell reaches for Eli's hands and holds them. "It's all right, Eli," he says. "It's only me."

When they are inside his office, he asks how eating is going.

"Mostly the same," Ruth says. "Snap peas are in season, and he's doing well with sweet potato mash."

"Very good," the doctor says, bending down to Eli's level. He checks his eyes with the light Eli has never liked, listens to his heart with a stethoscope. Then he knocks at Eli's knees with a rubber hammer Ruth doesn't know the name for. Sometimes Eli reacts, other times he doesn't, like today. "A little stiff," the doctor says.

For years, Ruth blamed herself for waiting too long to take Eli for treatment, but the doctor never suggests that himself. Like today, he assures her she's doing the best she can. He praises her for how well Eli is eating, how hard she works to procure the right foods. They don't talk about Emma, how Emma used to be the one to shop for Eli, but God was good, God had found a way for Ruth to procure turmeric this week at the market, when she'd hurried to the spice stand before closing.

Emma used to take Eli for checkups, too, when Ruth's heart rate elevated and she couldn't breathe. It happened less frequently now, but for years after the Happening, Ruth would find her body betraying her, turning uncontrollable—the way it had the day she entered the coroner's office, when there'd just been her own rapid breath in the room, dizzying thoughts, the tiles in the floor overlapping, the sound of Abraham shouting her name, the unrecognizable body of her child.

The doctor scribbles more notes on his pad. "How is Thursday for more bloodwork?"

"That's fine," Ruth says, thinking of the red circle in the painting, not a sun but a stain, or a gaping hole.

"Early, say seven o'clock? Before his breakfast?"

"Not a problem," Ruth says, realizing she's adopted this expression working for English families all these years. The endless requests they make, their preoccupation with making tiny changes to her weekly schedule around pickups and drop-offs.

Not a problem at all.

But sometimes it was a problem, wasn't it? Sometimes she agreed to things she didn't believe in, things she told herself she was doing out of courtesy because she couldn't say no. And what of all the times she'd accepted rides in English cars over the years when she might have walked instead, walked, like she'd urged Emma to do after the milkman, out of her own fear. It was a kind of contradiction, wasn't it, telling her daughter to do one thing, while she'd done another?

Later, as the doctor hands her a card with an appointment reminder, she almost asks, *Is it safe? Do you consider your wife a safe person?* But accusation is the opposite of absolution. Judgment belongs not in her hands, but in those of the Lord.

"Would you like to pay another day?"

He is looking at Ruth like the woman had the other day, waiting for her to follow through with the transaction. When Ruth had lost track of the minutes. How many had passed? "Oh," she says.

"I can wait," he says.

"No, I have it. Right here." She holds out the envelope with the earnings from the market, but as the doctor reaches for it, she finds herself holding on.

"Is everything all right, Ruth?" the doctor asks. "You seem distracted."

"I—" Ruth can't finish for fear she'll say the wrong thing. Blurt out Mrs. Caldwell's name.

"Take a seat," he says. "You look flushed."

"It's all right, doctor," Ruth says. "Really. I better get Eli home."

"But you're not feeling well."

"I'm fine. . . . Just tired. Last night I got little sleep." Before she adds anything more, she says, "I have something for Mrs. Caldwell. A pie to bring later."

"She's home most days," the doctor says, but he looks at her doubtfully. Why wouldn't he?

"It's just a small gift," she says. "To say thank you." She doesn't say that the pie is from Saturday, no longer fresh. That she still must make a new batch of dough and roll it to its proper thickness, but then later, when she's home, there's no time. Abraham is still stripping the tobacco to dry, and she has the preserves to finish jarring, and Eli's trousers to mend. Then Eli's needs his sponge bath, his lunch, his afternoon nap. Even the jarring will have to wait, she decides, for when Abraham can go to the cellar in her place, to check on the quantities of jam. Abraham agreed that she need no longer go down there, for fear of what else she might find of Emma's, like the first time.

Pages Emma had written as if they were her own stories, and yet she had taken lines from *Martyrs Mirror*, reconfiguring the old verses and placing them next to her own imaginings.

*Pardon me, O my Lord and my God, I, who am but dust and ashes, approach Thee, wash me of my sins, O Lord, wash me until I am whole.*

Ruth still recalls these lines, Emma's version of the sacred text, no matter how many times she's tried to forget. In quiet moments between things, the verses intrude, perhaps because some are too familiar, the lines from the original she'd learned by heart as a child. They are as ingrained as the Lord's Prayer, as the Nicene Creed, and for as many times as she prays each day, there is an adjacent line from Emma. Invading her thoughts when the wood clock ticks during dinner, just after she and Abraham have said grace and can begin, when she is pushing the food around her plate because she's forgotten how to sit still, how to eat instead of worry. She turns her focus to Eli, hardly eating himself, because it is better than remembering Emma's poetry.

*I have that which is Thine, yea, which is Thy most precious treasure, even the blood and offering of the saints; I must needs come and offer it to Thee. . . . I must needs come unto me unto me in the light.*

This night, after dinner, she is too tired to ask Abraham to check the jars of jam, to make her a list, so she sets Eli's chair by the kitchen window while she takes stock of the pantry. She finds two jars of apricot and one raspberry; she counts three jars of molasses, two tins of flour, and one large tin of sugar. When she finishes, she pulls out a chair and sits next to Eli. His eyes are open, and he is quiet, dreaming awake. Ruth reaches for his hand, presses hers over his, and says, "Rest now."

She stares into the void of the sky, the dusty blue of dusk over the cornfields that weave past their property. Washlines strung with her dresses and Abraham's shirts crisscross between trees. Once Emma said they looked like telephone lines. Ruth had stopped her and asked, *What do you mean?*

*I mean above the fields there are power lines, English lines, but these lines are for us.*

This was before the Happening, before the verses in the jam cellar.

*I don't know what you mean*, Ruth had said. *You aren't making any sense.*

But now, the longer Ruth looks at the lines over the fields, she can't help but notice how they stretch and bend, how the undulations of electric wire and washing wire are not so different. Can't help but think she could have listened, could have probed, could have said Emma had God's gift for imagination.

But it was too late now. Ruth has never shown Emma's writing to Abraham. Her husband doesn't know she hid the last page of verses she found in an old butter tin, that she folded the paper dozens of times, until it was as small as a pebble inside. All Ruth has left of her child.

# SARA CALDWELL

## SPRING 2018

Sara had been folding laundry when she learned of the shooting. She'd been rolling socks together, half watching the television, when she saw the shooter's face on the screen: pale and balding, blank eyes behind bent, oversized glasses. A local milk-truck driver, over thirty, alleged friend to the Amish through his family's business over the years. As Sara watched this collision of worlds—bonneted mothers draped in black, heaving before reporters and cameras and yellow tape—none of it seemed real.

Sara had called Peter, screaming, *Where are you!*

He'd been on his way to the hospital to identify those pronounced dead. There was confusion in the mortuary because of the sameness of the girls' dress, the sameness of their hair; Peter had been weeping, too, through the phone, and she'd begged him to let her come with him, but this was a private investigation. Ever the professional, Peter was the first to remind her to put her panic, her shock, aside. She tried, but over time, the horror only grew. News trucks and cameras and microphones everywhere, journalists swarming, ambushing the Amish, pressing them for statements. It felt like each day, in the weeks and months that followed, revealed something astonishing. Grandfathers offered forgiveness to the killer, Jon Williams, and his family. *We must not think evil of him,* one said. *Our hearts go out to his wife. We pray for her.*

There were countless interviews with Williams's wife, Emily. On the television, her face was drained of color, her eyes swollen and pink. She said there'd been no signs. Jon had been a good Christian, a regular churchgoer, a loving father. Later, she explained how they'd lost a daughter. A stillbirth. The suicide note revealed the secret resentment he'd been harboring against God, blaming him for their daughter's death.

No one knew how ill he was, not family nor friends. Emily's father owned a dairy that had sourced milk from the Amish for years. Jon had driven the truck for it. In the weeks leading up to the shooting, coworkers said Jon was distracted, his affect flat. But Emily maintained she had no way of knowing the extent of his sickness, weeping as she described his last desperate phone call to her from the schoolhouse before he began shooting. Before taking his own life at the scene.

Years later, Sara learned how Emily had changed her surname. She'd even authored a book under this name—Emily Anderson—on the healing power of Amish forgiveness, which of course Sara read but had trouble believing. Emily claimed to have devoted her life to caring for one of the survivors, a victim left comatose by the shooting—visiting Kathryn every Sunday, reading her passages from the Bible, bathing, spoon-feeding, and singing to her.

The schoolhouse had been dismantled, five trees planted in its place, one for each of the victims, and every year there was a picnic on the old plot of land to bring their families together. But what of the survivors, like Emma, and the four other girls who had come out of the schoolhouse alive? How did they grapple with what they'd endured inside that single room, their wounds made invisible?

Emma had witnessed firsthand every moment, had been lined up at the chalkboard and tied down with the others. Emma had heard her only sister offer her life first—to give the others longer, to give them a chance to live—and had watched Beth die. And then Emma, along with the rest of her community, had been asked to forgive Jon Williams and speak no more of him.

None of it made sense.

There were many books on the topic, not just on psychology and gun violence but inspirational titles, religious texts on the transformative power of Amish forgiveness. When we forgave others, we stopped the cycle of retaliation, the cycle of repeated harm. Seen this way, at least in Sara's mind, pacifism was not a goal but a stance—one that denied the healing process, which was different for everyone.

She'd seen the consequence of this denial in Emma—by the record player. Her senses heightened by particular sounds, her body readying for an attack that wasn't real. Sara had known what suppression looked like, what posttraumatic stress looked like, and now she saw it in Emma.

As the days pass between one Tuesday and the next, Sara finds she can't distract herself as easily with trips to the nursery, note-taking and sketching the next phase of work before her garden show. On Saturday, she decides to take a drive along the country roads with the windows down because it's a beautiful day, because it's May and everything is in bloom. She knows she shouldn't take the road to the Walsh farm—Snake Hill—yet she does, telling herself she's simply stopping by to say hello to Emma, as if she hadn't been planning this all along.

As she pulls into the Walshes' driveway, she hopes to remain discreet. Perhaps observe from a distance on the chance that Emma, doing a farm chore, will spot her and approach without risk of complication. But what is she thinking? Her black Volvo stands out on the property. Of course it does. What would Peter say if word traveled back?

Before Sara can turn the car around, her gaze falls on a figure in the vegetable garden. At first she thinks it's Emma, then realizes this woman's older, though she looks a bit like Emma. Her mother? A bonnet is covering her face, but for an instant Sara imagines their eyes meet. Then she detects movement and turns her head to find Emma standing by her car, holding a basket of cherries, fingers stained red.

"My brother isn't feeling well," Emma says. Her voice is distant; she's hardly the young woman in tears over "Eleanor Rigby." "I'd invite you in for tea—"

In Sara's periphery, Emma's mother has moved to stand by Eli's wheelchair on the porch. She looks at Sara, at the car, then looks away.

"Don't worry," Sara says. "I just wanted to see how you were doing since The Beatles." She tries a smile.

Emma only looks back at her silently, almost as if she doesn't know what Sara means.

"I'm good," she says, her eyes still refusing to soften.

"Oh," Sara says. "I'm sorry to bother you. I guess I'll see you on Tuesday, then."

"See you Tuesday," Emma says, smiling politely before hurrying over to her mother and Eli.

Once Sara turns out of the drive, she picks up speed, racing all the way to Hunsecker, where she notices a few boys pushing mowers across the field of another farm. A small blond boy stops and looks at her, or is she just imagining this too, the way she'd imagined Emma's mother staring minutes prior? Suddenly, she feels the same panicked estrangement. That she is an interloper. She isn't holding her phone, but still the second boy gestures to the first to get away. She's crossed some unspeakable line without even trying. She knows she should cut her losses now, and yet she can't. This shame, once acknowledged, was like a scab she must pick at until it bled. Impulsively, she swerves the car around, turning back not on Emma's road but to 896, a straight shot through Peaceful Valley to the old schoolhouse. She surges past stretches of farmland, past red barns and shimmering silos, past more fields wild with buttercups.

After Peter had helped identify the girls, he'd locked himself in his office for days. Told her it was for research, but she knew he was grieving. At last, when she brought him dinner one evening, he opened the door to reveal files upon files, stacks of books, and he broke, telling her he'd been reading about the long-term effects of trauma on a survivor. Not just on the girls, but the boys too—the boys who'd run when the shooter let them leave, who still blamed themselves for failing to protect the girls like God wanted. She had held her husband, tried to steady him as he wept. He told her about his nightmares, how he still saw the girls at the morgue: their long, blood-soaked hair hanging from metal tables; how he'd examined what remained of each victim, finding enough to confirm all five names for the coroner's report.

As the sharp sunlight pierces her windshield, Sara tells her herself to stay focused on landmarks. On Good 'N' Plenty when she passes it, the Sight and Sound Theater, the strand of pretzel and ice cream shops. On Quarryville Road, she sees a sign for Faith Mennonite School, then the ROD & GUN CLUB. Without conscious thought, Sara tightens her hands on the wheel.

When she reaches White Oak Road, she barely notices the turn. There's a swimming pool, a large public one she's never been to. Was this even an Amish neighborhood? she wonders, but then spots the sign for Mine Road, the one the school was on before it was dismantled. Where the milk truck would have been parked. In its place is just an empty plot of land, a barren meadow. In a news article, Sara read that the town had planted pear trees to commemorate the tragedy. Five on the site, for the five girls who had passed, and one near the home of the victim who lived on in a coma.

There are no farmers about. No children. Sara walks into the emptiness like it's a desert, her car parked under a copse of elms off the dirt track. Strange, Sara tells herself, they said there was a new school. Finally, she approaches the trees, planted in a straight line just a few feet apart from one another. Circling around them, she walks down another dirt path and sees it there: The New Hope School. Its white sideboards, freshly painted, are almost too bright in the sun. By the entrance, the school bell glints metallic. Sara draws her hand to her cheek and hears herself breathe.

# EMMA WALSH

## SPRING 2018

Mother and I are in the kitchen making rolled oatmeal cookies with raisins for market on Saturday. Flour covers Mother's fingers, a dash over her forehead and lips. She cuts a tablespoon from a stick of butter, and I add molasses to the mixture. Sunlight slices through the kitchen window in a way I want to write down. I'll remember for later. *Streaks like golden jessamine. Luminous skeins.* I wonder if Beth sees it too, if she's here with us in the room. If she'd want me to write it down. Would Mrs. Caldwell?

"We could try selling flowers," Mother says. "Rosalie has good luck with bouquets."

Mother is always thinking about profits, where we can expand to cover Eli's bills. "What kind of flowers?" I ask.

"I don't know," she says. "What does Dr. Caldwell's wife keep in her garden?"

Did Mother sense me thinking about her? What will she say if I mention English names for things from the nursery?

Japanese witch hazel. Spanish flag vine. Copper birch. Meadow rue.

I keep it simple. "She has peonies and forsythia, mostly."

Mother looks up and nods. "Good," she says, affirmed in her own choices, in what we have available anyway. "Will you start the other batch?" she asks. "I'll wash the blueberries."

I nod. Mother moves to the sink with the strainer. An eventual wedding present for me, the strainer—silver with small stars and hearts cut out of the metal.

"How is Isaac?"

This other topic I know she wants to get to. My wedding and how much money we are making, that we could be making for Eli, are always on her mind.

"He's well," I say.

"Lettie visited the other day. I have a hunch he'll be proposing soon." She smiles.

"Maybe so," I say. It will be quiet, the way all proposals are. After we tell the church we are getting baptized. No wedding ring like Mrs. Caldwell has, no silken dress like I saw in a photo she's displayed in the library, of her cutting a tall white cake with silver-lined frosting. I will wear a dress of black to absorb the light of God.

How does Mother know, how is she so sure, Isaac wants to stay? That I will? She assumes I'm only going through the motions of Rumspringa. Otherwise, I wouldn't wear my simple dress to work. I would accept more rides home. She assumes I will follow in her footsteps. Out of duty, out of love. We've never talked about Mother's Rumspringa, any doubts she might have had, what she might have tried.

I don't tell her about the party Isaac is taking me to Saturday.

*English drinking and cigarettes. Guns. One thing leads to the next,* Mother said once.

I didn't argue then, but now I want to ask her what is evil if it is temporary. Why is a taste of Captain Morgan more dangerous than sweet molasses? Why are English blue jeans dangerous? Why is a woman showing her hips, her bust, under tighter cotton?

Leslie Zimmerman went to the shopping mall off the turnpike. Tommy Girl, she said she got—this spray she wears to parties. Last week, outside the Zimmermans' horse barn, after Sunday singing, she let me smell her wrist. *Like bottled delphinium,* I wrote down later, after reading the word delphinium in a book from Mrs. Caldwell's library. *Mrs. Dalloway.* When I held it up and saw on its cover the English name written in red script, I marveled that a woman had written a whole book about another woman's life.

When I asked Mrs. Caldwell what it was, delphinium, she called it a fancy name for larkspur. When I asked what it smelled like, she said like fresh linens. I've memorized the passage about the first time this woman, Clarissa Dalloway, goes into Miss Pym's flower shop. . . . *There were flowers: delphiniums, sweet peas, bunches of lilac; and carnations, masses of carnations. There were roses; there were irises . . . how she loved the grey-white moths spinning in and out, over the cherry pie, over the evening primroses!*

When Mrs. Caldwell wasn't looking, I slipped the book into my apron pocket. She didn't ask me what was there, later, in the garden. Maybe she thought they were my shears, or my bottle spray. The book is in the cellar now, next to my pages. I'll return it to the library when I finish reading. I will, next Tuesday.

*There were flowers, Beth . . . delphiniums, sweet peas, bunches of lilac; and carnations.* . . . I want to whisper the words like a prayer, indistinguishable from Bible verse.

"Will you check the oven?" Mother asks. Her eyes are scolding, because she's already asked me this. She knows I'm distracted. That my mind is on Isaac—is that what she thinks? But what am I to be sorry for?

There is another book by Virginia called *A Room of One's Own*, with another line I've copied down for Beth, if she is watching me now, hearing me write in my head . . . *how unpleasant it is to be locked out; and, . . . how it is worse, perhaps, to be locked in.*

I think my sister is free now; she's in the angles of light on trees and flowers, passing over us, along the soft wing of a chickadee. I will write this down, too.

"Hurry up now," Mother says. "We don't have all morning to mix the flour."

*Flour* and *flower*, two words that sound the same yet stand worlds apart in my mind, the way I see the powdery feather dust of a swan's wings grazing a lake. *Beth, is it you?*

Six dozen pages of my own writing now, stacked up neatly and bound with string beneath two crates of empty jars. Has mother found anything? Would she tell me if she had? What would she say if she knew what I'd stolen? The pencils and paper from the schoolhouse, the book from Mrs. Caldwell's library?

I crack and whisk three eggs, add them to the second batch, while Mother fills another baking sheet with plops of dough. She works quickly, spacing each ball a perfect distance from the last.

As she sets the sheet in the oven, I go to check on Eli in the parlor. He's in his chair, sleeping by the window. His head angled over his neck. Carefully, I move him so he's without strain. I wipe drool from his lips.

*Do you know, Beth, that when light catches Eli's eyes, I try to hear the air passing through his lungs?* It has to be enough, the silence of him breathing. Alive. The greatest prayer there is.

I hear creaking then, outside. Father pushes through the door, home from work early. He hangs his hat. "Smells good," he says, looking at me.

"Another few batches," I say. "We're almost done."

He follows me into the kitchen, greeting Mother. He braces her shoulders, kisses her cheek.

"You wash up," Mother tells me. "We'll eat, and then we'll finish the cookies later. Make a list for the market bouquets."

"All right," I say.

At the dinner table, I feed Eli first, spoonfuls of mashed butternut squash, as Mother and Father discuss this month's expenses. The new shoes I'll need for work come July. The tissue paper and stem preservative we'll need for the bouquets. "They expect it," Mother says.

"Where do we get something like that?" Father asks.

"From the garden center," I say. "Where Mrs. Caldwell goes for supplies."

"Would she order it for us?" Mother asks, "subtract it from your wages?"

"I think so."

"Only if she doesn't mind," Mother says, sipping from her water glass.

After dinner, Mother makes another three-dozen oatmeal cookies while I read to Eli from *Martyrs Mirror* in the parlor. I read the story of Rutilus again, *Yea, torn asunder with manifold torments . . . committed to the fire . . . thanking the mercy of God for it . . . endured the suffering which had been his destiny.*

Father and Mother are certain Eli would commit himself to the church if he could, that he would let Bishop Yoder ladle holy water over his head while we rejoiced in the promise of his afterlife.

How can they be so certain? If Eli sees little more than light and shadow, senses life as a waking dream? *For we were born yesterday and know nothing; our days on earth are but a shadow*: from the book of Job. What would Eli say about what I've seen? Would he show me how to forget, how to watch shadows in place of memories?

*A clevis pin is missing*, the man had said when Teacher Martha let him in. He thought someone had stolen it. I recognized his face—it was the same man from the night by the milk tank.

*The violences of the English world*, Bishop Yoder would say, *are out of our hands.*

*But call to remembrance former days, in which after ye were illuminated, ye endured a fight of affliction*: from Hebrews. I read the words aloud like Father expects, this verse for the promise of the afterlife, the promise of unconditional forgiveness. *For what has man profited if he shall gain the whole world, and lose his own soul?*

Mother and I have never spoken of this—whether Beth would still be here had it not been for the book of martyrs.

Years after the Happening, I found the copy of the newspaper Mother bought without telling Father.

One night before bed, I told Mother I felt there was no sense to it all. Where was the sense in our wounds? She'd stopped me there, turning off the oil lamp on my nightstand. *Pray now*, she'd said.

Just as she does every night, after we've put Eli to bed and fastened leather straps around his arms to keep him from harming himself accidentally.

*Do you know, the other night I dreamed of Eli, and in the morning, I wrote it down before daybreak: Eli's eyes like silver fish underwater, his mouth moving forcefully with words. The water drowns every sound, while above, a roaring wind moves light over his face in prisms. Yellow gladiolus spreading its petals like wings, and I wait for the day to begin again. Again, again, I wait for you to arrive in the water, the sunlight.*

# RUTH WALSH

## SUMMER 2019

Ruth lies awake in bed, watching candlelit shadows tremble along the ceiling. In one, there is the silhouette of Emma's face. The black of her Sunday bonnet, as if the thin shadow could stretch to trace the clean curve of her child's nose, the soft bend of her upper lip. Long bonnet strings hang down, rippling in the dark. Ruth wants to rise to see them better. She almost does, but she can't risk waking Abraham from his deep, undisturbed sleep.

It's almost two o'clock, not long before he'll roll from bed to feed the cows, and her husband needs his rest. When he's in the barn, Ruth will go to the cellar to retrieve Mrs. Caldwell's pie. She's decided today is the day to bring it over.

She'd promised the doctor—it's too late to change course—but there hasn't been time to make a fresh one. The old one will have to do, even if it's over a week old now. When she last went to the cellar for more preserves, a ring of fruit flies had darted about the plastic wrapping. She'd done little to swat them away.

She is tempted to deliver it in the night, when no one would see her. This spoiled pie delivered of a dark mind. Her mind.

Ruth closes her eyes. She need only stay in bed and pray to the shadows along the wall, take comfort in their shapes. But each time she tries, her thoughts morph into the shadow, growing with the darkness. The sound of Abraham's steady breathing doesn't comfort her, in and out, like a mill churning feed. How easily he's always been able to sleep compared with her, even after the Happening. She wants to reach for his hand, just to feel his dry, blistered skin, but this too could wake him.

Abraham's hands remind Ruth of leather horse reins, of the pinch of nails between callused fingers. It was the first thing she noticed about him when they were courting.

They hadn't met during choir or at volleyball after Sunday services, as Ruth's mother and father might have liked, but at a local bar when they were eighteen and on their Rumspringa. Abraham had been leaning against a wall by the billiard table at the back, his hair cut clean across his face, his beard shaven. He was in blue jeans and a white t-shirt, his strong shoulders under the short sleeves. Ruth wore a plain gray dress; she'd decided not to buy English clothes like the other girls. She didn't have the money for that. Her father collected the whole of her earnings at the end of every week to pay for more horse and chicken feed, new farm equipment, the monthly paratransit.

The candlelight bends again, and now she sees the outline of her own face, sees herself just as she'd been that first night at the tavern. The way she'd let her hair down. Still, she'd refused to look at herself in the bathroom mirror. As afraid of her own image as the graffiti on the stall. When she was out of the bathroom again, she couldn't help but feel the weight of her hair down her back, the ends brushing her waist. How did the boys see her?

Abraham had introduced himself first, taking a seat next to her, in a wooden chair by the billiard table. They watched the game, speaking quietly about the roads they lived on while their friends drank liquor and clumsily poked at colored balls. Ruth sometimes closed her eyes at the crack of the balls colliding over the pool table, waiting for them to slow, stop, or fall into a net with the clacking sound of another point.

In these silences, Ruth wished for something to say to make Abraham laugh. Something to make her appear more interesting. Why was an English pool table green like grass? Why did the balls look like oversized marbles? But she didn't ask these things. She only watched, making peace with the long silences she was used to at home. The sound of the clock, ticking, ticking in the wallpapered parlor.

Later that night, someone called for shots of Jameson. A girl hung from a boy's shoulder. In the shadows of the bedroom, Ruth can see her now, laughing and carrying on. Beer bottles had accrued along the rim of the pool table before an English waitress cleared them away.

The whole while, Abraham held his sweating Budweiser. Ruth had almost asked him to get her one, but she wasn't sure she was ready for that. One drink might lead to another. If she agreed, when would it be too many? What if Abraham suggested taking her to his room, in the motel off the turnpike, where he was staying with the other boys? If she went to bed with him, she would have to marry him. There was no other way. So she'd sat in the quiet without drinking or risking speaking something unwise.

Though she'd been nervous and wary, something about Abraham's hands had let her know it would be all right. That home could exist outside the farm too, that you could feel at peace with someone even when another part of you felt afraid. That straying from custom like this, at the tavern, was only temporary. Ruth had understood Abraham to be who he was: someone else who wanted a family, a life in the church.

Two days later, Abraham had come to the house on Quarry Road. Ruth had been in the garden, helping just as Emma had helped Ruth on Rumspringa. Abraham had walked up in his wide-brimmed hat, in a clean shirt and broad trousers, Ruth could hear her heart beating.

*How about a walk on Saturday?* he asked.

Ruth had been holding a large watermelon. She blinked as though to clear her vision, like he couldn't be the same boy from the bar. Yet he was. They looked at one another for a little while, and finally, she nodded.

Ruth had spent several days planning what to wear. She chose a lavender cape dress; braided her hair under her bonnet. Her friends Mae and Annabelle had told her she should go with them to the outlets for English jeans. They wanted to pluck her eyebrows, do her up in eyeshadow and lipstick, but Ruth feared there would be no end to the shopping and preening. *Abraham likes me as I am*, she'd said.

On their first courting walk, they skirted along the edge of her family's farmland, and when Abraham asked if she wanted an ice cream from the Freeze & Frizz, she went with him. By the picnic table where they sat licking their cones, an English family stared at them. Ruth was used to it. She paid no mind, finishing her cone next to Abraham in the summer heat. When some ice cream dripped, he startled her by drawing her hand to his lips, catching the sweet beads. What did the English think when they saw? That she and Abraham were of the wrong kind? That they'd been corrupted?

The idea disturbed her, though in her heart, Ruth knew there was no sin in the flirtation. And Abraham quickly made his intentions clear. Three months later, they were married. And a month after that, Ruth was pregnant. While she was carrying, Abraham proved a gentle husband, a good father. He made her dry toast when she felt sick, built a crib and a dresser for their first child, named Beth after Abraham's grandmother, born on a Thursday morning after two days of labor.

After the delivery, when Ruth had still been in pain, Abraham stayed faithfully beside her in their bedroom, helping her mother apply cool cloths and running ice over her wrists. She'd held his hand, her eyes fluttering as day moved to night and night to morning. It took several weeks for her to recover, but Ruth had found comfort each time Abraham brought Beth to her bedside, so she could hold and feed her. In time, Ruth regained her strength, and both she and Abraham had prayed to the Lord, giving Him thanks.

Now, Ruth wonders if it's a dangerous thing to love too much? Invest too much in what God alone has the power to decide. It was his doing to take Beth, and Emma, too, to test Ruth's love for Him, her trust in a world without answers.

She is getting better at acceptance. She has made a pie for Mrs. Caldwell. She has plans to deliver it. She is good in the Lord's eyes. Always has been. Hasn't she? Unlike the other girls of her youth. The ones who did not trust in Him. Such as Joanna, Ruth's childhood friend who'd fallen prey to English drugs. At the tavern, Joanna tried crystal meth. She was not yet twenty. After Joanna left the community, there were rumors of heroin. Ruth had never seen the needle herself, but she knew there was no coming back—knew that heroin became your God, your only love and happiness.

Ruth sees Joanna in another shadow flickering on the wall, crouched somewhere on a street corner in a soiled t-shirt and jeans, begging for change. Why is it she can't turn back to the peaceful emptiness, forgetting all but Him? It's as if each time she pushes down a thought, a new one arrives in its place. Now, Ruth sees Joanna's skeletal arm, bruised by the needle.

*Heroin*. Not like *heroine*, the English word for a courageous woman, something Ruth knows she can ever be. Not in the material world. It's not something she's ever considered before. Reading novels or writing poetry like Emma did, secretly jotting lines in the jam cellar. The words Ruth saved in the butter tin. If Abraham were to open the tin, he might mistake the crumpled paper for refuse, something to discard like a crumb. Once more, Ruth fights the impulse to rise, to run and check that it's still there, the crumb, but she must wait. Another several minutes at least, another hour.

She watches the shadow cast by the candle flame, the distended line of a body in an alley.

"Gelassenheit," Ruth whispers. "Uffgevva, yield to the Almighty." She will rise with Abraham today, just as she's always done. She will start a fresh pie from scratch, as many times as it takes for the dough to reach the right consistency. When she finishes, she will draw a cross for Mrs. Caldwell along the center. All bitterness drained from her heart. In its place, only the Lord's forgiveness, for those who know not what they do.

# SARA CALDWELL

## SPRING 2018

With Emma's help, Sara feels more ready for her garden party. Though it's still weeks away, the begonia beds have been planted, along with the juniper and the larkspur, the helenium and the chrysanthemums. Emma remembers everything she's told, even the varieties that are foreign to her. She wants to learn the name of every plant by heart, their spellings too, because she is curious. Sara imagines it isn't easy to be this way in her community. To be in love with words, to hunger for the kind knowledge that Sara wants to provide during her Rumspringa.

Last week, when Emma asked about flower-arranging supplies for selling bouquets at the market, Sara suggested other things as well. Emma was an entrepreneur, Sara was sure, a creative, and they discussed what people might like from her mother's stand. Such as soap, or a body lotion or spray.

*Whatever you recommend*, Emma had said. *Mother is grateful for your advice*.

Today they will make soap. Sara has done her research, has already procured the necessary supplies. The aluminum pail and the birchwood molds, the silicone and apricot kernel oils, the cocoa-butter cubes, the oatmeal milk and honey fragrances. It's something Emma has done before, something that won't feel entirely foreign, and Sara can help Emma set the right price when they finish, tell her how to upsell her product for a bigger profit. She knows every penny matters for Eli, and that it's what Peter would want for the Walshes too.

When Emma arrives, Sara is on the veranda, staging their work area, and doesn't hear her approach. She startles, then laughs. "Oh," she says, "it's you."

"Hope I'm not too early," Emma says.

"Not at all," Sara says. "Always better to be early than late."

Emma blinks, and the sunlight catches her eyelashes. Sara hasn't noticed them before, so long, even without a hint of mascara.

"Don't you look pretty," she says, then corrects herself. "That color on you, I mean. Violet is so pretty."

"Thank you," Emma says, but Sara can sense her discomfort. The Amish were modest people.

"It's so hot," she says, changing the subject. "I should have picked you up."

"It wasn't a problem. Father drove me in the buggy."

For a second, Sara muses that if she and Peter had had a daughter, she might have resembled Emma. Not just her eyes, as inquisitive as Peter's, but her serious mouth, her calm tone when she speaks. Goodness, what is she thinking? The chance is long gone. At their ages, the risk of genetic anomalies doubled, percentages Peter could calculate in his sleep. And then there was his deep commitment to his work, long days at the clinic followed by long nights at his desk. All the caretaking would fall to Sara. The feedings, the sleepless nights, the disciplining as their child grew. The banality of suburban motherhood—none of it had ever appealed to her, especially when it came at the cost of the gardening and yoga that grounded her, and reading and rereading as many novels as she desired.

No, they never could have managed it, Sara thinks, and she should be ashamed for comparing an impossible future with the reality of Emma on her doorstep. She should be grateful for what she has, which right now is Emma's companionship, someone to occupy her for the better part of the afternoon.

"Come," Sara says, realizing she's forgotten her washing gloves inside, and Emma follows her through the sliding door to the kitchen.

"You must be thirsty," she says. "And you need gloves too."

"Thank you," Emma says, taking the glass Sara hands her. She gulps down the water so greedily that Sara laughs.

"Thirsty, are we?" she says.

Emma laughs then too, exactly as Sara had, softly, like they are becoming more similar, or at least more familiar. "I suppose so," she says.

When they are on the veranda again, Sara asks why the milk must be frozen.

"So the lye won't scorch the soap," Emma says.

"How long before it melts in the heat?"

"Soon," Emma says, "so we should start."

"I'll get some mats," Sara says, "for under our knees."

When they're both kneeling on the mats, Sara can't help but think once more: Is she too old to try for a child? Peter couldn't tolerate these maudlin musings, her menopausal provocations, as he called them, clinical as always. Last time, she'd been quick to correct him: *I will tell you when it's menopause. This isn't that.*

"Do you have a scale?" Emma asks, and Sara almost flinches at the sweetness of her voice. "We need to weigh the milk first."

"Upstairs," Sara says. "Let me get it." She gives herself a mental shake, but when she's there, in the bathroom, the same thought repeats—how in December she'll be forty; in March, Peter will be fifty-eight. She's thought about suggesting a sperm donor, but this too would aggravate him. He knew the risks to well, he'd say, and why put themselves through an unknown like this, especially now, when his private practice was thriving?

Back on the veranda, Emma weighs the milk and then adds it to the pail with the lye flakes. "Do you have a butter churn we can use?"

"Oh," Sara says. "I didn't think of that."

"Don't worry," Emma says. "A plain spoon will do."

"But it's so hot," Sara says. "I don't want you to overwork."

"I'm fine," Emma says. "I'm used to it. Besides, if we don't finish soon, the mixture will harden."

"Right," Sara says. "You know best." But she wants, at least, to reward Emma for her hard work some other way. "Can I treat you to something after this? How about an ice cream? Would you like one?"

"I can't," Emma says, but when she looks up, Sara senses there's a pulse of something else, curiosity, the same as when she asks Sara about English words.

"Pass me the molds?"

Sara does, but she's practically useless, no help at all as Emma walks her though the next steps. Maybe she can tell Emma something about herself, something she might like to know.

"I used to live in New York City," she says. "For just a little bit, after college. Have you ever been?"

"No," Emma says, but there is the same flicker in her eyes when she looks up, and she pauses her stirring.

"I could barely make rent on my publishing salary. I mostly worked the mail room, shipping books for the sales department. I hated it," she said. "So boring."

"Publishing?" Emma says. "What is publishing?"

"Basically, it's printing books to sell. Someone gets an idea for a book, writes it, and if it's a good idea, a publisher prints it."

"How do you know if it's a good idea?"

"Beats me." Sara laughs. "I only worked in the mail room."

Emma doesn't laugh; she's clearly still thinking, trying to understand. "You mean you just mailed books to people after they were printed, without reading them?"

"Sometimes I read them," Sara says. "The ones that appealed to me."

Emma has resumed her churning, more forcefully, as if she's running out of time. Or has the talk of books scared her? Something about printing, about reading?

"Do you like them?" Sara asks.

"Like what?" Emma meets her eyes again.

"Books," Sara says.

"Oh," Emma says. "I don't really read them. Just the Bible mostly."

"Right," Sara says. "Mostly. So you read something else?"

"*The Book of Martyrs*," she says, lifting the spoon from the pail. Her hands are shaking. From the effort? Sara wants to help, but she doesn't know what to do.

"What is it?" she asks, unsure if she is making things worse by asking.

"It's a book about the Christians who died for God," Emma says. "They suffered horrible deaths so we could be saved." Now her lips are trembling. "Like Beth did."

"Your sister," she says.

Emma nods, glancing back down at the pail, her hands still shaking visibly.

"I'm sorry," Sara says. "I shouldn't have brought it up. I didn't know."

"It's okay," Emma says. "Everything reminds me of her." She isn't crying, and when she looks up, right at Sara, it's almost as if she's glad.

"Let's do the molds later," Sara says. "I mean it. Or we can try again next week. I'll even order some soap wholesale, wrap it up and everything before Saturday. Your mother will be so pleased."

Emma looks startled. Uncomfortable and unsure. Has Sara offered too much again? Said too much?

"Thank you," Emma says. "It's so kind of you."

"I'd really love to take you for ice cream. If you have the time. It's on the way home, anyway."

"I guess Mother won't be expecting me yet," she says, "but are you sure? The garden. We didn't get to it."

"The garden can wait. We are in great shape for the show."

In the car, the radio starts louder than she wants, 96.9, popular music; Sara turns it down. Then she lowers the window, and Emma seems pleased, the breeze ruffling her bonnet.

Sara almost asks if she's ever had ice cream. But that's silly: of course she has. The Amish make their own. She wants to take Emma to the new place downtown, Bonnies, with exotic flavors like basil and lavender mint. But the burger joint with soft serve is closer, on roads more familiar.

"Have you ever been to the Freeze & Frizz?"

"Yes," Emma says. "Once."

"Really?"

Emma nods. "With Isaac."

"Isaac?" Sara says, trying, and probably failing, to hide her excitement. "Your boyfriend?"

"I don't really call him that," Emma says. "We are courting."

"Right," Sara says. "Of course."

Emma reaches her hand out the window then—Sara almost can't believe it—to feel the cool air on her wrist, her open palm.

"Have you been courting long?"

"Just a few months," Emma says. Then offers, shyly, "He's on Rumspringa too."

She doesn't look at Sara, fixed as she is on the cornfields streaming by, the farmhouses and barns, until they reach the strip where the Freeze & Frizz sits by the old package store, on New Holland.

Would Isaac have driven her? Sara wonders. Like this? Did the Amish drive cars on Rumspringa, or did they still take buggies? It's confusing to ponder which risks Emma is comfortable taking and which ones she isn't. Either way, Sara is glad she can get ice cream. What will she order? But when they park by the drive-in, Emma doesn't seem sure she wants to get out. Is she afraid of being seen?

"Would you rather I bring it for you to eat in the car?"

"Oh," Emma says. "No, it's all right. I'll come." She unbuckles then, unlatches the door.

"What did you have the last time?" Sara asks, hoping to put her at ease.

"A vanilla cone," Emma says.

"And what did Isaac get?"

"A vanilla cone."

Sara laughs, then Emma does. "That's a good sign," Sara says. "You like the same things."

"I guess it's what we're used to."

"What about sprinkles?"

Emma pauses as if she's unsure what Sara means.

"You have to get the sprinkles. I'll get some too."

"All right," Emma says.

Sara almost asks if they should be chocolate or rainbow, but that sounds too complicated. Better to decide for her. At the counter, she orders two vanilla cones, both with rainbow sprinkles.

The benches out back are empty. They decide to sit in the shade, under an umbrella.

"How are the sprinkles?" Sara asks.

"Good," Emma says, licking her cone quickly, so it doesn't drip.

Sara does the same, then says, "So—tell me about Isaac."

Emma seems embarrassed, but Sara senses eagerness behind her reluctance.

"Is he the same age?"

"A little older," Emma says. "Nineteen."

"Do you like him?" she asks.

"Yes," Emma says. "We're planning to marry."

"Wow," Sara says. "That's a lot. A few months of dating, and then you marry. But that's how it is."

"For you, too?" Emma asks.

"Oh—Peter and I?"

"Yes," Emma says.

"We dated for years."

"Years?"

"Sometimes it's fast. People fall in deep, they marry. Sometimes people aren't sure and they wait. English people, I mean."

"I know what you meant," Emma says, and Sara is surprised at how assured the statement sounds, like Emma's true self is coming out.

"Tell me about him," Sara says.

Emma hesitates. "He's Isaac," she says. "I don't know what else to say." Before Sara can ask anything else, she adds, "I should get home. Mother needs help with supper."

Inwardly, Sara sighs. Is Emma irritated with her? Sometimes it seems like she wants to open up to Sara, other times like Sara is prying. Sara doesn't know to gauge it right. "Of course," she says. She hasn't finished her cone but tosses it out anyway.

Emma seems perplexed by this, too—that Sara could be so wasteful—but when they are in the car again, Emma is the first to speak.

"Isaac wants me to go to a tavern with him this weekend."

"Really?" Sara says. "Which one?"

"The Stone Tavern," Emma says. "Where my parents met."

Her parents met at a bar, not at church as Sara had assumed, but that was presumptuous of her.

"What will you wear?" she asks, already mentally reviewing her wardrobe, trying to think of why she needs Emma's help another day this week, like Thursday, so Emma can try something on.

It's like Emma can sense her thoughts, the way she says, "I've never been to the mall." Finishing the last bite of her cone, she wipes her hands with a napkin, then her mouth.

"I'm sure I have something for you," says Sara. "How about you come on Thursday? The toad lilies will be in then. They won't take long to plant. Afterward, I'll show you some options."

"Really?" Emma says.

"Really."

"You won't tell the doctor?"

"Now, why would I tell Peter?"

"He's your husband."

"Well, one English thing you should know—we don't tell each other everything. There's a lot I don't know about the clinic, and a lot he doesn't know about the house, the garden. It's a fair trade."

Emma doesn't say anything. Only smiles. "I think I can understand."

# EMMA WALSH

## SPRING 2018

It's Saturday, and I'm wearing the dress of black silk Mrs. Caldwell lent me on Thursday. I am taller than she is, so the hem is above my knees. Mrs. Caldwell gave me lipstick too. Showed me how to apply it in the mirror. I almost couldn't look, but I didn't want Mrs. Caldwell to see me flinch again, like I sometimes do around her. I wanted to be calm, to look straight on for the first time at my reflection, holding the tube like she showed me, following the line of my mouth. *Another layer*, she'd said, handing me a tissue. *Now blot*. I do it this way again inside the bedroom Beth and I used to share. I have to use my dim reflection in the window, in the late afternoon light. *What do you think?* I ask her. *Do I look all right?* Then I wonder: Will Isaac kiss me again tonight? In other places besides my lips?

He doesn't come for me until after dark, in Joshua Fisher's rental car, when Mother and Father are sleeping. I meet him a little down the road—so no one wakes and sees the headlights. They don't need to know about the party, even if they went to them too when they were my age. Even if they know Isaac and want me to marry him.

When he gets out to open the door for me, he's wearing blue jeans and a white shirt that isn't buttoned all the way, exposing a thin gold chain at his neck I haven't seen before. Joshua is behind the wheel. He told Isaac he got his license last summer, but I'm not sure I believe it. I don't know much about him except that he wants to stay English. As I buckle my belt, Isaac smiles at me. "You look nice," he says.

At least I'll know some of the others, I think, when we get to Stone Tavern. Mary Ann Stoltzfus, another girl from Nickel Mines, works there as a waitress. Before she left the community, I'd to see her from time to time at volleyball, after services. She has grafting on her chin from when it happened, where her jaw broke. When it's bright out, you can see shadow lines around the scar, like the one on my shoulder, only hers is out in the open, mine hidden under my dress.

At the bar, my eyes meet hers briefly as Isaac orders drinks. We've never spoken about what happened. What we saw. But as Mary Ann collects used glasses from a nearby table, I want to lean over and ask, *What do you remember?* Same as I want to ask Beth, at night when I write in the cellar. I need only think the word *write*, and I see her there in my mind: Mary Ann, five years old that day, a year younger than me. I hear the sound of her breathing, her muttering as we prayed. *Our Father, who art in heaven, hallowed be thy name*, Mary Ann and I had whispered into our hands.

*Hallowed*, I think, then *hollowed.*

*Hollowed be the name of the English man who took you, my sister. I am alone now, without you.*

Mary Ann fills our water glasses and tells us the specials. As she says the names of English dishes, the lamb chops, the pork ribs, the salmon, I can make out the scar in the candlelight, and I reach for my shoulder.

*You have beautiful shoulders*, Mrs. Caldwell had said on Thursday, but I didn't tell her about the scar, the bullet wound she could not see.

Isaac finds my hand and holds it, as if he senses my distraction, my nerves, around Mary Ann. He orders the French onion soup, then the New York strip. Joshua's date, Naomi Lapp, orders the shrimp scampi. I have never had French soup, English steak, or shrimp. I want to ask about them, ask Isaac if he's tried any of these things, but I don't. I order the fish—filet of cod with wild rice—because maybe it's like the trout in the Susquehanna. This river I know, the one that flows into the creek Beth taught me how to swim in. The creek that gurgles under the bridge Isaac and I walk over, where I smell the wet stones and moss.

I don't find out about the cod, because by the time the food arrives I'm too unsettled to eat, though when Isaac offers a bite of his steak, I say yes. He passes his fork to me, smiling like he's testing what else I might say yes to, and I take it. I savor the salt on the meat, the smoky taste on my tongue, even after I finish my water.

Isaac and Joshua order Johnnie Walkers. "Neat," I hear Isaac say, and I wonder if it means clean, like Mrs. Caldwell's countertops after I spray them. But when the order comes, it's just whiskey, plain, in a small glass, and Isaac drinks it quickly before he slams the glass down. A *shot*, I learn—an English word I immediately want to forget.

When two other girls arrive, Becca Amos is wearing a t-shirt that doesn't cover all of her belly, and you can see the lace on Hannah Miller's bra under her tank top. I think it's silly, their need to make a show of themselves. Then I feel Isaac reach for my hand again. He nudges his whiskey for me to taste, but I say, "No, I'm fine with water."

Isaac doesn't respond, only takes another sip from his glass. When Mary Ann brings more bread for the table, she and Joshua joke like they've been friends for a while. "The English don't know how to do rolls," he says. Becca laughs loudly, but I don't know what's so funny. Is she flirting? But Joshua's girlfriend is already Naomi. Then Mary Ann says she'll join us when she's off in a few hours, for the party at the apartment Joshua's renting off 896.

Tonight, my hair is half down, half pinched-back with Mrs. Caldwell's ivory clip. She said she got in Paris, when Peter took her there, and it's still strange imagining the doctor in France instead of here. To think of him and Mrs. Caldwell walking past expensive shops where she might have bought dresses like the one I'm wearing. We are told English clothes are dangerous because of the attention they attract. Our simple dress is meant to protect us, but Isaac seems so happy with me, the way he keeps turning to me and smiling. At one point he whispers, "You look good." Is it because he's drunk or because of my dress?

Either way, he's losing control, and I don't know how to feel about it, what it means, whether to be afraid. But I can trust Isaac, can't I? Even when he's drunk? I can trust him because he's still the same person, and he loves me. What would Mrs. Caldwell say? That you have to try things to know whether you like them. This dress from her wardrobe, for instance, and her lipstick. Ice cream with sprinkles.

For dessert, Isaac orders us a slice of strawberry pie to share. Before it comes, Joshua tells a story about the auto shop where he works in in Lititz. Something about an English man, a businessman, who didn't know how to change a tire. "Lucky for him," Joshua says, and this time it isn't Becca laughing, but Naomi, his date—Naomi who'd taken a shot of whiskey with the boys.

When Mary Ann comes back with the pie, I work up the courage to ask her how she is, right there before everyone.

She pauses. Smiles. "Fine," she says. "How are you, Emma?"

"Fine," I say, then fall silent, though I want to ask her what it's like, now that she's left us. Would she tell me how she knew she wanted this life? Did Bishop Yoder understand her choice more than he would have otherwise, because of what happened, or is she judged the same? Do her parents act like she is an apostate—a child who might as well be dead?

I want to ask if she likes it better, even though she's without family. I think of how she can read whatever she wants, write whatever she wants. In public. On a park bench. Even take the train to the city, no longer worried about her hem length or bonnet. What was it like to let her hair down the first time and know she'd never have to cover it again?

I begin to feel strange. When Isaac nudges our dessert plate closer so I can try the pie, I can't feel my hands as easily. They aren't shaking. I'm not afraid, but there is numbness in me as I watch Mary Ann clearing another table. The sound of the plates when she stacks them on her arm is louder than usual. Even in this noisy tavern. At home, our farm is so quiet I can hear every clink of Mother's fork when she is pushing around her food, every chime of the clock in the parlor. In the summer, I can hear every bird's song, and in autumn the gentle rustle of the wind through the trees.

It's as if the tavern has stopped still, like it does at home when God shines His light over us, blessing our table. And yet God isn't here, not clearly. How can He be if I am English tonight, no longer pliable in his hands like a paper doll, or a piece of communion dough rolled between two sisters? Mary Ann is something like a sister, I think, the closest I have, and if I left, I would also be without family, a lone woman in the world, . . . and yet I wouldn't be alone, not like I am now with no sister to talk to in the open.

When it happens, the panic, the numbing, I've learned to scrunch my toes in my shoes to feel them there. To push down on the pads of my feet, knowing they're on the ground. Before the milkman came, Mary Ann and I used to play at house with our dolls in the schoolyard. We used to exchange hairpins when we lost them, so our bonnets stayed on.

Isaac wants me to take another bite of pie, and I do, though I wish it had rhubarb like we make at home. The tartness of the rhubarb balances the sweetness. "I'm finished," I say. "I'm full."

"You barely ate your dinner. Are you sure?"

His words don't slur. And he's paying attention. He can't be too drunk, then.

"I'm sure," I say, smiling.

"You're cute," he says, another word I've never heard him use. He leans in to kiss me on the cheek. Before Mary Ann takes our plate away, he forks up a last bite, finishing the pie.

In the car, Joshua rolls the windows down, and the breeze cools my face like in Mrs. Caldwell's car. How good the air feels on my skin. Isaac's hand rests over mine, as if he wants to prove I'm his. But how can I be anyone's but mine, if my thoughts and words are mine? I want to write about the breeze, the silk of the night, how I belong to the air when I close my eyes and turn to the open window.

At a long stoplight, Joshua lights a cigarette. I read the box he keeps in the center console. *Marlboro*. I won't ever smoke, but I like this English word, like Dalloway, like delphinium. Soon, the air turns bitter in the car, even with the rolled-down window. Joshua senses this, stubbing his Marlboro into the ashtray he's made of a drink holder.

When we pull up to his rental, the lights are already on, and I can hear music blasting through the speakers. Rap, I know, from the sound of the bass. The kind of music Isaac loves. On our third courting walk, he said the bass makes his heart beat faster, like it's vibrating. I know what he means, and I don't, because the music is too loud for me. But I expect it, at least, so it's not like "Eleanor Rigby," when the song started without warning. It was the sound of different strings, Mrs. Caldwell had explained later, showing me pictures from a book. Of a violin and cello, a bass and a piano.

Joshua is playing rap on the stereo, and when we enter he turns up the volume with a remote control. There are red, blue, and green lights blinking over the wall. "Strobe lights," Isaac says when I ask him. Like *autotune*—the other word he explains when the voices change behind the rap music, this electronic sin. It's only temporary, I tell myself. I am only trying it out. At a real English party, in a real English dress.

In the kitchen, boys stand over girls, talking close to their ears. Everyone is holding large red cups. Isaac pours two for us, from a tall clear bottle on the counter. Stolichnaya, it reads, a foreign language. "Russian," Isaac says when he sees that I am trying to understand the label. He watches as I take a sip, but even that's too much. I cough, and he laughs. "Goes down like water, doesn't it?"

More of the English joking I'm still getting used to. *Sarcasm*, Mrs. Caldwell called it on Thursday, when I walked out of the bathroom in her clothes. *You look terrible*, she'd said, and when I wanted to hurry back and change, she explained she was joking. *I'm being sarcastic. You look stunning.* It's like the English need to lie to say what they mean.

I don't know how the other girls afford their clothes. Most probably don't have medical bills like we do, but still. I also don't know how they choose what to buy. How they decide between shirts and kinds of makeup and the high heels they wear to parties. When I don't sip more of my Russian drink, Isaac says he'll make me something sweeter. Something I'll like. He reaches for a liter of Pepsi, which I've seen at the market, where they sell chips and candy. He mixes the Pepsi with what he tells me is rum, showing me the bottle. I try it, and he's right. It's easier to drink. Sweet like birch beer, I decide, like a molasses donut, except there aren't any crumbs.

Isaac starts talking to some boys I don't know. Joshua's friends, likely. One is from the auto shop where Joshua works. Another is a mason, and a carpenter like Father. Some of them can stay and work in the English world after their Rumspringa, like Isaac will when we marry, without dressing in English coveralls and hooded shirts. Some will wear blue jeans streaked with sawdust and paint, burning their plain, collarless suits, or leaving them for their brothers.

A boy who must have left the community already says he's going to a Phillies game at the stadium, same as last year. He's on a bar stool drinking beer. The girl on his lap is wearing a black shirt you can see through.

"I like your dress," she says, smiling. Is she being nice, or does she feel sorry for me? I realize I'm clutching my elbows instead of my drink. Isaac hands me my cup to hold, and I drink so she can see.

"Thank you," I tell her. This girl isn't afraid of showing her breasts like I am. She isn't afraid of what people think, what they might say. Isaac presses his hand along my shoulder blades. His hands are warm, though I feel cold.

Then another boy, this one in baggy jeans, offers Isaac a cigarette. Isaac nods, excuses himself. I almost follow, but I don't want him to think I depend on him that way. And yet I do, don't I? If we marry? He'll provide the food, and I'll bake the bread and raise the children and darn the socks for my husband, the one who keeps us safe.

"I love this band," the girl says, making conversation. She looks at me like she is waiting for me to say something else, tell her my favorite song. "The National," she says like she knows it's my first party. "They're so good."

"Like the United States, you mean?" I say.

"I guess," she says, looking like she might laugh. "But there are other nations."

"Yeah," I say, wishing I'd traveled to Paris like Mrs. Caldwell. Or Russia or England. A nation could be any body of people, any place. I know this, and yet I'd said something stupid.

"How long have you been together?" she asks.

"Me and Isaac?" I say.

"Yeah," she says. "Who else? You're funny."

I can't tell if she means a compliment, or if she's being sarcastic. Because the English like to laugh.

"Isaac, yeah. We've been courting for some weeks now."

"Seriously?" she says. "It's like you guys are married already."

"Maybe so," I say. "Our parents are friends." This sounds silly too. Of course everyone's parents are friends, or at least they once were, those who didn't stay.

"You should totally go to the drive-in. Have you been? They're playing *Jaws* tomorrow. I want to go, but I can't. Have to work."

I won't ask her what she means by jaws. A person's mouth for a movie, or if it's something else. But I do tell her I am going soon, to the movies, which isn't a lie.

"My friend's taking me," I say. I mean Mrs. Caldwell. On Thursday, when I tried on her clothes, she said she would take me to a show, as a treat.

"Cool," the other girl says, taking another sip from her beer.

I almost ask where she works, but I don't want to risk saying anything else that's stupid. I glance away, looking for Isaac. He's on the deck, and I watch him through the screen door off the kitchen. As he leans into another boy's lighter, a flame catches the small cigarette in his mouth. Isaac waves the smoke and laughs quietly about something between him and the other boy. For a second he turns, like he knows I'm watching. He smiles, and I smile back.

It isn't long before he's back in the kitchen, his arm draped around my shoulder. "Are you cold?" he asks.

"A little," I say.

"I'll warm you up." And then he's leading me upstairs.

"I'm good," I say. "Can we stay here a little while?" I don't want him to think I'm boring, or a prude like I've heard other boys on Rumspringa call girls who don't go along with the fun, but I'm not ready yet.

"That'll help," he says, meaning my drink. I give him this, another sip or two.

"Let's dance," he says, pulling me to the crowd of teenagers by the speakers. A girl nearby is wiggling backside into a boy, her hands reaching back for his neck. Does Isaac want this of me? I don't understand the difference, now, between dancing and having intercourse. I am ashamed to think what Mother would say, but then Isaac leans in to kiss me. My knees feel soft, my hands numb like before, but it's nice, the sweetness on his tongue. Someone whistles. I want to pull away, but everything ripples like water, and I clutch Isaac for balance. We drink more from our cups, and he holds me gently by my hips while we dance—slowly, not fast like the others, and I trust him better.

I drink more than I realize, with the music, in the strobe lights. After a while, my cup is empty, my cheek pressed to Isaac's chest, and I can hear his heart. "Come on," he whispers. "Let's go." He looks at the stairwell, and I nod. I follow him because at least upstairs it'll be quiet. Upstairs we can be away from everyone.

"Joshua's room," Isaac says when he opens a door. There are posters on the wall. A woman in an English swimsuit, her skin kissed by the sun, the tops of her breasts bare. On the nightstand a deck of playing cards and an ashtray brimming with cigarette butts. When I slip off my shoes, I can't feel my feet. I'm not ready, I think, but then Isaac reaches for my face and starts kissing me again. He reaches behind him and turns off the lights. He pushes some coats off the bed.

I'm numb again, clinging to the same sweetness of his tongue, forgetting where I am. When he takes off his shirt off, the muscles around his chest are carved. I reach to feel them against my palms. He kisses my neck, and his body feels as soft as the silk of my dress as he pushes off my straps. I am spinning with him, to somewhere I've never been, in the dark. I'm afraid, yet I feel at home.

He whispers, "You're so beautiful," and I want to believe him as he kisses my bare breasts and we melt deeper into the room. Then he unzips his pants and reaches for my face again, holding it in his hands. "I love you," he says.

"I love you, too," I say, warmth spreading through my stomach, around my waist and hips as he holds me close. I'd follow him anywhere, just the two of us, and it would be okay.

He guides me to the bed, lies on his back and pulls me over him.

Was this what it was to love someone? To hold their body as long as you wanted, whenever you wanted? Or was it only in the English world when you felt pleasure for pleasure's sake, not just because you were making children? If we were English together, we could do this after supper every night, and in the morning, hold each other instead of feeding the chickens and horses and cows.

Isaac's body is arching over mine, and I wince at the sudden pain. I don't remember when he slipped inside me.

"Are you okay?" he asks, pulling away. "We don't have to."

My body tightens. "I know," I whisper. "I want to." *I do*, this is true, though I am afraid.

"We'll go really slow," he says, "if you're sure." He kisses my ear, then my mouth again, and it's easier to relax like before. Reaching between my legs, he touches me gently there. I don't know how he knows what to do, like he's been practicing, when it's only ever been me and him. *Me and him* I repeat to myself, closing my eyes as he kisses over my stomach and between my legs. This time, when he eases into me, it hurts less. I feel our bodies learning how to fit together.

Isaac moves faster over me, moaning, and I brace him, hold him like we are falling off the edge of the earth. I'm wondering how far we can fall when he moans louder, tensing, and then he relaxes and slumps over me. I sigh, unsure what to feel. There are tears around my eyes. I wipe them away.

"I love you," he says, reaching for my waist again, pulling me still closer.

"I love you," I say, but the numbness is still there. I was holding him the whole time, and I don't understand why I can't feel my body against his in the room.

It isn't long before Isaac falls asleep. He breathes deeply, and I can smell the rum on his breath. I try to pray, to sleep by him like this, but I know I can't stay. Downstairs, the music is still playing loudly as I get up and dress. I walk down the stairs, wondering what people think if they see me. *Whore*, I've heard boys call girls who give in too easily. The girls who aren't boring prudes. But Isaac would never say this about me. He loves me.

The crowd is denser than before. To make my way past people, I have to push through clusters of them like something is wrong. I start to feel like it is. Faces turn toward me as I walk in my crinkled dress. I am alone in their eyes, and I can't tell Isaac. I won't. A girl in a checkered shirt laughs while she dances, nearly stumbling into me, and then I pass an older man with a white beard—an English man—and I don't understand why he's here.

The moment I'm outside, I run, sensing heaviness in my body even while I can't feel my legs or face or hands. It's night, and I don't know how far from home I am, but there are streetlights, and I'm running past the summer cornfields, then a flickering television in a window. I see an Englishwoman like Mrs. Caldwell; she probably watches movies or reads books into the later part of the night while her husband sleeps.

The longer I run, the more my toes hurt, blisters burning my feet. I take off my shoes and hold them. My legs ache, but I can't stop and risk being seen by a truck, by a man, in a dress like this. Gravel digs into my callused feet, but I don't stop running until I reach home. When I see our house, I almost don't believe it, and I nearly weep when I reach the cool grass, feel it under my toes.

Inside, I find I can't sleep right away. I have to stop and breathe. I go to the cellar to write what I remember of the dew in the morning grass. How it caught on webs between blades of green gleaming in the sun. How Beth used to run and run just to feel the dew. Finally, I crawl to some empty feed sacks and roll onto my side, tuck my legs to my chest. I'm warm, sweat along my neck and mouth, my cheeks hot, as my lids close. I don't know how long I sleep, but when I rouse, the house is still quiet. I can return to my room before Mother and Father wake for chores. I tiptoe up the stairs, change into my nightdress, and fall asleep wondering about joy and terror, joy and sin, how they live together in you, and in me.

# RUTH WALSH

## SUMMER 2019

She is still saving the pie for Mrs. Caldwell. It's been days since she last checked on it, though she meant to the other morning—after that night she couldn't sleep—but then she'd forgotten. Abraham had been the one to remind her yesterday, when he noticed it in the cellar, the fruit flies, perhaps even some mold under the wrapping, and asked if she was saving it for some reason. *Oh, I'll check and see*, she said. *I'm not certain what you mean*. Two lies. Ruth wouldn't check and see, and she did know what he was referring to—of course she knew. She kneels then, to pray, *Lord, please forgive my sins, for I have failed to tell my husband the truth about the pie I am saving.* Then she rises. Ties her bib apron over her dress, washes her hands. The Lord will be pleased she is making a fresh batch for market today—that there will be a new pie to bring to Mrs. Caldwell—that all will be well again, in a matter of hours.

The ingredients are already on the table. The flour and butter and milk, the cherries and sugar. Even the wax paper and baking dish. The scoring knife.

It's gray today, like it might rain. By the window, shadows pass over Eli as he sleeps. Easier for him to rest in his chair, she thinks, without too much sun.

She always starts with the filling, cooking down the cherries, which are ripe and full, newly pitted. She stirs slowly, thankful for the kerosene heat in the cast-iron stove, breathing in the cherries she has always found beautiful, not just their color and taste, but for the words that describe them. *Tart. Red. Sweet.* Moving the words around in her mind, she remembers Emma's writing, the rushed script, as if her daughter couldn't get the words on the page fast enough.

That Emma would write for the sheer pleasure of it—Ruth still can't understand why. And more than simply writing them, Emma had kept them. Had sought to preserve these words, this sin.

Ruth stirs the mixture again, peering into the red to know its texture better, and when the skins begin to overheat, juices boiling up from the flesh, she doesn't turn down the heat, not yet, inhaling the ferment the cherries until she can practically taste them. She wants to prolong these moments, her favorite of the entire process, Emma's too—but the last time they'd done this together, sharp words had passed between them.

*It's my choice*, Emma had said, *if I want to be baptized.*

Ruth had whirled from the stove. *What do you mean?* She'd raised her voice: frantic-sounding. Uncomprehending, and yes, angry.

Ever since she was a girl on the threshing floor, a girl among other unbaptized girls, she'd longed to work alongside the other sisters, kneading the dough with them, to prepare for the love feast. She assumed Emma had desired the same, that she had watched with reverence as a child, same as Beth had, the passing of the mounds, the scoring, and waiting for the heat and smoke from the oven to move to the forebears, while the men sang of a woman's duty, her humility in becoming of one body.

*If I want to be baptized.* Emma's words cut into Ruth again now. She presses a kitchen towel to her forehead to feel the coolness.

By God's grace Ruth had learned to control her emotions, endure discomfort without complaint, confront any unknown with impassiveness, pray when she became afraid. She wants to pray now. What is she afraid of? She turns off the stove. The cherries cooked too long, but there is enough mixture to salvage, adding sugar and lemon juice for the filling. She can work on the pie crust. In a large basin, she sifts the flour and salt and baking soda, then reaches for the cold butter from her tin, pushing pieces of it in. The flour tightens around the butter, forming little pebbles in her hands she presses into, kneading them like flesh, though she would never tell anyone this, never write it down—that sometimes the dough reminds her of a body.

She adds water, another dash of salt, then more flour a bit at a time, working to achieve the right consistency, something that bends and folds but doesn't collapse. A little dryness in the crust was good—but not to the point of brittleness. It wasn't like making bread on the threshing floor, when you had to work with the piece of dough you'd been given. During Pentecost, the night before communion, every baptized woman gathered before the table, while the deacon recited the sermon. For many years now, Ruth had taken her place among the other sisters, passing the dough in bits until they were combined into a single mound to be rolled and flattened, then scored into four separate pieces, pierced to represent the wounds of Christ, before the loaf was placed in the oven to rise.

*Worthy is Christ, the Lamb who was slain, whose blood set us free to be people of God. . . .* Ruth wants to sing, lift her voice to the heavens as she does in the sermon barn . . . but a woman was never to sing alone, never to eat alone, never to walk alone, not even in an open pasture.

She can almost hear the voices singing in praise, see the light pouring in beyond the forebay, through the doors, the light that once called to her, just as the light of the English world beckoned Emma—from the open pages of the books loaned to her by Mrs. Caldwell. When Ruth baked bread with the other sisters, she never questioned the thickness of the dough, not like she does now for the pie, the eighth of an inch she is determined to get right for market.

She tells herself she can make a perfect crust in her sleep, but today, when she coats the table with flour and rolls it out, it's off, too stiff. She scraps what she has, reforms the dough into a ball in her hands, adds water. When she fails again, she begins again, suppressing any doubt, her shame over the time she has wasted. But to form a body in Christ's image, it had to be right, the body, the flesh of the child. She almost doesn't think she's heard right, what she's muttered aloud for anyone to hear: *the flesh of the child.*

During the breadmaking ceremony, scrapping the dough wasn't an option, neither was adding more flour, more water, or salt. Once the dough had been kneaded, you couldn't knead it again. A sister received what she was given. Made the most of what she had, becoming pliable in His hands before her worktable, while the men sang *Alleluia . . . this is the feast of victory for our God . . . alleluia . . .*

And yet, Ruth keeps kneading—*kneading, needing*, she doesn't know the difference now, the sound of her fist resounding, pounding, she doesn't know how long, how hard, and when she stops her hands are aching. Bruised. She starts to sigh, but breath catches in her throat, and she drops to the floor again. Not kneeling; she is sprawled on the wood floor in the gray light. She presses her palms together and prays, but no words will come, no clear verse, the lamb who was slain, the victory of our God . . . blessing and honor and glory and peace, all of it escapes her as she weeps.

# SARA CALDWELL

## SPRING 2018

Peter works late most nights, and somehow, they've gotten used to this pattern: Peter at the clinic, and Sara getting dinner ready. For years, she's told herself she likes to cook, that she finds it relaxing. Gratifying, even. Especially when she uses fresh herbs from the garden, such as the parsley that went into the meatballs tonight. Or the fresh garlic and rosemary she's pressed into the focaccia with olive oil, the scent of it filling the kitchen as she takes a sip of white wine from her glass.

"How was your day?" Peter washes up at the kitchen sink when he arrives, greeting Sara as he would one of his patients. As he's drying his hands, he pauses to look at her, as though thinking, and she wonders if he knows. Had Emma mentioned the clothes Sara lent? The lipstick and shoes? She won't see Emma again until tomorrow morning; suddenly, the twelve hours that must elapse until then feels like a long stretch of time.

"Fine," she says. "Dinner is ready. I made fresh focaccia."

"Oh, that sounds nice."

He's already heading upstairs to change. He always works out before dinner—on the NordicTrack they keep in the sunroom. Doesn't matter how cold his food might have gotten, nor how much time Sara has put into the meal: His workout comes first. His reasons are health related. Men were most susceptible to heart disease in their fifties. Peter exercised at least thirty minutes a day, the equivalent of five songs from Eric

Clapton's *Unplugged* album, so Sara takes her time setting the table. She sips more wine than she should, oddly calmed by the sound of Peter's machine swishing at top speed in the other room.

*What's this?* Emma asked last week when she went to dust the elliptical.

Sara was sure she'd wondered before and was pleased she'd finally asked.

*Calories?* Emma said after Sara explained the machine's purpose was to burn them.

How did one begin to tackle that topic? Sara wondered. *You don't want too many*, Sara had begun, *or more than you need?* Not surprising that Emma seemed confused. *If you eat too much and don't exercise enough, it is bad for your heart*, Sara said finally.

Emma simply nodded and finished dusting the machine. Then she sprayed the windows, cleaned the floors with lemon oil.

Now, as Sara slides the cloth napkins through their wooden rings—the ones she and Peter bought on safari—she can't help but think it was ridiculous, not the napkin rings, but the elliptical. That Peter would exert so much effort, breathing audibly, sweating profusely, in his faded t-shirt from college, squeezing water from a bottle in short bursts. Peter looked like he was braving Kilimanjaro—all to stay in shape for his much younger wife? All so he wouldn't die too early, leaving Sara before she was ready. How to explain this to a girl such as Emma? Why even try?

When Peter is finished and showered, he returns with a healthy sheen on his cheeks. Sara has been keeping the food warm on the stove, and while she prepares their plates in the kitchen, she hears him say, "Dammit. Goddammit."

"What?" Sara enters the dining room to find Peter swatting at the air.

"Did you leave the windows open again?"

"No. Why—"

"I don't know why we have mosquitos in the house."

"I wasn't even out today," she says. "It was too hot. Besides, it rained all afternoon."

"Maybe the screen door is broken." Peter shakes his head, filling his own wine glass and taking a big gulp. Then he reaches for a large piece of focaccia.

"Good thing there's plenty," Sara says. She's being sarcastic, of course. The fact that he can't even wait for her to finish serving . . . and yet she doesn't speak her mind. Instead, she says without thinking, "I'm worried about Emma."

Peter finishes chewing. Swallows. Follows up with more wine. "Emma?"

They haven't really talked about her, not since Emma started working for Sara. It has felt important to maintain the boundary between personal and professional, but Sara can't help herself, can't hold it in: "She's so easily agitated. Nervous, you know?"

"I'm not sure I do," Peter says.

"Like the other day," Sara says, "I was playing some music to lighten the mood, but then her body seized. She went into a kind of shock."

"Sara," Peter says sternly. "What would you do that for?"

He swats at the air again, but she doesn't see anything. Not even a mote of dust.

"What do you mean?"

Peter rises and goes to the fridge for another bottle of white. "This is just what I was afraid of." He rummages in a kitchen drawer for the opener. "Emma's situation is sensitive."

Sara watches as he scores the foil with the corkscrew's blade, peels it off with unnecessary force. She can't take it anymore, this unspoken thing between them.

"Why didn't you tell me she'd been in the schoolhouse?" she says.

"What are you—"

"After her reaction the other day, I looked up the names of the survivors online."

"Sara," Peter begins, but still, she will not let him finish.

"Don't you think it's something I should have known before she started here? I could have taken more precautions."

"Precautions? Wait. What have you done?" Peter is gripping the neck of the wine bottle.

"Nothing," she says. "Nothing." But they both know this isn't true. That once Sara gets invested in something—a person, a cause—she becomes obsessed.

"You know as well as I do why I didn't," Peter says. "The Amish are private people." He takes a deep breath, applies the corkscrew. "Their boundaries are sacred."

"Boundaries?" Sara says. "Have you ever stopped to consider how absurd it is? How contradictory? That they are strict about their way of life, and yet they keep their doors unlocked, their schools and homes open to strangers. How else could the shooting have happened?"

"Sara." Peter is nearly yelling now. "What is wrong with you? They are God-loving people. What happened was unimaginable. Unspeakable. You're acting like some kind of authority on the topic, when you don't know the first thing—"

Sara stops him there. "That's where you're wrong, Peter. I do know the first thing. I know about abuse, about trauma. I know what it means for a woman to feel unsafe in her own home, her own community."

"Do you now?" Peter says. "Do you, really?"

"What about you? You think you know better—what it means to be a woman today?"

Peter pulls forcefully at the cork until it releases.

"Look," Sara says. "I don't want to make your work harder for you, or more complicated, but I do care about Emma. She is so impressionable, and she shouldn't have to carry her wounds silently, like she has been, for the rest of her life."

Peter refuses to speak. He refills his glass, then hers.

"If something like that had happened to you, can you imagine being told to forgive the perpetrator? Never talking or writing about it? Never grieving?"

"Of course I've thought about this," Peter says. He is looking down at his hands over the wine glass.

"I just think we need to support Emma in finding her own path. Through the gray area." Sara walks over to Peter, placing her hand over his. "What if it had been our child," she says, "in the schoolhouse?"

Peter jerks away. "Our child? Sara, you've gone too far. You're acting like—" Peter stops himself. Turns away.

"Like what?"

"Never mind."

"Go on and say it." Sara is still standing behind him, her muscles clenched.

"Emma has been through a great deal," he says. "There is no denying that, but talk therapy, or EMDR or mindfulness training, whatever it is you're thinking, is off the table."

"I never said any of those things," Sara says, her voice tight. "It's unfair of you to assume—"

"Look. I know it's been a while since you've felt connected, like you're helping teens the way you used to. But this isn't the answer."

"I'm not talking about that, Peter. I'm talking about a young woman who has her whole future ahead of her, a woman in the middle of making crucial decisions about her life, and she has no tools. These are separate points."

"You're right," Peter says. "I shouldn't have assumed that the two things are related."

Now he is the one being sarcastic, the one set on closing the subject, which he does before they've even taken a bite.

"I have some work to finish," he says.

"Whatever." Sara reaches for her own full plate, takes it to the kitchen and drops it in the sink. Then she drains what's left of her wine, holding the chilled glass against her throat. Her free hand grips the countertop as Peter brings in his plate, and before he can leave, she says, "There's something else."

"Something else?" He sounds shocked that she'd continue a conversation he's made a point to end.

"Can you sit down?" She meets his eyes, lets her expression tell him it's serious.

"All right," he says. "What is it?" His voice has changed to match hers.

"I know it's been a while since we've talked about it. But I've been thinking. What if we tried again?" She draws her hand to her stomach.

"What?" He shakes his head. "What are you even—"

"Try for a child," she says. "When we talked about it all those years ago, I was too young, foolish, really. To understand."

"No." He stands up, heads to the kitchen sink, braces his arms on the counter. He stares out the window, though there's nothing beyond it but darkness.

"Peter, please," she says. "Just hear me out. There are options."

When he turns to face her, his eyes are colder than she's ever seen them.

"Honestly," he says, "I can't believe you'd even bring this up, and—" He pauses. "—I don't want to talk about it again." As he spins away and heads for the doorway, something tips. A glass along the edge of the sink. It shatters.

"Fuck," he says. "Goddamn it." He reaches for a paper towel, wraps it around his finger, which he holds above his heart.

"What happened?" she says. "Peter." But her voice sounds theatrical now, even to her, and he is disregarding her, working with one hand to unlatch the first aid kit under the sink. When she moves to help him, he shoos her away, tearing the tape from a roll with his teeth.

"At least let me get the broom," she says.

"Forget it, Sara," he says, wrapping the tape around a square of gauze.

"It will only take a minute—"

"I said forget it!"

He turns his back to her again, grips the sink, his shoulders stiff. With anger or sadness? Sara can't pinpoint what he's feeling, why he won't even consider the idea of a child. Was he worried about his reputation, the risk of genetic complication? What kind of hypocrite did that make him?

"I have some work to do," he says again, already on his way to his office in the basement. Where Emma never goes to clean. Peter made a point of that in the beginning. His office was off limits, lest Emma read something, learn something she shouldn't know about her own, or someone else's, family.

The house suddenly feels suffocating, and Sara reaches for her car keys on the counter. A night drive always did her good, helped her to decompress when no tv show or novel or gardening catalog would do.

She's been doing it since they moved, taking long drives when she tires of their circumscribed suburban life. Sometimes she just goes to the nearest gas station for a cup of coffee; other times she drives until her mind is clear again. She's made it as far as Reading or Carlisle or Gettysburg before, especially on a clear night when she can roll down the windows. Tonight, as she blazes along the back roads, bluish trees fill her periphery. The road too: a deep gray-blue in her headlights. She passes through the bridge on Hunsecker, almost turns right to continue the loop, but at the stop she decides on Snake Hill, Emma's road, because the deeper one travels into the countryside, the more beautiful it gets.

She follows the long hill past barns and silos, farmhouses with wide front porches, unlit except for her low beams. She only flashes them on high for an instant around curves, to check for stray dogs, or deer. When she approaches the Zook farm stand, she can read the familiar sign for CUCUMBERS, LETTUCE, SUGAR PEAS. Pulling up to their stand, she studies the mounds of produce, then the small collection box illuminated by her headlights. Unattended, unmonitored. Anyone could steal from it. Truckers, English teenagers desperate for another pack of pricey cigarettes. The trust, she thinks, the continued trust in us, after everything.

The windows of the Zook's farmhouse are dark. No doubt everyone is already asleep. When you woke before dawn, you went to bed early.

Sara continues past the stand. She intends to keep going, take the longer loop to the creek, to hear the wood thrush, the crickets and bullfrogs. This means passing the Walsh house, which she also intends to do, yet when she's a hundred yards away, maybe less, she catches sight of Emma on the porch, backlit by the kerosene lamps. Without conscious thought, she takes her foot off the gas, turns off her lights, coasts until she is close enough to see better, then pulls off the side of the road, letting her eyes adjust to the dark.

Emma's mother is there on the porch too. Ruth, wasn't it? And a third figure? Sara can't be certain, and she finds herself exiting the car, walking stealthily toward the house until she gets close enough to see the boy in his wheelchair—the brother Peter is treating. She crouches behind a tree to study him. In the kerosene glow, his head is lolling. He's awake, but the two women pay no attention, focused as they are on some kind of ritual. There is a bucket involved. At first she thinks they are shelling peas, but in the muddled glow, Sara sees mounds of red.

Were they pitting cherries? The market wasn't until Saturday morning, but of course it took time to make all of the goods Emma's mother sold there. Sara can't imagine the preparation, this constant work at all hours.

Sara has never really asked Emma about her mother. Whether they're close. Was that even a question to ask? Was closeness, emotional intimacy, something the Amish thought about in their relationships? Or did such things remain unexamined, unspoken in their pragmatic world: a mother cared for her daughter until it was time for her daughter to care for her? A daughter cared for her siblings when her mother was occupied. A daughter helped her mother with whatever had to be done. It was that simple.

Sarah is afraid to linger, worried they'll sense her watching, look up and see her car. What then? Before she can retreat, however, Eli begins convulsing, making terrible sounds. It happens fast, with no warning, but Ruth's response is also fast. She reaches for a mason jar and tilts it to her son's lips. Water drips down his chin. He struggles for a moment, then calms and seems to take the water. Not a seizure, but a coughing fit. Now Emma is holding her brother's hand. Ruth waits, tips the glass once more to Eli's lips, until he is no longer coughing. Then Ruth stands, tells Emma something, and Emma steps inside. Sara watches Ruth brace Eli in the darkness, her hand at the back of his head while she soothes him.

There was a teenager at the prison who suffered from a form of autism—a boy who repeatedly pressed his thumb into the points of the miniature pencils until they bled. During her first visit, a guard came and took the boy away. Sara never saw him again. That was twelve years ago, her last term before writing her thesis, and she hadn't been back to work since.

Sara should turn away, leave the family to their own devices, and yet she can't. How many times has Ruth had to calm her boy? How many times since his first episode, since she'd started going to Peter for treatments?

Eli was at least five, maybe ten years younger than Emma. Born after the schoolhouse? Ruth would be in her forties now. Sara is certain that Peter would have warned her about having more children after Eli, about the risks. Had she, like Sara, been stopped in her tracks—allowed her doubts and fears to keep her from moving forward? What would someone like Ruth think of her? Assume about a woman like Sara? Perhaps how easy her life must be compared to Ruth's. If Emma told her mother about Sara's gardening projects, her garden shows, would Ruth assume her empty? Vain?

Sara is in the car again, breathing hard though she hasn't exerted herself. The windows are up, the engine idling. Sara backs out slowly, hoping to avoid notice. When she's on Hunsecker again, she tunes the radio to a clear station. Classical. 90.1 FM. She loses track of time as she drives on. At a certain stretch, trees encroach, their branches blocking out the moon, the stars, and Sara turns on her high beams. Then she keeps them on, forgetting everything but the road, suddenly illuminated.

# EMMA WALSH

## SUMMER 2018

Every Sunday, after church services I wash Eli's hair. He usually cooperates well enough after he's in the tub, but the getting him in is the hard part. He slaps at me, moans, and I tell him, "You're all right, Eli." But this afternoon I'm more tired than usual. Impatient, even.

"Stop, stop!" I nearly yell at him when he slaps at the sponge. I hold his hands down, then kiss them to prove he's safe. He relaxes a little. I squeeze the sponge over his neck, his back. "There," I say.

When I lean over the tub to reach under his arms, over his chest, to scrub his legs, his knees, I feel an aching in my breasts, a tenderness I'm not used to. I try to dismiss the discomfort, hurrying to shampoo Eli's hair, but the tenderness in my chest is deep and aching.

I tilt back Eli's head, pouring water over his scalp before he can slap the cup away. He cries, kicks in the water. "I'm almost done," I say, but then, when I try to lift him out of the tub, the pain is worse. I call Mother for help, and she comes.

"What is it?" she says.

"I think I'm getting sick."

"Oh," she says. "I can take over from here. Go on and get some rest."

"It's just the lifting," I say. "I can help you dry."

"All right," she says, reaching under Eli's arms to pull him out. I support him as best as I can, and when he is on the bathmat, we prop him up and wrap him, even as he squirms, resisting us, as usual.

It's usually easy for me to hold Eli's legs down, but now my grip is unsteady. I am dizzy. Lightheaded.

"Emma," Mother says. "Go on and rest now. Have you eaten today?"

"Just a little bread." I hadn't felt hungry. The bread tasted strange.

"I'll fix you something," she says. "You'll feel better once you sleep."

As I lie down in bed, my thoughts turn dim, blurry. I've been more tired than usual lately. After I do just one thing, I feel I must sit down, catch my breath.

I've seen Isaac only once since the party. When he called on me last, I said I had chores. I miss him, and yet I'm afraid to see him. I left early that night and woke up feeling sore the next morning. I woke up sick. Now I fear the sickness won't go away, as punishment for being with Isaac before we married.

The sound of the music, the sweet taste of rum, my silk straps over my shoulders, fallen as Isaac kissed there, made me a sinner before the Lord. Worse, I didn't repent right away. I had gone to bed without praying, still warm with drink. My head hot, as it is now, my eyes turning the shadows drifting over the curtains into gnarled branches.

The Tuesday after the party, Mrs. Caldwell told me about her college years in Massachusetts. In Boston, she said, a big city hours away. She'd described the parties in dorm rooms. When I asked her what a dorm room was, she said it was where college students lived during the school year.

*We used to eat pizza in the middle of the night. Dip the crust in ranch dressing. They call it the freshman fifteen*, she'd said, shaking her head.

*Fifteen?*

*Pounds*, she said. *From all the pizza and beer.*

I think I'll be sick. I reach for the edge of my bed, on the verge of vomiting, but the wave subsides. I breathe. Thank God, I can breathe.

The doctor has weighed me many times. I've never told Mrs. Caldwell about those visits—how I used to go every week after the Happening. I don't like talking about myself. I'd rather learn about her life instead. About her college years, about the campus she said was full of brick buildings covered in ivy. Libraries bigger than churches, filled with books.

She still doesn't know about my borrowing *Mrs. Dalloway*. Because I returned it already. But she knows I'm curious about books—sees me reading the spines each time I dust them. She has so many I've never heard of. Plays by William Shakespeare with titles in gilt lettering. More books written by women, even when I don't know they are. Like *Middlemarch*. When I spoke the title and the author's name, Mrs. Caldwell caught me; she said, *George Eliot is a woman, you know.*

*But George is a man's name, isn't it?*

*It is,* Mrs. Caldwell said. *But the author wrote under a pseudonym, at a time when it was very difficult for women to get their books published.*

*What is it about?* I asked.

*Marriage. About marrying out of obligation—or marrying for love. Women didn't used to have as many choices as they do now.*

Was marrying Isaac a choice? Or was it an obligation, especially now, after we'd sinned at the party? Because to marry anyone else after going to bed with Isaac would be a worse sin. I loved Isaac, and yet I didn't trust him enough to tell him how afraid I was to love anyone. He didn't even know about my secret writings, or the book I had stolen then returned to Mrs. Caldwell.

I know he's worried about me, worried something is wrong since the party. What would he say of my sickness, my punishment, my walk alone on Saturday, to our place by the bridge? Writing lines there about the eye that's always watching me, us, from outside the bridge when we think we are alone, separate from the world. What would he say of my curiosity for college, my desire to read as many books as I pleased? For my Rumspringa to be not temporary, as Isaac believes, but forever. What would it mean to read English books in a city like Boston?

Lately, I fear there is no end to my wanting, that maybe this is God prolonging my punishment, like Eve listening to the snake, eating from the Garden, only to realize eating one bite of the crisp red apple was to desire another and another until all the apples were gone. Poison red, I think, crimson lips closing over the sweet flesh.

My eyelids grow heavy, and I sleep. At some point, I think I feel Mother over me, pressing a cloth to my forehead, but when I open my eyes, no one is there. I look for the soft flicker of her face, but there is only the gray room, the same dance of light through the muslin curtains. I'm not certain how much time has passed when I head downstairs, still weak, famished, though the thought of food makes me ill.

Mother is at the kitchen table, mending a button on Father's coveralls.

"You don't look well, Emma," she says. Then she asks Father to draw up the buggy. She wants to take me to see the doctor. Before I can persuade her otherwise, Father is calling on Cousin Frederick to accompany us, then helping me into the carriage seat. When the horses start up the road, my head turns still lighter, my nausea growing worse. I try to doze, try not to get sick over Mother, who wakes me gently when we arrive. In the waiting room, there are dozens of brochures I don't remember seeing before. For genetic tests, for preventing heart and lung disease. *A closed gene pool*, Dr. Caldwell once explained to mother. *Overlapping strains, fraternal twins, cousins twice removed.* I can still feel Isaac's hand along my back, his mouth by my neck, warm hands along my aching breasts. This unnatural pleasure, I think, this sickness.

"Emma, this way," Dr. Caldwell says.

I rise and follow him. He closes the door behind us and helps me up onto the table.

"I'm sorry you aren't feeling well," he says. Then he takes my temperature, my blood pressure. "How long have you lacked an appetite?"

"A few days, maybe."

"No more than that?"

"I guess I don't really know," I lie.

"And you waited this long to visit?"

"I've been busy working," I say.

"Working too hard." He shakes his head, makes a note on my chart. "Do you have any nausea?"

"Yes," I say. Why lie about this?

"Are you vomiting?"

"A little." I don't tell him that the first time was last week in the garden. Mrs. Caldwell went inside for a pack of tomato seeds, and I hurried behind the bushes. When she returned, she didn't notice anything, not the stink on my breath, or the wet on my dress. At least, she didn't show that she did.

When the doctor asks me for details, I tell him it's only in the morning, after breakfast.

"Your baptism is in a few months, if I'm not mistaken?" he says.

"Yes," I say, unsure of what this has to do with anything. "In October. The first Sunday."

Dr. Caldwell sets down his pad on the table. He clasps his hands in his lap and looks at me for a few moments before he speaks. "Emma, I need to ask you . . ."

My thumbs tighten under my fists.

"Is there a chance you might be pregnant?"

My hands clench tighter. The words out loud make it real. What I've feared all along. My punishment. My sin. *Ich will dir viel Schmerzen schaffen, wenn du schwanger wirst. I will greatly multiply thy sorrow and thy conception*. Stiffly, I nod.

"Can you estimate the last time you had intercourse?"

"Several weeks ago," I say. *Und dein Wille soll deinem Mann unterworfen sein, und er soll dein Herr sein. And thy desire shall be to thy husband, and he shall rule over thee.*

"Did you use protection?" he asks.

"No," I blink rapidly, heat flooding my face.

"It's all right," he says.

*Du sollst mit Schmerzen Kinder gebären. In sorrow thou shalt bring forth children.* "Please forgive me," I say. I cannot stop the tears. My chest is heaving.

"It's all right," he says again. "You're human, Emma. These things happen. We just need to make sure, so we can keep you healthy. I'll need to take some blood."

He pricks a needle into my arm, and I close my eyes. I picture Mother's and Father's faces, the horror in their expressions. I have deceived them, dishonored them, in taking this risk. As Dr. Caldwell closes the vial of blood he's taken, I see the same red poison on my lip-sticked mouth, the same red wound in my shoulder from the bullet they had to cut out.

Paper along the examination table crackles under me. My hands search over it like the back of a feed calendar, but my palms are empty, my sickness worse. I dry heave while the doctor is gone, clenching the table, swallowing my spit.

"Emma," he says when he returns. By his eyes, I know. "It's going to be okay. Breathe."

I try to but I can only see Mother again in my mind, Mother ashamed.

"We won't know how far along you are until you have an ultrasound," he says. "Do you know what that is?"

I shake my head.

"It's how we check on the health of the baby."

"How?" I ask, wiping my eyes.

"We can see inside using sound vibrations. It's not a regular picture, but an impression that shows us the heartbeat and the baby's measurements."

"I don't know anyone who has gone for this other test," I say, thinking of Rosa Beiler, who was with child before she married Jonah Belier. Jonah's brother had Pretzel Syndrome, his joints too loose for him to walk without a cane. And Isaac's sister had died of the same disease Eli had.

"That's because not everyone comes to see me first. But anyone who does, like you, qualifies for preventive treatment. This will be especially crucial, given your and Isaac's medical histories. Usually, we'd wait until you were married and planning on children to have this discussion. But now that you've conceived, we have to take every precaution. A special doctor, an obstetrician in an English hospital, is the best person to see to make sure your child is healthy. Do you understand?"

I nod, but I can't stop myself from crying again. *Genetic disease* and *obstetrician* and *ultrasound*. These are the words of my story.

The doctor crouches beside me. "Don't worry. I'll write down the name of the doctor I recommend," he says. "Dr. Vivian Lee at Lancaster General. When you see her, she'll check for a heartbeat. It's normal for them to take your weight and blood pressure too. And more blood. And then there will be the option for genetic tests. It'll be your and Isaac's choice in the end, but I recommend you go down that path, so you know how to prepare."

I nod again, unable to speak.

"Is your mother here?"

"She's outside," I say. "With my cousin in the buggy."

"I think we should tell her," the doctor says. "To make sure she understands."

I want to tell him I'd rather wait and do it myself, but silence envelops me like a coffin.

Moments later, Mother takes a seat in one of the chairs pressed against the wall. Before the doctor, she is silent, too, stern and expressionless as listens to what he has to say—until he hands her a pamphlet, tells her the name of the doctor at Lancaster General. Then she cries into her hands.

I haven't seen her weep since Beth passed. I want to reach for her, hold her, but I'm too weak. I can't even look at her.

"Is it Isaac's?" Mother says, nearly shouting. I have never heard her raise her voice this loud. "Tell me, at least, that it is his!"

"Yes," I say. "Of course. Of course it is."

"Please forgive my anger," she says, looking at the doctor and not at me.

"It's all right," he says. "I know it's a lot to take in." His voice is soft, reassuring. The way it was when he examined my bullet wound the first time, and later when he removed the stitches. He'd traced the scar line then, told me it would heal.

On the ride home, Mother and I are silent. She keeps her eyes fixed on the window. Meidung, my shunning. I look out the other window, watching as we pass the gold fields, tall with corn. It will be autumn soon, almost thirteen years since the day the milkman came. Mother had forgiven the man that day, along with the rest of the community, with the sun shining through the maple leaves in the schoolyard, like it is now.

# RUTH WALSH

## FALL 2019

In the buggy's rearview mirror, Ruth's hair is turning gray. She almost doesn't look, especially not on this baptism Sunday, and yet she cannot help but notice wisps of fluttering gray.

At a two-way stop, a yellow car with the top down appears. A woman in a sunhat, the striped ribbon flapping, makes herself known to the world. Maybe it is all this exposure, more English cars on their roads in the mornings, that has made Ruth more self-aware. Just last year, Susanna and Jason Yoder lost their farm on Quarry Road to a development project. In its place: rows of brand-new houses with garages made for three vehicles. And the cars on their way to downtown go faster, and faster.

Each year, at least a half-dozen boys got in car accidents during Rumspringa. Someone driving under the influence. But they didn't usually die. Most suffered injuries, and sometimes the Lord's punishment went only as far as jail. Boys bailed out by their fathers. Restitution came in the form of baptism—in choosing to stay in the community to repay their debts. Jonas Zimmerman had been one such boy, and he was, in fact, getting baptized today.

Abigail Miller, Jonas's cousin, would also be baptized. A year younger than Emma, she had looked up to Emma like an older sister. Perhaps because Emma was a strong student who'd excelled at memorizing the Scripture, even after the Happening. Dr. Caldwell had noticed symptoms long before Ruth was willing to admit them. Such as the time Emma was clipping laundry along the wash line and her knees had gone weak and she'd fallen, frozen, to the ground. When Ruth brought Emma to the doctor, he'd used English terms—posttraumatic stress . . . anxiety—and Ruth hadn't known what to make of them. Trauma, the doctor said, was any severe event that trapped the mind and body in a state of perpetual fear. Fear that the event could happen again at any moment. Putting a person on high alert. While anxiety, he said, was a lingering nervousness that was hard to place, and that couldn't be easily cured by sleep or hard work or a meal.

Ruth supposed after Eli was born, she could understand some of what he meant. She'd had a fear that something horrible was going to happen, and then it had. His seizure, his near stroke. A kind of sadness had overtaken her that was both connected to and separate from fear, her thoughts spinning into the unknown that lay ahead. But it was God's way. His way of revealing his power to decide her future. Of reminding her to be thankful for what she had. She had one daughter still alive. One son, who was ill but still alive. Ruth recalled the first time she had doubted Him, when she had felt the sadness envelop her like shadows along the wall when she couldn't sleep, but she had told herself: *Stop now. To follow these thoughts is to accept the Devil's pain, and the Devil will destroy everything.* Better to be sad, she decided, than to question God.

She had assumed it was the same for Emma. That the Scripture had taught her to have faith in Him. That to take her pain away, she need only trust in Him as the only way.

Joanna had been sad, Ruth thinks then. Her best childhood friend. Before she'd become a woman, even, Joanna used to say things—about how she was ugly. She called herself fat. She wished she was a boy because it was easier to hide your body in coveralls. Ruth hadn't understood. She'd told Joanna what her own mother had told her: that all were beautiful in God's eyes. But it hadn't been easy for Joanna to suppress the thoughts, to stop them from creeping in at weak moments. Joanna had run wild during her Rumspringa. Had found refuge in drugs. Joanna had chosen not to be baptized and could never come back under the Bann. There was no undoing what had already been done.

As Abraham drives on, Ruth clutches the basket of bread she and Lettie baked this morning with the grain fresh from threshing. In October, Ruth and Abraham had separated the grain from the chaff in the barn, and Ruth then collected the grain to grind for flour. She can smell the yeast, the bread still warm under the cloths they'd used to wrap the three loaves for baptism. Lettie will meet her there, bringing the cinnamon rolls she baked, and the Angel cake.

This morning, the Millers are hosting. Esther Miller greets Ruth and Abraham on the front porch, which is newly painted with six rocking chairs—one for each of their children. Esther had given birth to Abigail, Susan, Jacob, Leigh, Tomas, and Luke. The children are spaced a few years apart, regular as a heartbeat, and all healthy. Eyeing the rockers, Ruth reminds herself to be grateful for what she has, for Dr. Caldwell, who keeps her boy, and her hope, alive.

The men work to lift Eli in his chair onto the porch. Once inside, Ruth wheels him to the window, parts the curtains so he can see into the open field. After she sets down her basket, Abigail, Esther's eldest daughter, hugs her, then leaves to cut some flowers, a mix of daisies and roses for the parlor table. Ruth gets to work helping Esther set out the dishes she and the other families have brought. A large salad with butter lettuce and tomatoes, pickled eggs and beets, sugar peas and ham. Ruth smells sweet molasses warming on the wood stove. Esther has made waffles for the children, and there are bowls of fresh berries and whipped cream ready to be spooned on top.

Eventually, more guests arrive, more food adorns the table, more feet creak over the wood floors. As Ruth pauses to admire the roses, she feels eyes on her and turns to find Abigail watching, whispering something to Hanna Beiler.

What are they saying about me? About Emma? she wonders, then stops herself. Gossip was vain. Gossip was wrong. If Ruth pays no mind, God will work through her. Even so, she's relieved when Deacon King motions for everyone to follow him into the barn. The unbaptized boys and girls sit along the threshing floor, while the baptized men and women flank them in the side pews. Ruth waits for Deacon King to be joined at the podium by Bishop Graber. No, Ruth reminds herself, it's

Bishop Yoder now. Bishop Graber was before, when Ruth was getting confirmed. Joanna almost had too. Another thought Ruth must banish from her mind.

When they were first married, Ruth and Abraham would sit on separate sides for services, but since Eli, they always sit together in the unbaptized section with the younger children. It is easier there to quiet Eli's cries during the sermon, keep him still, take turns leaving through the back when he had a fit.

The forebay doors to the barn remain open, letting in the sunlight. It had been the same on the day of Ruth's confirmation—the day Joanna had walked out, straight past the flung-wide doors, disappearing into the radiance beyond. Ruth can't help wondering if they had closed the doors that day, locked them, would Joanna had been saved?

Already, Eli can't sit still. Ruth moves his chair still farther back from the others, clicks on the brake. Abraham reaches for her hand over the handles. He smiles at her—with thanks, it seems, with tenderness. Or is it sadness? She doesn't know, but this thought, too, she decides, must be banished.

When everyone has found their places, the ceremony begins in the soft, shadowy light of the barn. Unthinkingly, Ruth grips the slick blue of the wheelchair handles tighter. She can't keep her eyes off the forebay, the deacon's podium. The image of Joanna, just as she'd looked twenty years ago, refuses to leave. They'd stood beside one another before the bishop, ready to commit themselves to the church, and then, without a glance at Ruth, Joanna had told Bishop Graber she was leaving.

Ruth had gasped, not loud enough for anyone else to hear, but still she'd felt the lapse in her breath, her heart's tick along her throat. She'd looked around at her peers, all of them wide-eyed. Ruth had waited for Bishop Graber to intervene, say anything to deter her friend, but instead he'd only nodded. With near indifference, he kept his eyes on the believers as Joanna walked through the doors in her white Sunday bonnet, two long strings hanging down, and stepped into the light.

Through the open doors now, Ruth thinks she hears wind chimes or clopping hooves; she hears leaving, she hears passage, not of Scripture, but of moving through, of moving past, or apart. When Decon King tells them to open their hymnals to "Blessed Redeemer," Ruth cannot absorb the words. Usually, she takes comfort in the familiarity of ritual, how it lets her forget, lets her become one with the others, but today, no matter how softly she sings, somehow her voice sounds too loud in her ears, distinct from the others. Like she is a single buzzing bee, separate from her hive. Even when Bishop Yoder turns to the story of Philip in Acts, Ruth's favorite section, she can't focus.

"As they traveled along the road, they came to some water and the eunuch said, Look, here is water. What can stand in the way of my being baptized?"

Already, Deacon King is holding the bucket filled with holy water, his eyes closed as Bishop Yoder continues to the Gospel of Mark—"Whoever believes and is baptized will be saved, but whoever does not believe will be condemned"—yet Ruth hears Emma's words over the bishop's: *It's my choice if I want to be baptized.* She could have slapped Emma then—how she'd desired to—but violence only begot more violence. Forgiveness was salvation; it had saved her people for centuries. She knew this . . . but if she'd said more, if she'd done more than blindly forgive—would things have turned out differently?

Ruth grips Eli's handles still tighter, feeling a weight on her chest no amount of prayer could lift. The open forebay doors summon her again, as they had when Joanna walked out. Though Ruth would never admit it, part of her had wanted to follow. Had imagined what the sunlight felt like on Joanna's face. Had wondered whether she'd taken off her shoes to feel the cool grass beneath her feet.

"Don't you move," she whispers, watching as all nine of the youth knelt in preparation for their anointment.

"In the Ordnung of this church," the bishop says, "in accordance with the word of the Lord, can you be obedient and submissive therein?"

But had she really forgiven? Ruth wonders. *A disgrace*, she'd called Emma the day they'd learned of her pregnancy. *How could you bring such disgrace upon our family?* Yes, Ruth had spoken up. She'd made her disappointment known. This other thought invades her now: Why had

Emma copulated in sin? Was it because she'd spent time in the English world, among people who pursued pleasure for its own sake? Or had Isaac pressured her? Taken Emma to more parties than Ruth could count? How many times had it happened? Had Emma discussed such private matters with Mrs. Caldwell?

As the youth take turns repeating their confirmation, Ruth almost forgets where she is—here at a baptism beside her unbaptized son. Abraham is, too, but he is not like Ruth, trapped in the past. Abraham's heart is free, she thinks, to bear witness to the others proclaiming their commitment to the church, no bitterness in his chest. No resentment. No regret.

*A disgrace*, the words return despite herself. Violent words. Evidence of rage. Over what? Her lack of control, when it was all in God's hands?

Ruth's eyes sting as Deacon King ladles holy water into Bishop Yoder's hands. The bishop pours the water over the head of each child with the words "Upon your Faith which you have confessed before God and many witnesses, you are baptized in the name of the Father, the Son, and Holy Ghost."

Ruth wipes away tears while other parents do the same, aware that hers are tears of grief, not joy like the others feel, knowing their children, unlike hers, will be saved in the end. Bishop Yoder has assured her many times that Eli is with God, but how does he know? How can anyone know what's inside a person's heart?

Jonas Zimmerman is last to receive the holy water.

"You are now no longer guests and strangers, but fellow citizens with the saints and of the household of God." As the bishop speaks, the soft light from the open doors falls upon his face, as it does along the faces of the children—these teenagers—by the grace of God, and yet Ruth cannot help but think: A baptism is only a ceremony.

Bishop Yoder completes his blessing by kissing each of the young men on both cheeks, while his wife, Carrie Yoder, does the same for the girls. Hanna Beiler turns toward the pews and smiles, and Ruth can hardly look. Quickly, she turns her hymnal to "Das Loblied," the last song she must struggle through before Bishop Yoder closes with Second Corinthians: "Therefore if any man be in Christ, he is a new creature: old things are passed away; behold, all things are become new."

Eli begins to thrash, and Ruth seizes the opportunity. "He's had enough," Ruth whispers to Abraham. "I'll take him home." But before she can unlock the brake on his wheelchair, Abraham insists otherwise. "I'll take him," he says. "You're needed here."

She closes her eyes. "All right," she says. "Thank you," but her hands shake without anything to grip on the way back to the Miller house.

In the family's dining room, she smiles benignly at the other guests, unfolds the calico cloth she used to wrap the loaves. Lettie has come to help. "I'm so glad for the bread," she says, but Ruth is silent as Lettie slices and sets it onto smaller plates. Why couldn't Ruth be more like Lettie Ames? Lettie, who has accepted Isaac's absence at the ceremony. Isaac cannot bring himself to attend events such as these, and Lettie does not force him. Strange, Ruth has barely thought of him today. Consumed by her own thoughts, her own selfish anger.

She suddenly finds she can't stand it anymore, can't take another breath in this stifling house. She only means to stop in the lawn, away from the sight of so much food she can't stomach. To gather herself before a maple tree, root herself as the tree does, no matter how bright and hot the sun is on this day in the middle of October. There had been a breeze earlier, in the buggy, when she had seen her hair in the mirror. And the ribbon on the women's sunhat wavering in the wind. At the stop sign, on the way to church.

Ruth becomes aware she's walking quickly, and even more quickly the closer she gets to Quarry Road, where she saw the topless car. She walks past this point too, all the way to the covered bridge, then to the creek, where she takes off her shoes. Her intention is to kneel, pray, but she doesn't. Instead, she wrings her hands over the muddy bank, as Isaac had done when she'd found him here alone on the riverbank. His beard long by then. Already, he was so thin. She might have embraced him, told him how sorry she was, but she hadn't.

Ruth cups cold water in her hands and rinses her face. She cups more water to drink. She sinks her feet into the cold mud, then forces herself to rise, ordering herself to regain her dignity, go back to the Millers where she belongs. But she doesn't. Instead, she goes home, where the pie is waiting. Where Abraham is all alone with Eli. Her husband needs her.

# SARA CALDWELL

## SUMMER 2018

What could be better than the movies on a rainy day in the late summer? The theater in Millersville is playing *The Graduate*; every Tuesday it runs an old classic—a half-priced matinee for seniors looking for something to do. Sara hardly falls into this category, but she is glad for the excuse to be a mentor, a retired social worker making the most of her time.

Given the weather, Sara is picking Emma up. An unspoken rule that when it's raining, Sara gives Emma a ride to and from work. Emma's mother hasn't objected, but then she doesn't know that today they're playing hooky. Ruth Walsh would never allow it, and Sara doesn't blame her: after what Ruth had been through, what she feared might happen again, it makes sense that she's protective, wants to know Emma's whereabouts. And yet Emma has her own life to live, doesn't she? Every woman has her own choices to make.

They meet at the intersection of Hunsecker and Snake Hill, Emma running in her cape dress, already soaked by the time she slides into the car, but that's okay. Sara has factored in some extra time so Emma can change at her house—into some Levi's she found at a thrift store downtown, and a camisole and cardigan like Sara would have wanted at Emma's age. Something light and versatile for the summer months, the sweater warm enough for air conditioning. She got everything a bit big just in case. Emma can borrow a belt if she needs to. If the cardigan is too large, she can always push up the sleeves.

Emma seems distant in the car. She barely said hello when she ducked in, like she's angry about something. At least, fretful. Did something happen with Isaac?

"Emma, you know you can tell me, right? If there's anything on your mind."

"I'm fine," Emma says quickly. She turns to Sara, half-smiling, but she hardly looks like herself. Her eyes are swollen with sleeplessness, her face pale.

Inside the house, Sara fetches a towel and drapes it around Emma. "You must be freezing," she says. "We have plenty of time before the movie. I gave us a buffer. Why don't you head upstairs for a shower? I have some dry things you can change into."

"Thank you," Emma says with another forced smile.

Upstairs, while the shower runs, Sara lays out the new things. She cuts off the tags so as not to make Emma self-conscious that she's gone out of her way—has spent money on her—even though she wanted to. Emma is like family now. In case the jeans are too big, even belted, Sara lays out a cream sundress with ties around the shoulder. The silk dress fit Emma so well that this one likely will too. And she could wear the cardigan over it if the theater is cold. Sara even has a vintage Coach bag, one in simple brown leather, to complete the look, but a purse is likely too much, too foreign—and Sara doesn't want Emma to think she needs to pay at the theater. It's Sara's treat. Just as the lipstick was last time. But today a lighter shade would be better. A softer pink gloss, and some perfume—a splash of Coco Chanel—Peter's favorite. It seems strange when she thinks of it this way, but it's more like nostalgia, like how she felt wearing perfume those early years with Peter, when they went out and it felt nice making an extra effort. Men responded to such things; Sara is only sharing what Emma might like to know—things she likely doesn't feel comfortable asking her own mother during her Rumspringa. What harm is there in that?

Besides, Ruth had asked her indirectly about selling flowers at market, and Sara had sent along with Emma some rose starts from the garden. Ruth had been glad for the soap to sell, too, and Emma finished another batch last week. The Walshes were entrepreneurs when it came to supporting Eli, and Sara is glad to offer her perspective in more ways than one.

When the shower stops, Sara heads downstairs to give Emma some space. She busies herself in the kitchen, unloading the dishwasher. Carefully, she wipes away any excess water from the glasses and bowls, aligning them neatly along the shelf. Outside, the rain beats harder, streaming down the windows. She can almost smell the wet grass, the trees thick with pollen, the sky over the greenery dark like purple petunias.

Sara readies her purse, packs her own lipstick, her compact. She folds extra tissues into the side pocket in case there are tears. She doesn't know what Emma will think of the movie, whether it will be the least bit relatable, but its themes feel relevant. Sara remembers how liberated she felt the first time she saw it as a teenager, falling in love with Dustin Hoffman and Katharine Ross on the big screen. Thinking of it, she can even see some of Emma in Elaine Robinson, in her simple elegance, her innocence turned wisdom by the end.

When Emma meets her downstairs, the thought returns to her: how elegant Emma is, how natural her beauty. She is wearing the sundress and cardigan; her wet hair grazes her waist.

"You look wonderful," Sara says. "It fits like a glove."

"Oh," Emma says. "I wasn't sure if it was too short?" She looks down to her bare feet.

"No, not at all," Sara says. "It's past your knees."

Sara remembered reading something about the Amish dress code, that girls were visited by local ministry for hemlines falling above the knee. When Sara was in middle school, there had been a rule against it too. In fact, her tech ed. teacher, Mr. Gray, had sent her to the principal for wearing a tennis skirt to class. It didn't matter that she was on the varsity tennis team, scheduled to leave early for a match.

The same old story, Sara thinks, men needing to control women so that they didn't attract unwelcome attention, when it was the men who had the problem. Why not send the tech ed. teacher to the principal instead?

"Have you used a blow dryer before?" Sara asks before she says anything else. Risks oversharing like Peter warned against. "I don't want you to catch a cold."

"No," Emma says. "You plug it in?"

"Yes, I can do it for you. I'll show you," Sara says.

Emma doesn't object, only follows Sara upstairs to the bathroom, where Sara starts the blow dryer, turning the setting to low.

"Flip your head over like this," Sara says, and Emma does, laughing. "It's silly, I know, but it goes faster."

Sara holds the dryer over Emma's hair, shows her how to ruffle the air through with her fingers. "That'll warm you up," she says.

"I'm still warm from the shower steam," Emma says. "Except for my feet."

Sara is glad for Emma's dry humor, that she's acting more like herself again.

"I have some sandals," Sara offers. "Flats with adjustable straps that should fit."

"I'll wear my sneakers," Emma says. "If you don't mind."

When Emma puts on her sneakers in the foyer, Sara is surprised by how good they look. White high-tops were coming back. Good old nineties fashion.

Inside the car, Sara has packed an extra umbrella and a raincoat for Emma. Maybe over the top, but Sara likes being prepared. She likes having checklists and facts for filling the silence.

"The theater is about twenty minutes away," she tells Emma. Maybe longer, if there's traffic. "The parking lot is small, so we can hurry in with our umbrellas." She's overexplaining, but if she were in Emma's shoes, she'd be comforted by these details. In graduate school, they'd said it was important to narrate, to answer a patient's questions before they asked, in case they were too afraid. Show them their fears and worries were understandable. That we're all human.

When Sara can't think of anything else to add, she says: "How is Isaac?"

"Oh." Emma jolts. Turns quickly to the window, focuses on the streaming rain.

“We don’t have to talk about him,” Sara says. “I just wondered.”

“Isaac is fine,” Emma says.

“And your family? Is everyone well?”

“Yes,” Emma says. “Can you open a window? I need a bit of air.”

“Do you want to stop?”

“No,” Emma says. “The movie is at noon—the matinee. Did I say it right?”

“That’s right,” Sara says.

“I don’t want us to be late.”

*Us.* Sara holds on to Emma’s choice of words, this sign of a mutual friendship. At the next stop light, Sara turns to Emma again, and Emma smiles the same half smile as before. Projecting the same unease.

“I think you’re really going to like this movie,” Sara says. “*The Graduate* is a cult classic. Have you heard of it?”

“No,” Emma says. “A cult?”

“No, not a cult. It’s not about one, I mean. Cult classic is a term for a popular favorite, and this film has been one since it first came out in the Sixties. Before you were born. Before my time, too. But my dad played it on our VCR at home when I was your age, and I never forgot it.”

This, too, seems to perplex Emma—that Sara was once a teen, or that she watched movies with her father? Or a VCR?

“A VCR,” Sara says, “for playing VHS tapes, before DVD players. Well, now no one uses those either. Now we stream everything.”

The more Sara says, the deeper she is digging the hole. But Emma isn’t asking her to explain; she’s looking out the window again.

“*The Graduate* is a love story, an American drama,” Sara says, “and the actors are really incredible. Well, you can tell me what you think.”

“I thought we were seeing a new movie,” Emma says.

“We aren’t going to a regular theater. I mean, it’ll have a big screen, but it’s not playing the latest blockbusters. This one focuses on independent films, and classics.”

“Independent?”

“Oh, they’re films made outside the mainstream production companies. They have smaller budgets, I guess.”

"Cool," Emma says, and Sara finds the response endearing. Something she's started since the party: trying out slang here and there.

"I think you'll be pleasantly surprised," Sara says as she turns into the gravel lot. The sign for the theater reads POINT-OF-VIEW (Est. 1923). She's never thought much of it before, but today the name seems apt, like it's been waiting for her to step outside of herself and see from Emma's perspective in this new context.

When they pull up in front, she's disappointed that Emma seems uncharmed by the old brick theater. Like it's just another English building, even if it sits in woodland a few miles outside the town center. The Amish community was extensive in Millersville. Perhaps Emma had been to the area already.

Peter had mentioned that a community of ex-Amish even went to the local university. There'd been a conference in the mid-'90s, on women of Anabaptist traditions, on histories that had been quieted. *Insiders know. Outsiders see*, Peter had said once, explaining why this scholarship was important. Wasn't Sara herself adding to that dialogue this very moment? If he found out about the movies, she would raise this point to him; his own point—how could he argue?

After they park, Sara hands Emma an umbrella.

"Isn't the door right there," she says, pointing to the entrance.

"Yes, but no use getting wet, is there?"

"I'm fine," Emma says. "I don't want to lose it."

Sara almost insists, but there is no point in arguing. Plus, her umbrella is large enough to spread over them both as they hurry inside.

They're greeted by a sea of red carpet around the old-fashioned ticket booth and popcorn machine. A family-owned business, Sara remembers from when she and Peter last came—to see *The Sweet Hereafter. Horribly depressing*, Peter had called the film afterward. She'd persuaded him to see it after she'd read the book, which was based on a real-life tragedy—a school bus that skidded on the ice, killing twenty-one children. The lives of parents and survivors, and even the private investigator determined to piece together how such a thing could happen, were forever intertwined. She'd thought it would resonate with Peter after his experience with Nickel Mines. It had with her, at least, and it's how she feels with Emma now, their narratives continually intersecting in unexpected ways.

"Do you like popcorn?" Sara asks as an elderly gentleman in a red bowtie hands them their tickets. The owner? It must be.

"I'm not really hungry," Emma says.

"Me neither," Sara says, though secretly she'd been hoping they might share some, for the real butter they melted over the kernels here. On their way to Theater 3, Emma stops before the Now Playing posters in the hall. She is studying the one for a film called *Never Rarely Sometimes Always* like a museum painting.

"Look good?" Sara says, examining the poster herself. Below the film title, a forlorn-looking teen with covered hair stares out at the viewer.

"I don't know what it's about," Emma says flatly.

Someone else might have found the remark flippant, but Sara is glad that Emma's being more assertive. That she's helping her find the confidence to speak her mind. "True," she says with a smile.

Inside their theater, there's only an older couple in the middle row. The seniors Sara would expect—replicas of her and Peter one day, if she's lucky. Or perhaps not. Peter had no plans to retire; in fact, she could see him working for the rest of his life: reading and reviewing the latest research on Amish genetics, presenting at conferences. She's surprised by the sadness she feels at the thought, the pang of longing. Would he travel with her to Paraguay like she's always dreamed? Try out a meditation retreat in the mountains?

Genetic medicine was Peter's vocation—how many times had he reminded her of this? And what did she have to say in return? That the garden was her haven, her raison d'être?

"You know," Sara can't help but ask before previews begin. "What do you think about some potted mums for the garden show?"

"I love mums," Emma says.

"So do I," Sara says. "But I'm not always thrilled about the ones at the garden center. Do you grow any?"

"We have a lot," Emma says. "I'm sure Mother would give you some after all your help with the market. We've made more money these past weeks."

"I'm so glad to hear it," Sara says. "But I'd like to buy them from her. Maybe two large pots, one for either side of the gate, if your mother doesn't mind putting something together?"

"I'll ask," Emma says, but her tone is noncommittal. Maybe Ruth Walsh isn't keen on interacting with her?

The lights dim, and Sarah doesn't have time to overthink it anymore. She notices how tightly Emma is gripping the arms of her seat when the curtains open, revealing the big screen. She almost whispers that the chairs recline, but this might make Emma even more uneasy.

The first preview shows a retired film executive diagnosed with Alzheimer's—this man in a three-piece suit—storming out of his corporate office in a city of high rises.

She'd have guessed it would be alienating, the sudden light and enlarged faces, the unfamiliar setting, but Emma seems captivated. She isn't taking cover like she had before the record player. Auditory desensitization, Sara decides—yes, they had achieved this together, over the past several weeks—within the safety of Sara's home. Through the next several previews—one about a family road trip to North Dakota, another for period piece about Queen Elizabeth—Emma remains calm.

As the Embassy Pictures logo spins into view, Emma gently clutches her wrist—possibly a sign, according to Peter, of pain related to tachycardia, inflammation of the radial artery in times of acute stress.

Sara wants to ask Emma if she's okay but, once more, she resists for fear of making things worse. Take it in stages, she tells herself. Try not to project worst-case scenarios.

When Dustin Hoffman's young, clean-shaven face fills the screen, Sara is relieved for this grounding image, for the calming music of "The Sound of Silence." Maybe she'll play Emma her Simon & Garfunkel record on Tuesday.

The camera pans to Hoffman—Benjamin Braddock—on a plane, about to land in L.A. Emma seems fascinated, remaining motionless as the scene gradually shifts to the suburban affluence of Beverly Hills. She watches intensely as Braddock evades guests at his graduation party, making comments about his new sports car, his red Alfa Romeo Duetto Spider. Even when Braddock changes into scuba gear and jumps into the swimming pool, Emma seems unbothered, rolling with the strangeness of this backyard party.

It isn't until later, when Mrs. Robinson enters the scene, that Emma's demeanor changes. Something about the older woman clearly unsettles her. Perhaps it's the woman's obsessive gaze, her refusal to let go?

When she insists Braddock drive her home, Emma turns to Sara and says, "I have to use the restroom."

"Do you want me to come?" Sara whispers.

"No, I'll just be a minute."

Before Sara can say more, Emma is hurrying toward the exit.

Sara waits in the silence, one exaggerated by the tension between Benjamin Braddock and his cougar neighbor, one Sara can barely tolerate, concerned as she is. She wants to respect Emma's privacy, and yet isn't it her duty to check on her, as someone older and more experienced?

Sara rises from her seat, rushes down the aisle toward the exit. Inside the small bathroom, she hears Emma retching in the stalls.

"Are you sick?" she asks. This stupid question. Of course she is.

A long silence follows, and then she hears Emma crying, sobbing.

"Can I come in?"

"Please don't," Emma says.

"I want to help." Sara sees Emma's feet shift over the tiled floor. "Will you let me?"

"It's not a good time," Emma says, her voice broken.

"Was it the movie?"

"No," Emma says. "I was enjoying it." A pause. "Can you take me home?"

"Of course," Sara says. "I'll bring the car around. Just meet me outside when you're ready. Take your time."

"Thank you," Emma says.

By the theater entrance, Sara lets the car idle. She wants to play the radio, but it will be too much, she thinks—anything would likely be too much for Emma at this point. She watches the rain, still coming down steadily, practices breathing from her diaphragm. In for two, out for two. She lets the air circle her pelvis, this balloon of air she imagines with her eyes closed. The breath is a bridge, she thinks, something she can teach Emma. A bridge between panic and calm, chaos and peace.

She is breathing like this, into the expanse of her ribcage, when the door opens and Emma slides in, newly soaked. Sara forgot to leave the umbrella, but she has the extra raincoat, at least, for Emma to spread over her lap.

"I'm so sorry," Sara says. "You must be freezing. And you're sick. Let's get you to the nearest gas station. Some ginger ale, maybe, or some hot tea—"

"I'd rather just get home," Emma says.

Emma has never been this firm with her before, this unapologetic. Yet this time, instead of pleasing Sara, the change worries her. "Do you think you maybe caught a bug?" she asks. "We could call Peter? I can try his cell—"

"No!" Emma says.

Sara is shocked. "I'm sorry," she says again. "I just thought . . . never mind." Her hand tightens over steering wheel.

"I'm pregnant," Emma says, erupting in tears.

"Oh my God," Sara says, her thoughts whirling. "Pregnant? I'm so sorry." She realizes she keeps repeating herself, wishes she could think of something else to say, but she can't. Instead, she reaches for Emma's hand.

"I drank too much that night. I was stupid." Emma sobs. "I hate myself. I'm so ashamed."

"Oh, Emma," she says. "Don't say that."

"I can't help it." Emma wipes at her wet cheeks with abrupt movements.

"What did you feel when it was happening? Ashamed, or like you wanted to?"

"I wanted to."

"So it was only afterward that you felt shame?"

"Yeah, I guess," Emma says. "The night's still blurry."

"We've all been there," Sara says. "Acting on impulse. It's being a teenager." She almost tells Emma about her first time, but Emma needs Sara to be a social worker now, not a friend.

"Mother called me a disgrace." Emma looks away, toward the window. "At home, after we saw the doctor, she said it. I've disappointed everyone."

"Not everyone," Sara says, reaching into her purse for a tissue.

Suddenly, Sara wants to gag. She hadn't noticed it before—the stink that's filled the car. Emma's hair must have fallen forward when she vomited. Now Sara sees the wet clumps caught in it.

"You can't put all the blame on yourself, you know," she says calmly. "And your mother shouldn't either. It takes two people. Where is Isaac in this?"

Emma just shakes her head, casting her a guilty glance.

"It's his child too, Emma," Sara says. "You have to tell him."

"Mother wants me to confess for the both of us. Before the church, so I can be baptized in good faith. Then we can marry."

"You still have a choice," Sara says. She used to tell this to the boys at the prison when they felt powerless. Alone. "I know it doesn't feel like it, but this is your life. Your future."

"What do you mean?" Emma says, like Sara's speaking a foreign language.

Of course, Sara is. One couldn't just tell an Amish girl she had choices when she didn't have them, not fundamentally, not in a culture that depended on female sacrifice.

"Let's backtrack," Sara says. "What are you feeling? Or where are you feeling discomfort in your body?"

Emma touches the side of her ribs.

"Okay." Sara nods. "That's normal. We hold a lot of tension there. If you could name the feeling, what would it be?" Emma remains silent, so she says, "The first thing that comes to mind."

More silence, and then finally Emma says, "Sadness, I guess. Confusion."

"Okay, good. What are you confused about?"

Emma's breath shortens again. "I told my mother I don't know if I want this life. Or if Isaac wants it either, but I didn't mean it. It was wrong of me."

"Why was it wrong?"

"I knew it would hurt her. That it was a threat. And I haven't even spoken to Isaac. Though I guess I think leaving might be what he wants. Since he likes parties. At least I think he does."

"Did you like the party?" Sara asks. "I mean, was it fun?" She tries to stay present in the moment. "It isn't wrong to have fun."

"I guess I did," Emma says. "But I don't remember everything. That's the worst part. I drank too much." She looks at Sara like there's something more she wants to say.

"You can tell me anything . . . the first thing that comes to mind," Sara says. "What do you feel?"

"Afraid." Emma meets Sara's eyes squarely.

It's almost too much for Sara, but it's what Emma needs most. This loving, mindful presence Sara spent years honing, during graduate school and after. Peter didn't give her enough credit; he underestimated her, assumed a lack of boundaries when she, like he, was a trained professional.

Another car pulls up beside Sara's, still idling in the rain. Emma jerks away from the window, panicked.

"Don't worry," Sara says, "no one can see us."

The woman steps out of the adjacent car, hurrying to unbuckle her child of four or five.

"I just want you to know," Sara says, "I'm here for you. Whatever you need. Just say the word."

"You're suggesting I leave my family?" Emma holds her stomach with trembling hands.

The words come as a slap to Sara. "Where are you getting that from? I never said that."

"But I can feel it in your eyes, in what you're trying to say. . . . I never asked for that." Emma's voice rises. "I just told you I failed my mother. That I threatened her unnecessarily, and I feel horrible about it—" Emma begins to cry again.

Sara tightens her grip over the wheel once more. "I'm not trying to suggest anything. Of course not. I just want you to know that you have options, that this is your body. Your life to decide." Without thinking, Sara continues, "You know I used to work with teenaged boys at a prison. I ran a writing workshop." She's slipping deeper, she realizes, perhaps foolishly, but she can't seem to stop herself from speaking. "There was a boy who was fifteen. He watched his brother drown while they were running from the police. They jumped in the pool so they wouldn't get shot, but the brother couldn't swim, and the boy couldn't save him from drowning."

Before she can finish, Emma says, "I don't understand. How is my life similar?"

"The boy blamed himself for not saving his brother. He made himself responsible for something that wasn't in his control. Who knows what would have happened if his brother hadn't jumped in the pool, what the police might have done, or the reasons they were running in the first place?"

"I still don't understand," Emma says.

"I'm just saying that the stories we tell ourselves aren't always true. They're not necessarily what happens."

"I know this already," Emma says. "God controls what happens."

"That's not what I mean," Sara says. "Not exactly. God may decide what happens to us, but we get to choose how we respond."

"It isn't so easy," Emma says. "I can choose to stay and marry Isaac or I can leave, but if my baby is sick, what then? My baby might have what Eli has. Isaac's sister had it too."

Tears stain Emma's cheeks, but she won't take another tissue from Sara. She stares out the window, beyond the rain, to the woods.

"The first weeks of any pregnancy are uncertain," Sara says.

"But the doctor told me the risks—" she begins and stops herself. "Never mind," she says.

Sara wonders if it's wise to say anything else, if she can still reach Emma. "Tell me, what are you most afraid of?" she tries.

"I have to go to the hospital to make sure everything's okay. To see if there is a heartbeat. But what if my baby is already dead? I feel so sick." Emma's whole body starts shaking.

"Come here," Sara says. She tries to hug Emma, dry her tears, but Emma pushes her away.

"No," she says. "I'm okay. I'm sorry," she says. "I didn't mean to sound rude, Mrs. Caldwell." She takes a deep breath.

"You don't have to apologize, Emma. You're going through a lot. I understand."

She pauses. "When is your appointment?"

"On Friday," Emma says.

"Let me drive you," Sara says. "I can help if you have questions. I won't tell Dr. Caldwell."

"Mother won't like it," she says. "I'm taking a van, anyway."

"That's all right," Sara says. "I'll meet you there, then."

Emma turns back to her, visibly calmer. There's more color in her cheeks and lips, and her eyes are clear. "Okay."

"We'll get you through this," Sara says. "I promise." She puts the car in reverse.

They don't speak on the drive home, and the rain is oddly calming. Sara can't help but sing Simon & Garfunkel silently, against the tempo of the wipers. The lyrics emerge in fragments, and she thinks of Hoffman again, of Benjamin Braddock and the gurgling sound of the fish tank inside the void of his bedroom.

The silence had been part of the point of the movie, just as it had been the point of being with the incarcerated boys—to sit there with them as long as they needed, without talking or even writing like she'd planned. Her last visit there had been like that, with the boy who lost his brother. She'd listened, then simply kept him company in silence. When he'd asked if she was coming back, she'd said yes, the next week. But then she hadn't come back. Peter's grant had come through, and there hadn't been time before their departure.

That last day, unknowingly, she'd driven through the prison gate into a different life. No way of knowing that a door had closed behind her. Heading home from the prison, she had only stared at the gray road, with no thought of a child or a private office of her own—the road long and winding before her, just like it is now.

# EMMA WALSH

## SUMMER 2018

Isaac flashes a light into my bedroom. When I go to the window, he begs me to meet him outside. I haven't seen him for some time—weeks, really—and I can't go on ignoring him forever. I put on my dress and thick black stockings. I'm too tired to fasten my hair covering, so Isaac will see me with my hair down to my waist. He will see me as I am. Just as he saw me at the party, in the English bedroom.

Outside, he's dressed in his collarless suit, as if he thinks this is what I've been waiting for, to know it's safe for me to see him again, because he plans to marry me. Yet I long for the other Isaac, the one in blue jeans, the one who drinks Captain Morgan and shakes hands the English way. I might as well have told Mrs. Caldwell this: that I liked the version of him I saw at the party.

"Did your mother tell you I stopped by yesterday morning?" Isaac asks.

"No," I say. A lie, but if I tell him why I've been avoiding him, he'll likely change his mind. I know Mrs. Caldwell wants me to be honest, but she doesn't understand that telling the truth means taking away my choices.

"What's wrong?" Isaac asks. "Is it something from the party? I fell asleep," he says. "I don't remember much."

He's looking down at his work boots, not at me, and I'm glad. That and the darkness make it harder for him to notice the weight I've gained, my dress straining at the bust. When I don't reply, he starts walking, and I follow as he shines the light before us, leading to a path along the field between our farms. The only sound is of us breathing as we move through the grass.

In my head I hear Mrs. Caldwell's voice: *Where is Isaac in this? It's his child too.* And then I can't keep it in anymore. I stop suddenly, turn to face him. "I'm pregnant," I say. "Seven weeks." My calm surprises even me. *It takes two people*, Mrs. Caldwell had said. Why should I take all the blame if the sin is on both of us?

Isaac looks at me. Stunned. "But we only did it once."

"I know, but this is what happened." I almost say it's God's plan, the way it was with Beth, with Eli. Things happened. *We get to choose how we respond*, Mrs. Caldwell said.

"What did your parents say?" he asks, looking at his feet again.

"Only Mother knows. She expects me to confess to the bishop before we're baptized. To get married before everyone finds out."

"We should, don't you think?" Isaac says, after a long pause. "Confess." He lifts his head, locks his eyes on mine.

I'm surprised, relieved that he sees his sin as the same as mine. That he will confess to the church beside me, show me I'm not alone. My eyes sting. Maybe because of his time in the foster home, Isaac knows how harsh the world can be. He is wiser than other boys.

He leans in to kiss me, and I close my eyes.

"I love you," he says.

"I love you," I say back.

When we kiss again, I taste the salt on his lips, his sweat.

I want to tell him the risks, but I don't want to worry him. I consider asking him to go with me to hear the baby's heartbeat. But if I do, and the baby isn't healthy, there's no going back. No unknowing.

"We're going to have a child," Isaac says. This time he's smiling. "We're getting married."

"That's what you want?" I ask.

"Of course," he says. "Why wouldn't I?"

"I don't know," I say. "You seem so happy on Rumspringa. I can't imagine you'd just want to go back. With me."

"Emma," he says. "Where else would I go? Who else would I want to be with?" He reaches for my hands, holds them in his.

"You want to stay in the church? We don't have to."

"I don't get what you mean." He's looking at me like I'm someone else, like something's wrong. And it is; something *is* wrong. I'm not sure of anything anymore. What I want. Who I am.

But I stop myself from going on. I only say, "It was stupid. I didn't mean it. I just know it's a lot all at once."

"It is," he says, "but it'll be okay, because we're together."

I nod, hiding the doubt that persists, what I can't let him see. At least not any more than I already have. "Let's wait to tell your mother," I say. "Until I'm further along."

"But my mother—she'll want to help us prepare. Like your mother is."

He isn't wrong. Lettie Ames would be as quiet as Mother, as careful as she wants us to be. "I just want to make sure everything is okay," I say.

He squeezes my hands. "Okay," he says. "Let's wait, then."

In the dim light, his eyes are hazy, how they looked when we were together at the party. I have nothing to doubt, and yet I do. I'm deceiving him by not telling him how afraid I am—that after the milkman, I'll never be right again. After I met Mrs. Caldwell and started writing, I began seeing things for what they are. Different from what Mother sees, what she believes about forgiveness. About happiness. About salvation.

It can't be so simple for Isaac either. Forgiving himself for what he's been through, for what the world has put him through. How hard it is to turn our worries to God when things cease to make sense. But after Isaac kisses me goodbye, tells me he'll see me tomorrow, I feel the weight of what I am holding for both of us: our blind faith. Our innocence after everything.

Tomorrow, Isaac will go back to his carpentry work. He'll put in extra hours, saving his wages for our future. In some ways he's like Father, calmed by the monotony of working metal and wood. After we lost Beth, Father started cutting trees. He said there was a rot in the elms, that the disease would spread if it wasn't stopped.

Once, I went looking for him in the woods. Mother needed his help with Eli. I found him weeping into his hands. It was November, the cold air on my face as I watched him cry before a tree stump, his saw shining in the wan light. Our men aren't allowed to cry. Not before the church, not before their families. They bury their grief. Even so, I wish now that I had held him then. Told him I understood. But I stayed silent, just I did before Isaac today, not wanting to risk making things worse than they already were.

I know Father wants me to marry Isaac, just as Mother does. He wants grandchildren, for his line to continue through me. Father, like Isaac, has no reason to doubt me. I've only ever fulfilled Father's wishes, handing him my earnings from the Caldwells. He keeps a ledger in the barn, silently writing the numbers down, balancing our earnings against our debts.

Will Isaac expect the same of me that Father does of Mother? Handing over my earnings? Mending his clothes, preparing his meals, tending the garden, the babies?

When I'm in my room again, I think about the boy in the movie, the boy staring at his fish tank, unsure of his future. It was so clear to everyone else but him. I can still hear the bubbles gurgling, feel this emptiness I can't find enough words to fill. I lay on my side for several hours, too tired to write, trying to sleep. Eventually I do, and the days bleed together until it's Friday, the day of my checkup.

Mrs. Caldwell meets me at the hospital, just as she promised. I don't tell her that Isaac knows, not yet, or that he wants to get married. We don't say anything in the waiting room. When Dr. Lee comes to greet me, she says Mrs. Caldwell can join me, if I want her to, for the visit. The doctor is a tall woman in a long white coat. She asks my age, when I had my last period, and some things about my medical history. Nothing about the schoolhouse, nothing about Eli. Today, she tells me, we are checking for a heartbeat, and to see if we can tell the age of the baby. "Project a due date," she says.

Inside a room with a padded table, I change into a paper dress, then the doctor comes in to rub a clear jelly over my stomach. She points to the computer, tells me we are looking for the picture there. A necessary machine, I think, just as tests are sometimes necessary to survive. Strange that it's Mrs. Caldwell who squeezes my hand, not Mother, when a little bean begins blinking white on the screen. A heartbeat. I gasp, wishing Mother could see this too, that the baby is alive. But how do I know the baby will stay this way?

"Based on the measurements and gestation, we're looking at April 12," Dr. Lee says.

This second date—APRIL 12, 2019—I will write down in my diary. Thirteen years since the schoolhouse, time continuing, even after the doctor tells me there will be other tests to check for a genetic condition. She doesn't say which ones, only that we'll know more after ten weeks.

I decide not to tell Mother this, because I know she'll fret over it. I try to forget her worry, and mine, wondering about the English word *gestation* instead. And another term the doctor used: *shadow heartbeat*, which makes me think about this shadow life I am leading outside of home. Such as how I use the money I don't spend on the van for the return trip to buy a turkey club sandwich with French fries at an *American bistro* downtown. Mrs. Caldwell has a chopped salad with strips of bacon and egg. Later, when I'm home, I write about the truffle salt on my French fries, and the *aioli* I devoured because it felt good to be hungry again. *I have never been so hungry*, I write, *or thirsty, for the kind of water Mrs. Caldwell ordered for us, sparkling in a glass pitcher with lemon.*

I don't tell Mother anything. We speak of only practical matters. On Saturday, when we're laying out the broadcloth cotton for my wedding dress, she says, "Here," handing me the tape measure. She shows me how to estimate the width of my waist, seeing that it is bound to grow. "Another three inches," she says. "To be safe. We can always take it in." The fabric is blue for simplicity, for humility. The dress I'll be buried in if I stay. *This bruise*, I want to write, *like rain-soaked violets.*

Mrs. Caldwell let me borrow a play by William Shakespeare. *Hamlet*, it's called, about a woman shunned for her longing. *Get thee to a nunnery*, Prince Hamlet says to Ophelia. She drowns herself at the end, in a river of flowers.

Her hair is long like mine, and when she lies in the river, I imagine she's at peace. To think this is a sin like all else, and yet I cannot stop myself from going to the jam cellar to copy what I must remember.

*There's rosemary, that's for remembrance; pray, love, remember; and there are pansies, that's for thoughts. . . .*

As Mother and I tack the first pieces of blue fabric together, I hear the words as rhythms, this song I can't erase. . . . *You must wear your rue with a difference. There's a daisy. I would give you some violets, but they wither'd all—*

When Mother finishes pinning the outline, she says, "Shall we start them for the side sitters?"

"We might as well," I say.

I don't know what I look like in blue. I'd look in the mirror if I could, at Mrs. Caldwell's. I am less afraid than I was to see myself as I am, less ashamed, and this must be a worse sin. Instead, I imagine the side sitters in their matching dresses with high collars. The same blue, with white aprons upon them, though theirs won't be organdy like mine.

Isaac's younger sister, Grace, will be a side sitter, and Lydia Yoder, another youth from our district, who works at the market fruit stand with her mother and two sisters. Lydia went to another school, but her mother and father, Ellie and Peter, visited with us frequently after we lost Beth. They sat in our parlor and read the Scripture.

In the weeks following, our neighbors and cousins brought us food. They sent their sons and daughters to do the milking and mowing. Lydia kept me company when I was still getting back my strength, but we barely talk now. She didn't want to go on her Rumspringa. It's Mother's wish to include her, and I don't say anything while she sketches the shape of Lydia's apron.

Yesterday, after I told Mrs. Caldwell I was going to be married—while we trimmed the edging along the stone path—she asked me about flowers for the wedding, and I told her there wouldn't be any, just as we didn't have them for funerals. She was confused. "But bouquets are wonderful?" she said. I told her I didn't know why. Told her I'd never been to a party with flowers.

Then she showed me her own wedding pictures. Bouquets of yellow roses and lilac and calla lilies. And then there was the lace trim on her dress, the diamond drops that hung from her ears. She still had her white satin wedding shoes. I didn't tell her about the black top shoes I will wear, nor about my plain black bonnet instead of a veil.

After Mrs. Caldwell showed me her photographs, I kept thinking about how it had felt to wear silk for Isaac that night. *The "s" sound of English words like silk and suede and satin*, I wrote in my diary. *There is nothing more lovely.* I scribbled them in pencil, too, next to the lines about Ophelia. Perhaps one day my child will read them. Sometimes I speak them aloud in case the baby can hear them somehow, words swooshing like wind through the trees.

I've started writing *you*, my child, addressing my thoughts to you as I do with Beth.

When we finish cutting the side-sitter capes, I almost tell Mother that I saw you. That they printed a picture, a *sonogram*, for me to take home.

I want you to know that I think the word *sonogram* is beautiful in its own way. This picture made of sound waves—*echoes*, Dr. Lee explained—and it seems right, the way the sounds of words cast shadows, ripple out in my mind as you grow inside me, a little more each day.

I don't tell Mother, and I won't show her the words I write; I can't, because they draw pictures, and though I want her to know the baby is healthy, I don't know what she'd say about a sonogram, or all of these medical tests I need. Would she feel bad knowing she might have been able to make Eli better before he was born? It's all too much to weigh. I won't say anything to Mother unless she asks. If she does, I'll say my appointment went well. That I have a due date. I won't admit to the night terrors that persist even after I saw you on the screen, my fear that somehow no matter what we do, we are still powerless to fate. That the most we can do is learn to accept what we can't understand. I'll never know what Eli sees in the shadows or smells in the rain or hears in the wind chimes. Only that God passes through him, just as he passes through you, shaping you into His love.

"I've spoken to Lettie," Mother says once all the hem lines are pinned, the fabric folded into the sewing basket. "We'll have a roast turkey and ham. Mashed potatoes and butter beans. And at least fifty loaves of bread. A love feast," she says, like nothing could be funnier.

"Yes," I say, wishing I thought the same—that jokes about baking and cleaning were funny, not English jokes or double entendres like Mrs. Caldwell showed me in Shakespeare. In *Hamlet*, before she let me take it home, she showed me a line she had underscored.

*It would cost you a groaning to take off my edge*, Hamlet tells Ophelia. Mrs. Caldwell said "edge" could mean two things. *To be on edge was to be irritable*, she said. *But Hamlet means something else. He means he desires Ophelia. His edge means an erection. There are tons of these in Shakespeare's plays*, she said. *Phrases that can be construed in different ways, depending on the context.*

It's like a game to me, to find the double meanings. I've never been given the chance for this, to see beyond the lines. We are taught to read what is there, in the Scripture, the Word of God, not to look for hidden meaning. In these borrowed books, I fold the pages with passages I want to remember. I've read the line about Hamlet's edge many times. How free English books are to name this part of the body rather than hide it.

We act as if our bodies are for making children only. Not for the pleasure I want to feel on our wedding night. Not for seeing if it will be easier the more times I try. For learning Isaac's body, as he is learning mine.

At the appointment, Dr. Lee had urged me to be safe. *You'll want to avoid intercourse*, she said, *until you're further along.*

*She's only saying that as a precaution*, Mrs. Caldwell explained later over lunch. *Because you are a higher-risk patient, she is focusing on safety, so things can go smoothly.*

I wanted to ask what she meant—what could go wrong. I didn't, even though I know Mrs. Caldwell wants me to ask her questions, to read as much as I like from her library. To learn other words for sex, other words for being human. *Hamlet is human*, Mrs. Caldwell said. *And Ophelia, too. Imperfect. No matter how much the world might have expected otherwise.*

The more I read, the less afraid I am of darkness. Of sadness and pain, of desire and sin. Books give me names for things, tell me I'm not alone. When Isaac and I marry, I don't know what he will say about the books I still want to read. The writing I still want to do. Not apart from him, in hiding, but in plain sight. Would he react like Mother if I showed him my writings, or would he listen to me because of what we've both been through? Will he let me read as much as I like, let me be more than my family sees in me, more than what others think they know of us? Would he read with me if I asked?

*Reading helps me through life transitions*, Mrs. Caldwell had said after she explained the line of Shakespeare. *Every story has its own situation*, she said. *Its own context, and once you know the context you can interpret lines within that world. Find new meanings again, and again, so the story never gets old.*

Mrs. Caldwell has a whole shelf of more plays for me to read. *Not just tragedies*, she said. *Comedies. Lots of double entendres. But I'll warn you, things people found funny then might not seem as funny now. See what you think.*

The more books I take, the harder it is for me to hide them. I'll give *Hamlet* back and take *As You Like It*, one of the comedies. I'll see how many I can get through before November. I want to see if I laugh, and how it will feel to laugh about different things than Mother thinks are funny. The breadmaking for the love feast. For communion. For Pentecost. For getting married. Our work never ends, and yet we are supposed to make light of it always.

I've begun to write down what I'm afraid of naming, such as the shadows that follow my feet when I walk in the sun, not so different from the ones that cover your face, still forming in the sonogram photos the doctor printed. Such as how when I can't sleep, I trace you on my naked body, your shape like a sound inside me. *Like a wound. A womb. They can be the same if you look closely. Both voids, vacancies at the beginning of our story.*

When I write to *you*, I am writing into the absence, tracing its outline as I once did the stitches on my shoulder. *I am searching for wholeness. To feel my body again as you fill the hole in me. Your head and limbs, hands and feet. Your little heart and lungs, learning to beat and breathe.*

The Sunday that Isaac and I confess before the congregation, I wish Mrs. Caldwell could stand among the others bearing witness, just as my writing lets me bear witness to who I am becoming.

I have written it all for you, in my diary. How we stood before our mothers, our fathers, in Bishop Yoder's living room. How when we confessed, Isaac and I bent our heads, our hands covering our faces. How we asked to be forgiven separately, and together, in time to be married. How the congregation held on to the silence that followed until Bishop Yoder, with his white tufts of hair around his ears, his long beard grazing his chest, finally nodded and blessed us, and we waited for the others to join in unison. *Amen.*

Afterward, when we stepped through the forebay doors, the sky was blue and open, the fields glittering gold.

To you, I write, *Why should we ask to be forgiven for our love? Our happiness? Why must we be forgiven like the milkman who hurt us was?* I think, *Unnergewwe*. To give under, always, but why?

There's a cross-stitch Mother keeps in Eli's room that reads: *Friendship with the world is enmity with God*, the words of James. Mrs. Caldwell will always be "the world" in Mother's eyes. My giving under to the Lord is for Mother, for all she's suffered. I need Mother's love more than Mrs. Caldwell's friendship. I want her sacrifice to be enough, to carry on through me, through Isaac, through our child.

# RUTH WALSH

## FALL 2019

After the baptism, after Ruth goes home to check on Eli, she finds herself reaching for the cherry pie and setting out for Mrs. Caldwell's house. A mile into the two-mile journey, she realizes she forgot her shoes. On her shoulder she carries a bag with extra money and a change of clothes that she's been keeping under her bed. She doesn't recall grabbing it. When she arrives at the Caldwells' driveway, she slows her pace.

Is it too late to turn around? She asks God for strength, keeps walking. As her bare feet pass over the warm cement, she senses the grit of a few small stones through her callused skin. She reaches for the doorbell and presses down, hears a faint rustling as she waits. In a moment she realizes it's not the wind but the sound of human hands among a branches, a tool clipping.

Ruth follows the sound until she sees a figure along the garden path. Mrs. Caldwell, bent over a bush with her garden shears, doesn't notice Ruth, not even as Ruth steps into her shadow, praying her tongue will move when she reaches this woman. "No turning back," she whispers to herself, gripping the pie in her hands.

Finally, Mrs. Caldwell turns, startles at the sight of her. "Can I help you?" she says as if Ruth were a stranger. But she does know Ruth—*Ruth Walsh*, rising from the ashes this woman left behind.

Ruth opens her mouth to speak. Several long seconds pass, and when she gets her lips to form words at last, she cannot stop them, calm them in the way of the Lord. "Where is she!"

Mrs. Caldwell sets down her scissors in the grass. She rises, approaches Ruth cautiously. "Who?" she asks.

Ruth wants to seize her, shake her. Instead, she recites Galatians in her mind. *Be glad, barren woman, you who never bore a child. You who were never in labor.*

Mrs. Caldwell crosses her arms, sleeveless in the sun, and their bareness nearly makes Ruth sneer. She cannot hide any longer. God would not redeem this woman, unlike the desolate one of Galatians, not after what she has done.

"Can we go inside, to talk?" Mrs. Caldwell asks. "Lighten your load?"

She reaches to take the pie, but Ruth hugs it to her chest. "I've got it," she says.

They walk toward the back patio, and then through the glass doors into the house.

*I forgive you, Mrs. Caldwell.* How many times she had repeated it—morning, noon and night—as if saying it enough would make it true.

"Take a seat," Sara says in the kitchen, then walks to the cabinet above the sink for two glasses.

Cabinets her daughter dusted, glasses she drank from while she worked, Ruth thinks, setting the pie on the kitchen table. She pulls out a chair, but when Mrs. Caldwell brings over their glasses, she decides the pie isn't safe there. She reaches for it, sets it in her lap—not understanding her own impulse.

"Is water okay? Or do you want some iced tea? It'll only take me a minute to make."

"Water's fine," Ruth says. As Sara gathers ice from the freezer, she wonders: Did Emma like iced tea? Did she listen to music or the television, this din Ruth hears now in the background? Distractions Mrs. Caldwell planned, no doubt, as if she had nothing better to do than entice Ruth's daughter with these luxuries. She feels stupid—yes, this is the word that comes to her now—for including Sara in Emma's wedding dinner. Not to have seen the signs sooner, and then to have condoned this woman's influence with the invitation!

Mrs. Caldwell places long half-moons of ice in each glass and sits across from Ruth, drinking the water, taking her time, seemingly unaware of Ruth's gnawing urge to knock the air from her lungs.

"Did you walk here?" Mrs. Caldwell says. "You must be so tired."

Ruth nods, though she isn't playing dumb. Mrs. Caldwell had always been so eager to pick up Emma in her expensive car. Even when Abraham would have driven her in the buggy, Emma said declining the offer was rude.

Ruth had agreed they should be grateful, that there wasn't any harm in Emma accepting these rides. She couldn't have been more wrong. A barren woman was jealous. A desolate woman lacked remorse.

Outside, a truck pulls up—a delivery truck, by the sound of it—and Ruth tenses as she hears footsteps, and then the ring of the doorbell.

"Will you excuse me for just one minute? I have to sign for this."

"No problem," Ruth says, though she can't help but shiver, thinking about how the milkman had driven a truck. How Teacher Martha had opened the door to a stranger.

The English did it all the time. Anything for the sake of transaction. The exchange of services. Now Ruth hears beeping, sees lights blinking through a gap in the curtains, then the sound of Mrs. Caldwell signing for the package, thanking the stranger.

Ruth had forgiven *him* years ago. In a matter of days. She had forced herself to imagine his pain in losing his child—his stillborn daughter—what he could not make right with God. She had thought of his infant's motionless face, her closed eyes. Peaceful. Not how Beth's had been, unrecognizable on the coroner's cold table, in the metallic room of the morgue.

"Thank you for waiting. I'm so sorry. I had these perennials overnighted, and I'm worried about them getting enough sun. I'll just to set them on the porch, and then we can talk. When it rains it pours, you know?"

Ruth feels herself nodding, but she is still inside the morgue, shuddering in the chill air, remembering how even as Abraham signed the papers, she'd insisted it couldn't be her. It wasn't her, *not Beth*, and then Abraham had held her, calmed her, said it would be over soon.

When Mrs. Caldwell enters the kitchen again, Ruth is standing, the pie once more in her hands. "Where is she?"

"I don't know," Mrs. Caldwell says, the color leaving her face. "Let's sit down and—"

"No. Just tell me where she is!" Ruth is shouting just like she'd done at the morgue, where the weight of her grief had pulled her to the concrete floor, leaving her to grasp for Abraham's ankles.

"I said I don't know."

"*But you do.*" Ruth manages to lower her voice, yet still she wants to throw the pie on the floor, see the rancid cherry filling, molded green and gray, spill over the ceramic tile for Mrs. Caldwell to clean.

As if Mrs. Caldwell senses this, she backs away. "I wish I could tell you—" she says softly, her eyes filling with moisture.

"Who else could have driven her? Shown her the way?" Ruth can't hide her rage, her desire to do injury, now that they've made themselves known.

"She must have called a taxi. From a public phone—"

Ruth waits for her to finish, to shame herself, condemn herself with these falsehoods. But the woman cuts herself off, straightens as if she's come to some conclusion.

"I told Emma . . . I wouldn't disclose her whereabouts," Mrs. Caldwell says. "I'm sorry. I made a promise. I do wish I could tell you, and you deserve to know she's safe, but I gave her my word. I hope you can understand—"

Ruth's arms begin to tremble, then her legs follow, and she's forced to sit so as not to embarrass herself by collapsing. All the while, she refuses to look away, holding the other woman's gaze.

"I tried to find out," Mrs. Caldwell says. "But she didn't send an address after she left, and when I looked . . . She might have changed her name."

"Why would she?" Ruth asks, relying on bitterness to keep her steady.

"I don't know. She bought her own ticket." Mrs. Caldwell pauses. "But I did take her to the station."

She looks away after this last statement, and something in Ruth is appeased. At last. A show of guilt.

"Without a place to live?" she says. "Pregnant?"

"I knew she'd find work," Mrs. Caldwell says. "And she said she had savings."

"Just tell me where you sent her," Ruth insists. "Tell me who helped her!"

"I can't," Sara says, tears trickling now.

"I am her mother. You are *nothing*." Then Ruth lunges—it's no longer only in her head, this terrible violence—but instead of reaching for Mrs. Caldwell, she falls to the floor, still clutching the pie.

Mrs. Caldwell is immediately there beside her. On her knees. "It's all right," she says, but her breath is as shallow as Ruth's. "Let's get you more water." She reaches out her hand to help Ruth up.

"No," Ruth says. "Don't." Slowly, she rises on her own. She fixes her bonnet, reapplies a pin. Then she hands the pie to Mrs. Caldwell, and without another word, reaches for her bag and walks to the door. She is running by the time she reaches the road, barefoot along the warm asphalt, her bag hitting her side. As she labors on, she imagines Mrs. Caldwell unwrapping the pie. Under a green sheath of mold, the red cherries have turned black, like the rotted eyes of a fish. The thought of it is enough to make her stop, breathe, off the side of the road. She doesn't know how long she's there until she hears, "Ruth."

When she turns, she finds Mrs. Caldwell in her long black car with the window rolled down. Strange but also familiar; before, it was Ruth watching from the kitchen window, all those times Mrs. Caldwell had picked up Emma.

"I'll help you find her," she says. "She's in Philadelphia."

Ruth nods slowly, struck by an emotion she can't name.

"If you hop in, I'll take you to the train station."

Reaching for the car door, Ruth slides inside.

Mrs. Caldwell tells her she doesn't know Emma's exact address, only the name of her friend, a realtor, who helped Emma find an apartment in the city.

"The truth is I haven't heard from her since she left," Mrs. Caldwell says. "I wish I had more I could give you."

As she speaks, her eyes seem softer, her sympathy more genuine—

or maybe it's Ruth's relief, her hope, that lets her see there is still some good in this woman.

"We have thirty minutes till the next train," Mrs. Caldwell says, gripping the steering wheel. "If we hurry, we can make it."

Ruth nods once more, holding tightly to her bag as Mrs. Caldwell speeds down the backroads, her neighbors' farms slipping farther away. After praying for the strength to take the train into the city, she counts her savings in her mind, the cash she's kept folded in an envelope for a day like today. She has enough for a hotel and food for several days, enough to give Emma as a gift for the baby. Ruth's hidden the growing sum from Abraham for over a year now, working extra to pay both for Eli and save for this—for finding her daughter.

When they reach the station, Ruth doesn't have time to second guess her decisions. Only ten minutes to buy her ticket and look for the right platform as Mrs. Caldwell instructs. Hurrying out of the car, she begins to run for the entrance.

"Wait," she hears behind her. Mrs. Caldwell is getting out of the car, unbuckling her sandals. "You'll need these," she says. "It'll be a lot of walking when you get there."

Ruth doesn't know what she was thinking, how she forgot about the problem of shoes. "Thank you," she says, taking Mrs. Caldwell's sandals from her and slipping them in her bag.

"Be safe," Sara says.

These words echo in Ruth's mind while she races up the stairs to the main concourse. Her breathing is jagged as she passes a blur of English bodies clutching much larger bags than her own. While she waits in line for her ticket, she buckles on Mrs. Caldwell's shoes. She feels the eyes of strangers on her, but then she remembers this is all part of God's plan. He wants her to bring her daughter home.

# SARA CALDWELL

## FALL 2018

Sara has always liked her garden best this time of year. Now Emma gets to enjoy it too—after all those hours hunched over in the sweltering summer heat. Now that it's September, shades of orange and plum and scarlet adorn her property like a dream. The caladiums, purple fountain grass, sedum, and coxcomb. Last week she and Emma hung fresh baskets of mums from the front porch, and they'd planted another row of asters and marigolds along the path to the back patio where the guests will gather for mulled wine with homemade cinnamon buns.

Before the party begins, Sara asks for Emma's help with the final set of party favors, little bars of goat-milk soap with a mixture of sage and lavender.

As Emma slips the soaps into sheer, dainty sachet bags, Sara can't believe she's already three months along. Emma isn't showing yet, at least as far as Sara can tell. She seems happy, eyes gleaming as she ties silk ribbon around another sachet. At Emma's eleven-week appointment, the genetic tests came back normal, and Sara is so relieved for her. At twenty-weeks, she'll have a comprehensive ultrasound to check for deformities and any other complications they wouldn't otherwise be aware of. Of course, Sara hasn't told Peter how much she knows. And he doesn't bring it up, doesn't convey his own analysis of the situation. Sara is certain Dr. Lee sends him updates, but so far she hasn't said anything about Emma's friend who accompanies her to appointments.

As far as Dr. Lee knows, Sara is just someone who wants to help, maybe even a social worker because she walks the walk and talks the talk.

Sara is so glad she can support Emma—can't imagine the isolation she'd feel at that age, expecting a child and unable to talk to her mother about it, at least not in a real way, outside of preparing for the wedding. At the appointments, Sara gets a taste of what it would have been like in more ways than one. She can see her past self, her naïve teenage self, juxtaposed against her adult self now—a woman who's never had to go through the uncertainties of pregnancy.

Part of her feels a little jealous. Or maybe this isn't the right word. More like sad, because no matter how many times she tells herself it isn't too late, it is. Peter has made this clear. She could imagine all she wanted, fantasize all she wanted, about surrogates or in vitro, but she's married to a geneticist thirteen years older than she. How many times would she have to remind herself of this very fact, bring herself back to reality, all while living through Emma, imagining the future through her eyes?

She might never be a mother, not in the way Ruth Walsh is or Emma is soon to be, but she knows what it means to sacrifice your hopes and dreams for someone else. In Emma's case, it was her community, and Isaac was part of that. The reality, if she left the community, would be finding work and pursuing an education as a single mother. If Sara were in Emma's shoes, would she really think she could brave such a life alone?

She stirs the mulled wine, adds some extra sage, some star anise and cranberries. The rolls are already in the oven, the kitchen warm with the scent of brown butter cinnamon. Sara fills a copper mug to taste the wine. She drinks it quickly, then fills another, feeling the room soften a little, her nerves settle.

Peter is catching up on some "weekend paperwork" at the clinic. His excuse, she knows, for not wanting to mix their worlds too closely. Such hypocrisy. What would the neighbors say to him putting Sara up to hiring Amish help, given his connections? Would they ask for Emma's services, too, seeing this line had been crossed? Sara doesn't know. But she's protective of Emma, especially now.

"I was thinking of making an herbal tea," Emma says after tying the last bag. "With the leftover lavender."

"Good idea." Sara sets her wine aside and starts filling a basket with the party favors while Emma chops the herbs, along with some fresh lemon for the tea. As the tea water boils, Sara prepares the patio table. She sets the party favors around a vase of fresh-cut flowers. Some dahlias and late-blooming roses. Luckily, the temperature is mild today, and if it drops later, she'll light the firepit for the guests to gather around.

When she returns to the kitchen, Emma is already stirring the tea.

"Let it simmer," Sara says. "There's something I want to give you."

"Me?" Emma asks, drying her hands on her apron.

"Yes, *you*. Who else?" Sara fetches the gift from the living room and hands it to her.

Carefully, Emma unwraps the paper. She looks up and smiles when she sees what it is. "Another book?"

"A journal," Sara says. "I thought it could be good for keeping a pregnancy log. How you're feeling, things you want to remember. What you're reading."

"I don't have any books on that," Emma says.

"Oh, not necessarily pregnancy books," she says. "But the ones you're borrowing. Poetry. Novels. Whatever you want. I know how much you like to read."

"Thank you," Emma says. "Thank you very much." She looks at Sara like she's about to say something else. Like there's some other secret she's hiding. But maybe it's just that this will be another secret between them—that she has her own journal now, a proper diary.

Without another word, Emma goes back to the tea. She presses her other hand to her belly, as if she can feel the baby move. But it would be too early for that, wouldn't it? Sara had read that the first kicks happened around sixteen weeks, and Emma was at twelve.

Inadvertently, Sara places her hand on her own belly. She blinks. Too much wine. She reaches for a banana, something to fill her stomach before her guests arrive.

When the first pull up a half hour later, Sara asks Emma to fill the water cooler with ice, then pour the tea so they can take it out with the wine.

Sara's neighbor, Melinda Herr, finds them on the back patio.

"I didn't know it was Amish themed!" Melinda says, kissing Sara's cheek.

Sara glances at Emma, embarrassed. "It's not," she says. "This is Emma."

"Oh, my mistake," Melinda says, unaware of her gaffe. "You're so pretty."

"Thank you," Emma says.

"I am always telling my husband," Melinda goes on, "that Amish girls are so lovely. No makeup. Perfect center parts."

Sara changes the topic quickly. "How are you, Melinda?" But before Melinda can answer, Debbie Wright, another neighbor, greets them.

"I love what you've done," she says.

Both Melinda and Debbie live in the newer neighborhood off Mondamin Farms. Large four-bedroom households with finished basements and decks. Melinda's son, Cal, was headed for Colby in the fall, while Debbie had two high-schoolers, Annie and Rachel.

Before long, Wendy Muller and Lisa Bernstein arrive. Both women lived on Pine Ridge, closer to the border with Amish country.

"How did you find someone capable of this, if you don't mind my asking? Through Peter?" Wendy says, as if on cue—but at least this time Emma is in the kitchen, taking out the cinnamon rolls.

"Sort of," Sara says, which is a lie but not entirely. Yes, it was Peter's idea to provide Emma with the extra work, but not to reimagine Sara's garden party, at least not to this extent. When more guests arrive, like Georgina Muller and Emily White, Sara is tired of answering questions about Emma.

Everyone wants tips on Amish soil, Amish color palettes, Amish calm, certain as they are that Emma's peaceful nature, and her connection to the earth, are good for the plants. At the same time, though, Sara is glad for the affirmation. To finally be seen by neighbors constantly lording it over her about what their kids are up to. About lavish vacations at four-star hotels. Husbands who buy them expensive jewelry for milestones. Unlike Peter, whose work is everything. She supposed she should be grateful that her companionship has always mattered more to him than how well she dresses, or how socially connected she is to the Lancaster scene.

Sara has never cared about these things, of course, and yet for these women to be so curious about her suddenly . . . she finds she doesn't completely dislike the attention. Without thinking, she says, "Emma is getting married, you know."

"Really?" Debbie says, reaching for a warm roll from a basket Emma has brought out.

"How old are you, Emma?" Debbie asks.

"Eighteen."

"Oh, to be young again," Wendy says.

Wendy was notorious for drinking on antidepressants. She carried with her a large Yeti cooler that was filled with white wine at all times.

"Can't say I'd want to get married at that age," Debbie says. "No offense."

"Debbie. Please," Sara says. But what did she expect, bringing up Emma's personal life like this? Was she really willing to lose her trust over people she didn't even care about?

"I'm sorry," Debbie says. "Am I out of line?"

"Hardly," Lisa says, raising her eyebrows at Sara as if to say: *Why did you invite Debbie in the first place?*

"I've never been to an Amish wedding," Lisa says. "But I'm intrigued. Tell me, what will you wear? Or is it taboo to say?" She looks to Sara for reassurance that she is *not* out of line, and though Sara should stop her, at least change the subject, she doesn't.

"I've been to an Amish wedding," Emily says. "When our girl, Gladys, got married. Do you know Gladys?" she asks Emma, as if all Amish women are all the same.

"No," Emma says.

Sara can't tell if she is annoyed or simply shocked.

"Isn't everyone a cousin?" Wendy says, already slurring her words. By now, Emma is hurrying to the kitchen like she's forgotten something. Sara rushes after her, reaches for her arm. Emma is crying.

"I'm so sorry," Sara says. "My friends have had too much to drink." Even hearing the words, *my friends*, feels wrong. Over the past few months, Emma has filled Sara with a sense of renewed purpose she didn't think was possible, not since her work at the prison. These women, her "friends," could have cared less about Sara's previous life in Philly, or the time she'd spent hustling in New York City before grad school. Anytime Sara mentioned the boys at the prison to Emma, she really listened.

As if Emma can read her thoughts, she reassures Sara. "It's okay."

"To be honest, I've had too much to drink myself," Sara adds. "I don't know what compelled me—"

Emma cuts her off with a wave of her hand; she doesn't want Sara to say it again—that she's getting married.

But Sara can't help herself. "I didn't mean to make you uncomfortable. I know your wedding is a private matter."

"It's all right," Emma says again. "I'm not angry."

"I'll make it up to you. Please—if you'll let me?"

"No," Emma says. "You don't have to. You've already helped me so much." There are still tears in her eyes, which she wipes with her apron. "Really, I'm fine."

Then Peter enters the kitchen out of nowhere.

Sara startles. "I thought you were working?" she says.

"I needed a break," he says. "And I couldn't miss this. You've both been working so hard. How are you, Emma?" His eyes look concerned, skeptical.

Before Peter can say anything else, Sara hands him a glass of iced tea. "Can you take out another basket of rolls?" she asks Emma.

"Yes," Emma says. And then: "Would you like one, Dr. Caldwell?"

"Oh," Peter says, "they look so delicious. But I really shouldn't."

"Are you watching your figure or something?" Sara laughs.

Peter shakes his head.

"Don't be rude, Peter," she says. "Emma's been slaving away at this all morning. And believe me, you haven't tasted a cinnamon roll until you've tried one of hers."

"If you insist," Peter says, reaching into the basket.

When Emma is outside with the guests, he sighs audibly.

"Go on," Sara says. "Try one." She watches as Peter takes a bite.

"Wow, you're right," he says. "This is really something."

Before either of them can talk—or rather before Peter can reprimand her, which she knows he wants to do—Emma is back again.

"One of the guests is feeling sick," she says.

Peter quickly heads to the door to see what's going on. Outside, Wendy looks like she's about to vomit. And yet she is laughing, unaware of herself.

Sara shakes her head. What was she thinking, inviting Wendy?

"I'll call Don," Peter says. "Have him pick her up."

While Peter makes the call in the living room, Emma asks Sara what's wrong. If maybe it was the food.

"Oh, no. Definitely not. She made poor choices," Sara says, surprised that this is turning into a lesson.

"Like me," Emma says. "Too much drinking."

"I don't mean it like that," Sara says. "This isn't something that happens to Wendy once in a while. Or because she's still learning her limit for alcohol. Wendy has a problem. She can't stop drinking. She does it every day."

"Oh," Emma says. "Until she's sick?"

"Yes," Sara says. "I guess so, when you put it like that."

Before Peter finishes the call to Don, Emma pulls Sara aside.

"I was going to ask earlier," Emma says. "When you gave me the journal. But it was a busy time."

"Oh," Sara says. "No problem. What is it?"

"I've been meaning to ask you—if you'd like to come to my wedding dinner?"

Sara can hardly believe she's heard correctly. That Emma would still extend an invitation, after this?

"Dr. Caldwell too," she says. "Mother and I are both hoping you can come. And Isaac would love to meet you."

"We'd be honored, Emma. Really. When is it?"

"In three weeks. The first Tuesday of November."

Emma's eyes are bright again. Sara opens her phone, checks her calendar. "November third," she says. "I'll have to double-check with Peter, but so far we're clear. He'll be thrilled—as I am." Then Sara asks what time the dinner will be.

"Lunch is dinner." Emma laughs. "At noon."

"Like Thanksgiving dinner, if you're traditional," Sara adds.

"Yes, like that."

Sara almost asks what she should wear but doesn't want to appear ignorant. She'll look this up online later, or in one of her books. "Let's get you home," she says. "Peter can take care of the cleanup. Least he can do." She's joking, but Emma doesn't seem to get it.

"Oh, I don't mean he's responsible for our mess, if that's what you're worried about. But you've done your work for today."

"If you say so," Emma says, but later, when Sara's home again, Peter is, in fact, cleaning up the kitchen, visibly angry.

"What's the matter, Peter?" Sara asks. "I've got it. I just had to take Emma home while you took care of things with Don."

"Yes, Sara," Peter says. "This is about Wendy. And Don."

"Okay, what is it then? Why don't you just come out and say it for once. I'm not in the mood for games."

"Games?" Peter says, opening the closet for the broom.

"Honestly," she says. "I don't see what the problem is. It was a lovely afternoon. The show went smoothly. I guess I thought you'd be happy for us."

Peter pauses. Takes a deep breath. "Us?"

"What?" she says. "I don't understand."

"That's the problem. You don't understand." He's sweeping forcefully, pulling the chairs out from under the kitchen table. "You don't think I notice what you're doing? How much time you're spending together?"

"She works here," Sara says. "She's going to get married and have a baby. She has no one to talk to about it. I didn't know I was committing a crime by being there for her."

Peter sweeps harder, fills the dustpan. Empties it into the trash. "I guess after our last conversation, I thought you'd take things more seriously."

"You mean after you tried to set me straight? Telling me what to do, like I don't have a brain of my own. Really, Peter. You do your job. I'll do mine?"

"Your job? This is social work to you?"

"Last time I checked, we talked about getting Emma some therapy. At least giving her that option. I thought you were clear on that part."

"Clear? You act like we agreed about what you're doing. Sara, we've never been on the same page on this. If I'm honest with you, I wish I'd put a stop to it in July."

"Jesus, Peter. Do you hear yourself? How you're talking to me?"

Peter just looks at her, like a parent who is both disappointed and stunned.

"Fine," he says. "Tell me? How am I talking to you?"

"Like I don't have any volition. Like I'm your assistant or something. An assistant who gives your patients work but can't have her own opinions, her own experience about what she's been asked to do. It's mind-boggling, really."

Peter sets the broom against the kitchen counter. Sits down and reaches for another cinnamon roll from the plate of leftovers. He peels away the outer layer and stuffs in the middle, barely able to keep his mouth closed. Sara watches him in the sustained silence as he chews, wiping his hands, then his mouth, with a napkin.

"Let me put it another way," Peter says, clearly struggling for calm. "I just think she's filling some kind of need for you. It's like—" He stops himself. "—never mind."

"What?" she says. "Go on, just say it."

"It's like you think of her as a kind of daughter. A child you never had."

Sara laughs. "You're projecting, Peter. You want to control the narrative. This is the easiest way for you to explain things to yourself. There's a lot you don't know."

"You mean like the fact you've given her your clothes to wear? And I know *you know* more about her pregnancy than you let on."

Sara wants to stop him, but what can she say?

"Look," he says, "this isn't some hippie experiment, Sara. This is serious. We have no right to interfere with Emma's life. Sway her one way or another. We don't know the first thing about what it's like for her—to grow up with a very specific set of values and ideas about the world."

"I'm fully aware of that," Sara says. "What if I told you that Emma has revealed things to me she's never told anyone else, completely unprompted?"

"Really," Peter says, shaking his head. "Unprompted, huh?"

In his voice, she can hear the anger rising again. The frustration.

"Fine," he says. "What was it, then? What did she tell you?"

"I swore I wouldn't tell anyone, especially you."

"This is juvenile, Sara. I don't have time for it."

"Right," Sara says. "You don't have time. Hasn't that always been the problem? You don't want a child when we could actually still try for one. You accuse me of pouring my repressed desire to be a mother into one of your patients. And now you don't have time to talk about it. About any of it, after I've been the one to set my life aside, all these years. My needs. My hopes."

Peter looks away, out the window to the garden, illuminated in the patio lights.

"Look," he says finally. "I get it. I'm sorry. I know it isn't easy for you. But the Walshes are a very sensitive case. They've been through a lot, Emma's mother especially."

Sara says, "You think I don't know that?"

"I don't want to fight with you. Don't want us to accuse each other of things and get defensive. But I do need to ask that you stop what you're doing. Please, for the sake of the family and my practice.

Peter looks at her sternly in the same authoritarian way he always has. And she's put up with this. But she knows nothing she can say will change his mind. Nothing she does can make him see from her point of view. Better to play along.

"Fine," Sara says. "I'll spend less time with her. If it's that important to you."

"Thank you," he says.

As Peter goes upstairs to change for his evening workout, she returns to the party—a few guests still remain even after the drama—and she's not about to let her and Emma's hard work go to waste. Even so, while she circulates among the stragglers, she makes other plans.

She decides Peter's jealousy, his selfish insecurity, is his own problem to solve, not hers. She won't bother him with the wedding invitation. She'll simply tell Emma he can't make it. That work has gotten in the way. Friday, they'd continue as planned—with Sara taking Emma to her twelve-week appointment. Afterward they'll go to lunch again, to the new Thai place she's been wanting to try.

# EMMA WALSH

## FALL 2018

The day of the wedding, Mother washes my hair. When it's dry, she parts it cleanly down the middle. The muslin curtains of the parlor are radiant with morning light. *Mourning light*, I think—something lost, something gained. Everything is about to change for me. The clock ticks into the silence, but my heart is louder, and I hold my left wrist, counting the pulse along the veins.

Mother works gently as she twists my hair into a smooth low bun, then fixes the pins. Without mirrors, we might as well do it with our eyes closed. The last pins are to secure my black hair covering, tight by my ears. My apron is organdy. The closest we have to lace—what Mrs. Caldwell had worn. I picture her dress, her veil, and wonder why my costume must be different. Why can't I carry flowers? Katy Fisher, who had been at the schoolhouse like Mary Ann Stoltzfus and me, works at the flower shop with a greenhouse. Katy, unlike Mary Ann, plans to be baptized next year. Katy's eyes were damaged in the shooting, but she got surgery and can see better now. I've thought of talking to her, too, about what happened. Of asking if Mrs. Caldwell would take me to visit, but I don't think Katy would like talking to me while someone she doesn't know is there.

I didn't like it in the beginning, either. It didn't feel natural, or right, to talk to Mrs. Caldwell, but now I think it's the only reason I'm still writing. The only way to be less afraid of having a child. If I saw Katy,

I'd ask for a bouquet of calla lilies and red roses and baby's breath. I wouldn't tell her why, because to tell her would suggest I've been writing words that are forbidden, reading books she might never read. That I've been granted the opportunity to see myself and our world in a different way.

Katy's brother Solomon was one of the boys the man sent to his truck to get supplies. He stopped eating afterward, blamed himself for failing to protect us—though at the time, he thought he was. He thought if he followed the man's orders, we would be safe. Instead, he helped the man hurt us.

Solomon was the same age as Beth. If she'd lived, Beth might have married him or another boy in our class. But Solomon had married another woman in Leola, Elizabeth Schrock, and they already had three children. All that's left of Beth are the trees where the schoolhouse used to be and a grave with a wood cross etched with her name, the year she was born, the year she passed. Nothing like the graveyard off Plum Street Alley that Mrs. Caldwell pointed out on the way to the hospital. We didn't stop, but the stones haunt my periphery, as well as the mounds of flowers, bursts of red and yellow that suggest a forgotten dream.

We don't leave flowers before our graves. I wish to plant eucalyptus for Beth or cut roses and calla lilies from an English bouquet for her. I wish for there to be some special word or shape or scent to set her apart from the others. To renew her memory, the way morning light renews the curtains, or shadows remake the floor.

You remake me too, in the gray vibrations of each sonogram over the course of many weeks. Same as my diary does, by my pencil marks, or in the lines from Shakespeare and Virginia Woolf and Edith Södergran and Emily Dickinson. I hide my diary in my bedroom now, in the blanket chest, because Mother doesn't want me going to the cellar anymore, not for anything, lest I fall.

On my wedding day, after Mother has pinned my cape, I almost don't recognize myself, not even my outline in the window glass when I part the curtain and look out to our front yard, watching the buggies come in. It *is* me, same as always, in my uniform, only in blue and organdy instead of black cotton, but I am not me. Not anymore.

The ceremony is held in our living room, and even this feels strange, like I am both home and not home. Familiar people appear like strangers as they find seats among the chairs Mother and Father have set out, leaving room for Eli in the back. Isaac meets me in his Sunday best, his newehockers too, their vests fastened with matching hooks and eyes. Isaac wears a pressed white shirt, short-brimmed hat, and black high-top shoes like mine. His beard is starting to show, and after we are married, he'll grow it long.

Sitting beside him feels safe, even as everything else is strange. *We have done this before*, I think. Two weeks ago, when we were baptized. *We have given our vows like this before the church.*

As Bishop Yoder blesses us, asks us to promise to love each other, in sickness and in health, my side sitters watch from along the wood bench, in a stretch of dark blue. In the dim lighting of this room, they are bearing witness. Lydia and Judith and Pricilla. I long for Beth to be among them. I think of Mary Ann and Katy. Why aren't they here with me instead? *We, who are survivors among the dead, and the living.*

Isaac turns to me during Bishop Yoder's long sermon. His eyes are soft and kind, as always. He grounds me, and when the bishop asks us to stand, his feet are firm on the floor, his shoulders back and straight, gaze fixed as the bishop reads from Genesis, then Corinthians, and the Book of Ruth.

*I give you every seedbearing plant on the face of the whole earth and every tree that has fruit with seed in it.*

*If I speak in the tongues of men or of angels, but do not have love, I am only a clanging cymbal.*

*Do not urge me to leave you or to turn back from you. Where you go I will go, and where you stay I will stay.*

Something about these lines, their certainty, chafes me. How can I be so sure, how can we both be so unquestioning about the rest of our lives?

We do not know *you* yet. We hardly know each other. We love each other, but it's our first time loving anyone not our family. Our bodies came together that night, but it was one time, and that doesn't mean love, does it? That Isaac is the only one for me, and I for Isaac?

I hate myself for this thought, how it edges into me, stops me still, no matter how much I want to believe in the words of the Scripture. To submit same as I always have to the Word, to Mother, this other Ruth watching us wed.

*Therefore, as God's chosen people, holy and dearly loved, clothe yourselves with compassion, kindness, humility, gentleness and patience.*

Bishop Yoder reads from Colossians. He reminds us to be loyal to one another as we grow old together, until we are separated by death.

"Bear with each other and forgive one another," he says.

This word again. How many times have I heard it, uttered it, prayed for it? Hoping one day I would believe in it—forgiveness—so my pain, so Beth's, could stop.

It's as if you hear my questioning, my reluctance to believe in a single word for absolution. I feel you kick, your tiny flutter under the loose fabric of my dress.

The doctor said you can hear already, that in a few more weeks, you'll know my voice. For now, my voice is one with my blood coursing through you, and my breath. Sounds are echoes in a cave. What do you know of this room, now?

Do you understand silence? And then hear the gentle sigh of the room as Bishop Yoder places his hands over your father's and mine, to bless our future? Can you sense the others, how they move about me, wanting to embrace me, congratulate me? Do you hear my breath grow short, then long, in the room that is my body, my sanctuary?

*In you, light and shadow flicker at once, like a school of fish caught within my body, waiting to break free.*

When we have lunch, I'm hardly hungry, but I want to give you the strength to swim. We sit at a long table in the barn, Isaac and I holding hands while Lettie Ames and Mother bring out the dishes. The roast chicken and stuffing, the mashed potatoes and creamed celery, the coleslaw and pepper slaw, the corn and carrots and baked bread. Mrs. Caldwell comes, sits alone because Dr. Caldwell couldn't make it. After we finish eating, or after I finish what I can manage, she comes to hug me. "You look so beautiful," she says as she had when I dressed in

English clothes. How could I be the same amount of beautiful, different as I feel, divided between two worlds?

But I only say, "Thank you." I say, "Thank you for coming." And I mean it. It's right for her to be here. But I also wonder if she thinks I'm a coward. How can I enjoy English restaurants and books and music and still go through with it? Why am I so afraid to be independent like she is? She has a husband, and yet she is almost always alone, keeping herself busy, not because she must, but because she wants to.

Of course, we do not dance at our weddings. We don't have a favorite song to choose like she and the doctor did. Sam Cooke, she said, and she'd played it for me on the record player: "Nothing Can Change This Love." She showed me the picture from her wedding album of her and the doctor dancing close in a ballroom, her cheek pressed to his chest. She'd called it that, *ballroom*, at a country club, like something from a fairy tale, something I would never experience myself. My wedding is without dancing or flowers, or a diamond ring, or kissing at the altar, or photographs to print and frame. At my wedding, the most we have is singing songs together and playing volleyball outside in the November chill. I like playing, but not today; I feel heavy when I run, and the doctor said I shouldn't risk throwing off my center of gravity. I could fall, she cautioned. My ligaments were looser, more prone to injury. I could overheat.

Isaac plays, at least, and I watch him laughing, the sunlight catching the stubble along his cheeks. The afternoon slips away. Mrs. Caldwell has already gone home, Mother and Lettie are busy cleaning up, and Eli sits beside me on the bench, happy to be outside where he likes it best—even when it's colder, like now, when we wrap him in an extra blanket. Like me, he watches while the others slap at the ball and laugh. After the sun sets, a sharper chill in the air, I wheel Eli inside. I wait for Isaac to come and meet us, wait for the cleaning to be finished. Mother won't let me help. "Rest," she says, because everyone is afraid of what could happen. Of you sharing Eli's fate. I could relieve their concerns, of course, show Mother the sonograms, or share the reports from the city clinic where I go now for appointments, but I do not. If they know you're healthy, that you don't suffer from a genetic condition, as I learned after the *amniocentesis*, they'll want me to stop going to the English doctor.

In the barn, Isaac and I have a few gifts to open. The clock Father has carved for us, with a gleaming pendulum to chime at noon and midnight. I know how much he labored over it—years—because he cherishes this kind of carving. The detailed parts set in place, gears clicking, ticking, like a heart he put together. Lettie gives me a new eggbeater, and a quilt to seal Isaac and me on our wedding night. I thank her, tell her I love it, because I do. I love the blue diamond in the center, set off by the lavender triangles along the border, mixed with bright green, like a prism reflecting out.

We don't go away on a honeymoon, like Mrs. Caldwell and the doctor did. *In Italy*, she said. When I asked where it was, she showed me on a map. She traced her finger along the coast of Amalfi, where the water was bright blue, she said, and the sand was soft. I've never seen sand. Nor the ocean. The closest thing is the dirt by the creek, where it's finer under my bare feet, and I can feel the water lapping over my toes when the current is strong.

What Isaac and I have for a honeymoon is visiting our family for six days. Aunts and uncles and cousins. We take turns staying at their homes, sleeping under our new quilt as the weather gets colder. By our sixth night, our last supper with Isaac's cousin Judith and his aunt Barbara and uncle Thomas, we are full of macaroni and cheese and fried sweet potatoes and pumpkin and lemon sponge pie. I'm hungrier now, eating as much as I can for the both of us, but I can't help thinking of the foods I had with Mrs. Caldwell. The coconut curry we'd shared at the Thai restaurant downtown. The naan and tikka masala I tasted another afternoon, savoring the stewed tomatoes and spices. I want to tell Isaac about it, but I can't. He wouldn't understand. He might try and put a stop to it, even, because our Rumspringa has passed.

After we finish visiting, we return to live with Mother and Father and Eli until our new house is built in the spring. Though my bed is familiar, and I like sleeping beside Isaac, our bodies next to one another, we must be safe. We can't risk an early labor, the doctor warned. My placenta is close to the cervix, she said, terms I'd needed her to explain.

The placenta is the barrier between you and me, she said. How you receive food from me, and enough blood for your heart to thrum at double the speed of mine.

I should feel calm next to Isaac, comforted that he'll never leave me, that you are safe and healthy and growing, and yet most nights I lie awake, watching the moonlight sharpen, then fade, through the window. Sometimes, I go down to the kitchen for milk and honey toast. Or else I try to stay busy, get a head start on the winter preserving and cooking, the cleaning and milking, before daylight. Still, when night comes around again, I can't sleep.

It bothered me at first when I couldn't see Dr. Lee anymore. Mrs. Caldwell found a city clinic—a low-cost clinic, she called it—for the remaining tests and checkups. I didn't know how expensive it could be—a whole year of market earnings and housecleaning, even more—to cover doctor bills without *insurance*, this thing Mrs. Caldwell says you need as an English person, for everything, in case something goes wrong. When I realized this, I thought it would be too hard for us to keep seeing doctors, but Mrs. Caldwell assured me she knew about these things, from her job before, as a social worker. She told me social workers were people who helped those without resources move through the world, that she wouldn't let anything happen to me.

When I was twenty weeks and the clinic asked for my insurance, Mrs. Caldwell showed me what to do. *She is self-pay*, she told the woman at the front desk. These words scared me. How could they be true when I couldn't pay for myself? At least not yet.

Mrs. Caldwell sensed my worry and said, *It's a city clinic. They see everyone here, knowing not everyone can pay the full amount. Don't worry about that now.*

I nodded, watching as the woman behind the front desk typed quickly into her computer.

In the waiting area, Mrs. Caldwell showed me where to write my name and date of birth. *They just need something on file*, she said.

What would Mother say, I wondered, that the care she thought I was receiving through Dr. Caldwell wasn't real anymore? Even the doctor—what would he think when Dr. Lee's office stopped sending bills? I'm relieved Mother and Father no longer have to pay from our savings, money that should be for Eli, but I keep waiting for them to discover I've begun making decisions without them. To confront me with my lies.

Mrs. Caldwell says not to worry. *The doctor hasn't mentioned anything about it. Trust me, he doesn't know.*

At the clinic, she sits patiently with me while the doctors tell me what to expect the further along I am in my pregnancy.

Each visit, there is a different doctor, but this is normal, too, Mrs. Caldwell says—for the doctors to rotate, sharing my file with each other, talking regularly to plan next steps. *You're in good hands*, she assures me. And I believe her.

When I'm at thirty weeks, the doctors say it's normal for my sleep to be disrupted because my body is changing so quickly, making space for the baby to grow. But it isn't just you kicking or flipping around in my belly that keeps me awake. No, it's my doubt about the future, my guilt over all I am hiding from Isaac. Not just the appointments, or that I am going to a clinic instead of a hospital, but that I am reading books he'll never know about. Poems by Sylvia Plath and stories by James Baldwin and Marguerite Duras, because Mrs. Caldwell says I have a *penchant* for classics. *Penchant*, I learned, is another word for love. She is certain one day, when you are old enough, I'll go to college. That I might even study literature. She says there are scholarships, and I like to dream about this too. At times, when I am thinking of such things, I know Isaac senses my distance.

"Where are you going?" he asked the other night when I rose from bed.

"For chores," I said.

He didn't believe me. I knew it from the way he looked at me, like I was hiding something. What makes it worse is that my hiding is more than stolen moments at night; it's that my happiness is an illusion. He seems so pleased with our new life, so content with where we're going. That so far our baby is healthy, that we have our families to support us in all things, but for me, it will never be so easy.

By the time I'm seven months along, in late January, I must put more effort into pretending, concealing.

The other night, when it was snowing, I watched through the window as flakes fell, softly at first, then at a slant in the wind. When I went outside to feel the cold on my cheeks, I heard the snow creaking under my shoes like an old floor. I walked into the landscape, making tracks, and then I wrote about them. *Blue hollows of snow in the night.*

When the journal Mrs. Caldwell gave me is full, I write along photocopied passages she made for me, filling each margin in tiny cursive, folding them in among my bound pages. When Isaac sees me with it one day, I tell him it's my baby book.

"It's a surprise," I say, pushing the journal down in my bag, under the fabric scraps.

"What do you mean? Isn't it just things like how big our baby is, the different names—"

"Yes," I interrupt, "but the surprise will be best when you can see it all at once. For our baby too."

"Assuming our baby can read." Isaac laughs, and then I do too, trying to make light of it all.

"Did you add any Bible passages?"

"Yes," I lie. "But of course that's a surprise too—for you and the baby, I mean." I am talking too quickly, chasing my words, but Isaac doesn't seem to notice.

The other day he saw Mrs. Caldwell's car on the road by our farm, and he asked why she was hanging around. I explained she sometimes took the back roads to the garden center.

It feels wrong denying Isaac a chance to come with me to the clinic, to know the doctors are good there, that they'll take care of me, and of you, no matter what happens.

Every time I call the van to ride into town, Isaac assumes it's headed to the same place. I make sure each pick-up and drop-off overlaps with the afternoons he works at the Zucker farm, so he'll never see Mrs. Caldwell's car or know about our meeting spot down the road. Sometimes I think I'm only truly happy during these trips to the city, not just because of the clinic, where I can learn about you, but because of all the places Mrs. Caldwell takes me after checkups. All the things I get to see and taste and feel that Isaac doesn't. It feels selfish, but I can't let on about this either.

Just before my twenty-four-week checkup, Isaac and I get into an argument because he wants skip work to go with me. I lie again and say he's not allowed, that English rules are strict, when the truth is I don't want to give up my day of freedom with Mrs. Caldwell.

"But I'm your husband," Isaac reminds me.

"It doesn't matter. The examinations are private." I use words the English use to keep him from asking more questions. But it's no use.

"What about when you give birth?" he asks. "You'll at least tell me, won't you?"

"Tell you what?" I ask.

"When you're in labor. I want to be there." I remind him that Mother will help me, my aunts and cousins, the same as it was for his mother, and her mother before her. And yet I sense he suspects I'm concealing something. I am. I plan to call Mrs. Caldwell when I go into labor, so she can drive me to the English hospital for your delivery.

When Isaac asks how he can be sure he knows it's happening—that I'm giving birth—I assure him that my labor will be unmistakable. That I'll have *contractions*, intense muscle pains he'll be able to see.

"I want to see a picture," he says suddenly. "Don't they give you pictures at your visits?"

"No," I say. "They respect who we are."

"I know you have one," he says. "I saw you tuck it away."

I wait for him to say something about my writing, but he doesn't, and I stay calm. "I should have showed you before," I say. "I'm sorry. I was weak and let them take one. Lord, please forgive me." This is yet another lie, but I think he believes it.

I pull out my journal, careful to conceal the other pages so he won't ask about them. The last sonogram is easy to find, a thick page toward the back of the book. Your feet show first, translucent little toes.

"Isn't it supposed to be head down, not feet first?"

"Oh, that's just the angle of the camera. And anyway, the doctor said things will change before I'm due."

"But is it normal?"

"What do you mean?"

"The shape seems off," he says. "In his foot."

"It isn't," I say.

"How can I be sure? You haven't shown me any of the tests."

"It'll be okay. I promise," I say, just as Mrs. Caldwell has been telling me this whole time. When I asked about how it would be to give birth at the hospital among strangers, she said, again: *Everything is in your medical file. They'll know what to do. I promise.*

I have to trust in what I don't know, which is the opposite of tradition. Tradition is the thing you can predict because people have done it before you, showing the way. Tradition makes Isaac feel safe, cleaving to what he knows, just as his father did, and his father before him.

I don't blame Isaac for this, but it means I must continue to hide the truth from him to preserve what freedom I have. It isn't same for Isaac. In choosing this life, he is giving up freedom too, but as a man in our society, he will always have more.

The other day, Isaac said he wants to name you Elijah, after his great-grandfather. If you're a girl, he wants to name you after my great-aunt Margaret, the one who died at nineteen, in childbirth.

"We must honor her," he said, but I offered nothing in reply, because I never met my great-aunt. Honor, I think, means little when you don't know a person. How to explain this to Isaac without him doubting my own sense of duty?

It's only when I am in the car with Mrs. Caldwell, when we are heading to the clinic, that I feel this story, this grip of honor and duty, release. When we are on the highway, I can become anyone I choose. A woman who takes care of herself and her child without anyone else getting in the way. A woman who can be curious. A woman who can speak her mind.

Isaac isn't like every man, but he's an Amish man all the same. An Amish husband and soon-to-be father who expects me to be like other women in our community. One night, through the window, I watch him work in the cold, pacing our frozen lawn in search of another tool, another task to finish before climbing into bed. As he circles the snow, it's as if he fears the ground will break beneath him if he doesn't keep moving.

Like Father after Beth died. Father, who refuses to let himself feel anything beyond duty, beyond serving family and community. That's his world, but it's not mine. I want to feel everything; I want to be free.

"Do you know yellow is forbidden?" I say to Mrs. Caldwell after my thirty-four-week visit.

We're eating ice cream at Penny's downtown, our favorite place.

"No," Mrs. Caldwell says. "I haven't heard that before."

"It—" I start, then stop myself. "It doesn't matter.

"Of course it matters," she says.

"Yellow is considered fancy," I say. "Like pink. It's too bright. But I love yellow."

"I do too," she says. "You can still love yellow. There can't be a rule against that."

"But there is," I say. "I want to sew a yellow border on the baby blanket. I can't." Though I start with the blanket, these words send me somewhere else. *I can't*. My mind fills with images of goldenrod and summer corn. Of running with Beth and hiding behind stalks until we collapsed, her hair gleaming in the light of an open field.

"I'm so sorry," Mrs. Caldwell says, reaching for my hand as she did that first day.

Suddenly, I can barely breathe. "I don't want to feel ashamed of the things I love, or forget them. And I never want my child to feel this way."

Mrs. Caldwell squeezes my hand tighter. "Is that so wrong?" she asks.

"Yes, it is," I say.

We take our ice cream to the car, where she lets me cry in private, for as long as I need to. Mrs. Caldwell has seen me crying more these past months than Mother has in my whole life.

I barely hear myself when I say the words, but I say them aloud: "I don't think I can stay."

# RUTH WALSH

## FALL 2019

It's dark when the train pulls into Philadelphia. Ruth hears ticking, and there's a sign rolling out departure and arrival times. Track numbers.

Inside the main terminal, people hurry about with luggage and shopping bags. They grab small packs of food and bottled beverages. Potato chips, hard pretzels, and cans of soda, the same brands Cousin Rosalie sold at the auction house snack stand. At the store in the train station, there's a rack of postcards. Ruth sees pictures of her own people in buggies, behind horse-drawn plows—the same kinds of postcards the English liked to buy at market, but the stand has more images to choose from. Or is it because she's never stopped, not like this, to look up close? All this time, she's forbidden herself pause. Busying herself with Eli, with the farm and with church and the market.

She peers into the photographs, touching each image. Men working their fields under a setting sun. Women clipping their laundry to lines. Buggies entering and leaving covered bridges. There's a close-up of a small girl with braids like Beth once wore around her head. Her eyes innocent and unknowing. Where was the child's mother to shield her? Where had Ruth been, the day that it happened? She'd been mending at home, like always, but there isn't time to think about it. Not now.

She peruses a tall stand of folded maps. One for Pennsylvania. Another for the city of Philadelphia. Another for New Jersey. New York City. Washington, D.C.

Ruth takes the map of Philadelphia to the register. English faces watch her extract dollars from her bag. After the woman behind the counter gives her change, Ruth folds it back into the envelope.

In the central terminal, she opens the map in her lap. She traces roads and rivers depicted in red and blue like the veins of a body, the inside of a body she's never seen. Dr. Caldwell has an anatomy chart in his office. Whenever he tells her things about Eli, about the intricacies of his brain, his heart, he refers to the chart, and she tries to follow along with her eyes, memorizing the words for things as the doctor names them. *Ventricle*, she remembers. *Artery*. Nerves and nerve endings, she thinks. The map is like this, too. The city is a body with many systems, filled with chaotic activity.

Ruth's hands are trembling as she refolds the map. Despite her apprehension, it's time to push through the doors of the station, to find *Eveline Mitchell*. This is Emma's real estate agent, according to Mrs. Caldwell. The map has shown her to way to Eveline's office: *45 Walnut Street*.

It's late already, but this city is illuminated. She's used to dimmer lighting at home, to reading in the near dark. By a streetlamp, she studies again the distance from where she is, 30th Street Station, to Walnut Street. She must use the key at the bottom to measure centimeters in miles. It's a long way, close to five miles. She's walked much farther in her lifetime, but never in a place so unfamiliar. Even so, she understands the numbers for city streets go upward past 30th Street—31st Street, 32nd Street, 33rd . . .

*Be brave*, she tells herself. *Trust in God*.

By the exit to the street, lights flicker red. *Axons* and *termini*, she thinks—these other terms the doctor had tried to explain to her. Because she'd been curious. Like Joanna, her childhood friend who didn't stay, Ruth had always been curious. When the shape of a body in green appears and others begin to cross, she follows. The cars are stopped, and now people—pedestrians—can go. *WALK WALK WALK*, the sign flashes.

*Take your time*, Ruth tells herself. *It'll be all right*.

She'll find a hotel on Walnut Street. Sara had assured her Walnut was a safe road, a main road, and hotels were open late. That way she'd be well rested for finding Eveline Mitchell's office in the morning.

Ruth continues on slowly, stopping at every street sign, looking up to confirm its name on the map. The English walk past her quickly. Horns are constantly blaring, but she doesn't know what the trouble is. A mile in, Ruth passes many restaurants and bars. Outside, people are holding cigarettes. Wrists flick little bits of red; ash glowing by their shoes. Evidence of Satan, of things she should stay away from, but people she loves live here. People she still loves.

*May God keep them safe, along with me.*

After Ruth walks a few more blocks, she sees a large sign for RED LOBSTER. The claws are enormous on this glowing creature; she's only ever seen one in an advertisement for fish. But it's just a sign, isn't it? Ruth closes her eyes as she walks past it, clutching her bag. She keeps walking, walking, until she reaches Walnut Street. She doesn't know what time it is, but there's a small grocery store with a lit-up OPEN sign. A blue sign, haloed in pink.

Inside, she finds the supplies she needs. A toothbrush and paste. A pack of tissues, some cleaning wipes. Above the register, a clock reads 10:06. Eli would be asleep by now. But not Abraham. Ruth cannot think about him, how worried he must be, alerting the others, shining oil lamps through the fields?

And Eli? What if he woke in the night? What if he needed her? Part of her feels shame. Another part of her . . . the part that kept the bag packed under the bed, the part that tucked away money . . . does not. This journey feels as important to her, as necessary, as her next breath. She tells herself she'll be back soon enough, before Abraham goes to the phone shanty to call the police. Before alarms sound beyond the borders of home. And Abraham knows how to tend Eli. How to keep their son alive.

The man in front of her in line is asking for cigarettes. *Marlboro Golds*. They're expensive, more than she thought they'd be. Ten dollars and seven cents. More than the cost of a pie. The man behind the register moves behind thick glass, the kind she read about after the shooting—the kind of that might have kept her children safe. Ruth had wanted Abraham to bring it to the elders, the possibility of this kind of glass, but he had feared it would suggest they wanted to be more modern than they were, even as he said he wanted a way to stop the violence. Put an end to it before Emma came of age.

"Help you?" the man at the register asks from behind the glass. Ruth puts the items she needs on the counter.

As the man scans her things, she asks, "Do you know the Holiday Inn?"

The man laughs. "Do I know it?"

Ruth doesn't understand why this is funny, but she continues anyway. "Do you know where it is?"

"Not near here." He pauses as if he's trying to picture one. "Not that I know of," he says. He smiles with yellow teeth. *Cigarettes*, *nicotine*. These are words that go with *Marlboro* and *Gold*.

"Do Amish folk like hotels?"

The man's voice is raspy. As though he's ill. Ruth opens her mouth, but before she can speak, she feels a tap on her shoulder. She turns to find a teenager in a green baseball cap. A young man.

"It's not far," he says. "A few blocks south. Make a right out of here and then another right on 38th. Keep walking, and you'll see a big sign for it."

"That's a gentleman," the man at the register says. Then he points to the total on his machine.

Quickly, Ruth opens her bag, but when she looks down, the envelope is gone. Her cash is missing. She kneels to search all the pockets, feeling around her map and extra clothes. Then she checks her apron pockets, patting along them, but they too are empty.

She looks up at the man behind the glass. "I'm sorry," she says. "I can't find my envelope."

The man just looks at her like she is the one who is ill. Crazy, maybe. A woman excommunicated? But she isn't. She wants to tell him she isn't. Someone must have stolen from her at the station, after she bought the map.

The man dismisses her with a wave, and with the same hand motions the teenager forward to pay.

Inside the station, there had been a man in a business suit, his hair greased and shiny. He'd glanced at her like he was looking for something, hadn't he? People could be deceptive. She's hurrying out of the store now, looking around the door in case the envelope had fallen out there, but no. Again, she thinks of the grease-laden man.

*Lord, Father*, she prays. *Please forgive me. I know not what I say, not what I do. I did not know that man. I do not believe in his evil intentions. All your children are good, and I have made a mistake. I was careless. Father, will you forgive me?*

And then He answers her. Tells her what to do. *There is no shame in asking for help*, He says. *No shame*. His voice is strong, filling her with light despite the darkness on Walnut Street.

The boy had given her directions to the hotel, she decides. This had been a sign. *A right out of here. Then another right on 38th Street*. She follows the words, trusts that she might find another woman like her. Or someone who will take mercy on her, like the innkeeper of Bethlehem, who offered a place for Mary to sleep in his stable.

She looks for a woman or a man with kind eyes, but no one meets her gaze. The English, even at this hour, are so busy. Their ears are plugged with devices. They are talking out loud to themselves, or into phones. She has heard about them. *Smart phones*. How you could talk on them with your hands free. And the phones could even talk back, tell you where to go when you were lost.

When no one stops for her, she decides to enter the hotel alone. To simply enter and ask for a place to sleep. But when she gets to the glass doors, she sees a man behind the counter like the man at the grocery, and she hesitates. She can't imagine he'll be any different. Won't this man, too, simply laugh at her? Consider her ill, or mad, dressed as she is, alone in this city?

There must be another way, she thinks. Another place she can stay through the night. And then, as if God has willed it, she sees a structure with a yawning opening and bright lights, red and glowing: PARK HERE. Ruth's pace quickens, her heels burning against Mrs. Caldwell's thick leather sandals. Strange she hasn't noticed them until now, the blisters, but maybe it's because she has made it here—to this place of shelter—that her feet are finally speaking, asking for rest.

Inside, she smells gas and hears the dripping of pipes, hears a man yelling something to another man about a *Toyota SUV*. There is a small glass room beyond the opening, but no one is inside it. Cars are entering a few feet from her, the drivers rolling down their windows to take tickets from a machine that continually spits them out. She considers trying to get the machine to give her ticket, but she isn't a car. She's a person who can walk, by the grace of God, past the lever that rises and falls into the car-filled cavern, where men continue talking amid the jangling of keys, the beeping of an alarm. Now that she's here, on the other side, an engine starts close by. She flinches, reciting the Lord's Prayer as she hurries past row after row of vehicles, more than she has ever seen in one place, all empty. She realizes that the structure is a shelter for them, not for the people who own them. It's an inn for cars.

She recalls the one forbidden book she'd read as a child. She'd taken it from a pile of books outside of an English home on Hunsecker Road. FREE, the sign had read, and though she was not English, she'd still taken the book, attracted by its cover with the shiny face of Alice, the blue ribbon in her hair, lured by the idea of *Wonderland*. This book she'd read in secret, one page at a time before bed. Now she thinks this tower full of cars, winding around her, is like the maze Alice finds herself lost in. Ruth had never told anyone about the book. Not even Joanna, who would have understood—not just that she'd read it, but what she thought about it, how the story had dizzied her, taking her far away from home and everything she thought she knew about the world. How she had loved the book for that very reason.

Joanna, the only person who would have forgiven her, accepted her, but had she done the same for Joanna? No. She had shunned her, pretended her dead like the others had after she left.

*God*, she prays, *I am sorry. Please do not forsake me now, knowing my sin, my pride in assuming myself better than Joanna.*

Ruth senses Him once more giving her strength as she pushes through the door to a stairway, the one that runs secretly, invisibly, between the floors of this tower. The stairway smells of dust and old concrete, but lights buzz on the ceilings, so she is sure it leads to a place of rest, if a humble one. Like Mary and Joseph, sleeping on a bed of straw. The miracle of Christ came without luxury, in a manger, among the animals.

Ruth has slept in a barn many times. During threshing season, when the cows and horses needed the most tending. She'd watched over them as a girl, and even after she and Abraham married, when they had to separate the grain from the chaff, Ruth spent had at least one night in the barn.

On the third level of the structure made for cars, she finds a little patch of open concrete behind a pillar where she can make a pallet. She spreads her spare dress to lie on and uses her cape for a blanket. Then she folds her hands by her cheek for a pillow.

In the barn, she was always as still as the animals. It kept them calm, made them feel safe. Assured them of the reward that was to come, after the threshing was over, when she and Abraham would feed them sugar apples in thanks for their work. But each time she hears another engine rumbling from below, or more beeping, or the voices of strangers coming and going, she can't help but fear. What would people do if they found her? Would they ask her for money? When they saw she had none, would they harm her, arrest her?

At one point, the shadows lengthen along the cement. Is this real, or is she imagining it? Then she sees a rodent, a rat, skittering down the steps, its eyes black and glinting.

She closes her eyes, thinks again of the threshing season. How last time she and Abraham had fulfilled their duty without Emma to help. Of course, they'd had the words of the Scripture to guide them as they spread the sheaves of wheat. *Separate the good grain from the chaff*. Their livestock did this work, pounding over the sheaves. *Thou shall not muzzle the ox when he treadeth over the grain*. They never used machines, only animals, because the animals were sacred. *Bread corn is bruised; because he will not ever be threshing it, nor break it with the wheel of his iron cart, nor bruise it with his horsemen*. As Ruth tries to sleep, tries to pretend she's home, she almost smells the grain, the sweetness of the hay in the barn while the animals worked. She almost hears the bells at their necks, louder than the sound of their hooves crushing wheat.

She recalls the Book of Ruth, her namesake. *So she gleaned in the field until evening. Then she beat out that which had gleaned, about an epah of barley.*

God wants her to stay here. Ruth knows this now. Some things, some work, must be done alone. Perhaps, the thinks, Emma understood this too. Ruth has been telling herself these sacrifices she's making are for Emma, for her child—a child Ruth has never seen. The Lord has shown her differently. It is Ruth's own lack, her own *need*, that has brought her to this place. Sleepless over the cold concrete, she prays and waits for morning.

# SARA CALDWELL

## WINTER 2019

On a cold morning in late February, Sara pulls up to their meeting spot just before daybreak to find Emma already waiting, eight months pregnant, in the wool coat Sara's given her to wear with a warm pair of boots she found on clearance at the mall.

As Emma slides into the car with only a small bag, Sara fights the urge to offer money again—enough for Emma get by until she finds a job—but Emma has already refused, and Sara doesn't want to spoil their last moments, so instead she tells her stories about her friend in real estate, Eveline Mitchell.

When she was still in graduate school at Penn, they'd met at yoga class and discovered they loved many of the same things. They'd kept in touch by email over the years, with Eveline filling her in on the best new restaurants and plays in the city, the latest installations at the art museum, as well as any changes to their old haunts.

When Sara emailed Eveline to ask for the favor, she'd felt an unexpected pang for her old life. Was it really that unexpected? Well, she guessed it was expectedly unexpected—how deeply she'd buried her love of the city. How, no matter how often she told herself she was making the most of her life here with Peter, she missed the way things used to be.

Her morning routine, for instance. Getting up early to work on her thesis, then drinking a second cup of coffee and eating breakfast while drafting lesson plans, writing prompts for her teens at the correctional facility. She used to dread the long wait before the guards let her in to do her job, but now she misses the anticipation she felt in those moments. The sense of purpose in doing this work, and of accomplishment after making it through another session. Making a difference.

It comes back to her now, all of it, in driving to the train station, in helping Emma leave: her stacks of notebook paper and miniature pencils, the cheap timer she set on the table inside the ward, beside the officer who oversaw the lesson. The look of the boys' faces when she came in, and as she was about to go, when they asked if she was coming back.

They arrive with ten minutes to spare. The station is small and crowded, but it's cold out, and Sara doesn't want Emma waiting on the platform, so she gestures to an open space by the service elevator. "We can wait here."

"What if the train leaves without me?" Emma asks.

"After the horn blows, it stops for a bit, so everyone can get on."

Emma is watching out the big windows, waiting for the lights to appear on the tracks.

"The city is only a short drive . . . if you need anything," Sara repeats for what feels like the hundredth time, but Emma seems less worried, less afraid, than she. It's Sara, not Emma, who's about to cry. Though Philly isn't far in distance, it feels far from where they started, at her house, less than a year ago.

When the horn sounds, it's too soon. Sara presses the button for the elevator, and when Emma turns to hug her, she feels the rounded belly against hers for a moment.

"I'll miss you," she says. "Thank you for everything."

"Be safe," Sara whispers, wiping her eyes.

As Emma steps into the elevator, Sara presses an envelope into her hands. Emma's eyes widen, and she tries to give it back, but the elevator door closes, preventing the return of the money Sara pulled from her private account, the one that covers her gardening expenses. Money Peter never has to know about it.

Through the window over the platform, Sara sees a man in uniform extend a hand to help Emma board the train. As if she knows Sara is watching, Emma looks up and waves. Sara does the same. And then she is gone.

*Be safe*. The words echo in her head as she walks back to her car, like an accusation, and she can see clearly this other way she has lied—lied to herself. Telling herself she was taking a risk in marrying an older man when, really, she'd only ever played it safe. She had stayed home, been cared for by her husband. A kept woman in Lancaster County. A woman without children to raise.

When she pulls the car into the driveway, she thinks of the last clinic visit with Emma. During another routine ultrasound, as the doctor had zoomed in on the baby's heart and lungs, they had both watched with excitement. He was healthy. Perfectly healthy, still.

Now, Sara can't imagine Emma giving birth alone, even though she'll receive the best care Sara could locate for her in the city. She'd steered the intake process too, finding financial assistance and low-cost programs to help Emma navigate her first months as a new mother. She'd reminded Emma many times that when it was time to give birth, all she had to do was show up at the hospital and say she didn't have insurance. *They won't turn you away.*

The truth is, even if Sara could be there, she wouldn't know what to do—how to advocate clearly. She's never been in a delivery room, unlike Peter, whose stories increased her anxiety. Such as that one about a baby born with Crigler-Najjar syndrome, a condition in which toxic levels of bilirubin built up in the blood after birth. The only remedy was intense phototherapy: lying under a bright blue light for at least ten hours a day. Peter had reminded her how light-beds were expensive, especially for Amish families.

Sara thinks of the blue light now as she exits the car and glances up at the cold sky. In it, she sees Emma's blue dress on her wedding day. How stunning she'd looked, despite Emma's claim that blue was modest and didn't attract attention. Sara stands on the porch, looking out at the road and the farmland that stretches beyond. The sun has risen now, and there is a slow dance of shadows over the driveway.

There was a prayer Emma used to repeat to herself sometimes, while dusting the bookcases, when she didn't know Sara was listening: *But where you hear of a poor, simple, cast-off little flock, which is despised and rejected by the world, join them.*

On a kitchen pad, Sara had jotted the words. Later, she learned they were from *The Book of Martyrs*, attributed to Anna of Rotterdam before she was sentenced to death by drowning.

Sara had found other references to this text. Though one website listed it as *Martyrs Mirror of the Defenseless Christians*, another called it *The Bloody Theatre*. It didn't make sense, the violence inherent in a volume embraced by people who were pacifists. But Anabaptists were outsiders. They'd fled persecution, vowing to dress uniformly to mark themselves as dissidents, though now in our eyes—English eyes, Sara thinks—they were conformists. They were all simple and all the same.

But not Emma. Emma had escaped the cycle, the expectations of sacrifice to the point of self-erasure. And what would Sara do now? With Emma gone, what did she have to look forward to? What darkness, what secrets, were hers to hold apart from the world?

# EMMA WALSH

## WINTER 2019

When I am thirty-six weeks along, Mrs. Caldwell comes for me. In the early morning, I wait by the creek. The sky is a cold gray, the sun barely visible beyond the horizon.

I'm wearing the black wool gloves she gave me to stay warm, gripping a pair of shears. What will Mother think later, when she discovers them missing? What would she think now as I stand by the stillness of the water, about to cut my hair? It's early March, not icy as it was in February, and the water casts enough of my reflection in the dim sun. I can follow the line of my chin, where my hair will end now, the English way. Easier to tuck under a hat when I'm in Philadelphia. Easier to hide who I am, who I was, when I'm looking for work in the city.

Mrs. Caldwell says she's just a phone call away. She's made a list of the things I'll need to do to get started. To make it on my own with you these next few months. I keep the list folded in your baby book, my journal, in a canvas bag with some soap, a change of clothes until I can get new ones, and a box of pencils.

The sound of the scissors in my hair is like corn pouring down the chute. The echo hangs in my memory, marking before, and after, same as the sound of gunshots marked it. Before the milkman came for us, we'd no reason to worry. In the late summer, when the corn was tall, and we could zigzag through the rows, laughing. Our border collie, Maddie, liked to chase us. The light had circled Beth's hair, had cast a soft sheen over Maddie's mottled back. We used to joke about how her ears flapped when she ran, her pink tongue lolling in the heat. Beth held her hands to her head like ears, and I did the same. We both stuck out our tongues and laughed. This was the last time we ran with Maddie. I never thought Beth would leave before her, or that I'd bury our dog alone, when she was eleven years old, in the yard, with a little stone to mark her resting place. I etched the years into the stone like Beth would have wanted, just as we had on the cross that marked Beth's grave in the field. As I watch my hair fall to the ground in pieces, I'm sure they're both at peace now, in heaven.

Mother wore only black the year after we lost Beth, as is customary, but she won't be buried in black. She'll be buried in her wedding dress, blue like mine. I don't know what Mother will do with my dress. Will she keep it to remember me by? Or will she bury it to forget me, now that I am an apostate under the Ordnung? I can never go home again.

And yet, in this continued silence by the frozen creek, I sense time moving forward, in *you*, this rush of current within me. When Mrs. Caldwell pulls up in her car, my cap is in place, and I don't look back at the heap of my hair. I can't. I don't think about Isaac, about our farm on the other side of the covered bridge. About how wrong of me this is, to leave him without warning, when you are his child too. I've told myself it's more merciful this way, harder for me, but better to leave before he has seen you in the world, held you in his arms. One day, you'll wonder why I didn't ask if he wanted to come with me. My answer: What if he'd said yes?

I've gone through all the ways I could leave, including with Isaac, praying for an answer that means we could be together, but every sign points the other way. Though I fear what he will imagine after I'm gone—that maybe I am dead on the streets, that *we* are dead—I fear more that he would try to persuade me to stay, persuade me we could never survive in the English world alone. Without a college education. Without a clear line of work or place to live. Worse, he'd likely tell Mother and Father, who would try to stop me. I don't know the lengths they'd go to. A swarm of buggies blocking my exit. This is what I imagine.

I'll find a way for him to know you, even though we can never see each other again. I'll write to him, send pictures. But writing this only brings more sadness for me. Each night I fall asleep, only to wake to the same reality of fracture.

My last image of Isaac will be of him shoveling the driveway. We'd thought the worst of winter was over, but it had snowed in March. Yesterday, he cleared a path for the buggy. Halfway down the drive, he stopped to pull his coat tighter against his chest. I almost called out to him, *Isaac, you need another layer on*. But to do so would have been misleading. My concern for him wouldn't have made sense this morning, when he wakes and discovers me gone.

In the car with Mrs. Caldwell, I keep my eyes fixed on the last silo we pass, tall and silver in the morning light. Mrs. Caldwell and I speak little. There is nothing left to say. We made a plan a month ago—for me to live at first within walking distance of the clinic, and then get set up with an apartment, an *efficiency*, after the birth. Mrs. Caldwell helped me complete all the applications for the social services I'll need, and we've gone over everything repeatedly. What it will mean for me to go into labor. That I can call her to meet me at the hospital, though I told her I needed to do this alone. I couldn't leave any trace in my file that she'd been there. I don't want Mother and Father and Isaac to blame her for my decision.

Mrs. Caldwell looks like she has been crying. Like she hasn't slept. She must think she's guilty, that she has done something horrible to my family, and after everything we've been through. But the opposite is true. This is my will. My life, like she's told me from the beginning. I want this all on my own, and I will raise you to be strong, to know your life is yours to live, not anyone else's, from the moment you're born. But I'll be here to watch and keep you safe and care for you as long as you need. I'll answer your questions, talk to you about everything when you ask. I will love you unconditionally. Forgive you unconditionally, even if your version of forgiveness is different than mine.

My contractions start when I am thirty-nine weeks. I'm staying at the motel Mrs. Caldwell found for me off the turnpike. Lying on a bed that smells of humid air and old cigarettes. Around two 'o clock in the morning, a dull pulse begins at the base of my stomach, rising into my back.

I have a timer on the phone Mrs. Caldwell gave me, an old phone to use until I can buy my own. I am terrified, more than I thought I'd be. I want to call her, but I don't. I stick to the promise I made to myself, for better or worse, not to leave traceable evidence of my new life.

When the contractions are every twenty minutes, I know I'm truly in labor. A week early. How long until they become sharper, shorter, five minutes apart? This is when the clinic doctors said it's time to go to the hospital. There is a book on my bedstand about this, another gift from Mrs. Caldwell. I try patterned breathing. In for five, hold at the top, out for five. I'm groaning when the contractions worsen, but they're not yet five minutes apart. I take a hot shower like the book says. Take a walk down the block, holding my belly, steadying myself, letting gravity help me, like the book says.

Finally, I call a taxi, a wad of bills folded into my palm. I can smell my sweat, feel my skin sticking to the leather seats. The bills are warm, a little wet, but I have enough to pay.

At the hospital, after I give my name and date of birth, and they ask for my insurance, I do just as Mrs. Caldwell told me. "I don't have insurance," I say. "I'm self-pay."

When they ask for my address, I tell them the one for the motel. They don't say anything, because this is the English world; you could live anywhere, raise a child anywhere.

"Is your husband coming?" the nurse asks me.

"No," I say, not explaining why.

I'm moved to a different waiting area, where I watch the sliding doors open and close as the nurse checks my heart rate and blood pressure. There are other women in labor, English women also giving birth. *I am not alone*, I tell myself. I will never know their specific stories, but our pain is shared. I watch a woman brace herself against the wall, moaning louder than I want to. I am not as far along, *not as dilated*, the doctor might say. The worst of my labor is still coming.

I helped Mother deliver Rosalie's baby, and she didn't scream. We don't scream when we give birth, not that I've seen. We hold it in, trust in God, wait for the pain to pass.

When the nurse asks if this is my first child, I say, "Yes, it is." An hour later they give me a room. I share it with another mother, further along in her labor. A curtain separates us, but at one point, while I am bracing against my bed, wires tied from my arms to the monitor, I can see her hair is black. She is howling like an animal when the doctor comes to give her an epidural. *An anesthesiologist.* I know I have this choice too, but I've decided against it. There's a chance of nerve damage I won't risk. I imagine Mother again, and Rosalie, and all the women I've ever known to have given birth without a needle in their spines. I'm apart from them, and yet I can be near them in choosing to feel in these next hours what they have felt. Mother's not here, nor Mrs. Caldwell, but nurses take turns holding my hand. Finally, a woman doctor I've never met arrives and tells me to hang on; that I'm close to meeting you. The room turns hazy, a mixture of overlapping light as I push and rest, push and rest, time passing slowly and quickly at once.

"You're almost there," the nurse says. "Nine-and-a-half centimeters dilated."

Sounds are as blurry as the light is when she announces, "I can see him!"

I grunt, pushing harder, breathing faster. When the doctor says I can reach down and feel you, I grope your fuzzy head and begin to cry. Then you arrive, slick with fluid from my body. In the mirror I watch you sliding into the world. My blood is blended with your blood, but we're apart now, and though your blue eyes flicker bright in the light of the room, you're quiet.

"Is he okay?" I ask, alarmed. "Is my baby all right?"

"He's fine," the doctor says, smiling. "A beautiful boy."

When you're clean and the nurse hands you to me, you finally find your voice. You're red and screaming in my arms as a nurse parts my gown and helps you to my breast.

"It's normal," she reassures me. "They cry like this because it's all so new," she says. "He'll learn."

I'm nervous still, certain something is wrong with my breast when you won't latch right away, but then you do. My milk has come, and you're feeding, suckling and pulling at me.

I name you Leo, an English name short for Leonard, a name to grow into. I sing you German lullabies while you nurse through the night—the only songs I know by heart. It's the first time I've heard myself singing outside of church. My own voice not among others'. I take comfort in thoughts of our future. *We'll go to the art museum when you're older*, I say. *We'll try the movies and the shopping mall. Take walks in a stroller around the park.*

I continue my journal, writing of your early months. I start with small notes, but as the days pass, my words flow. There is never enough room on a single page. I must buy paper in packs of three at the supermarket—*legal pads*, the packaging reads. Yellow paper with blue lines that English lawyers use. As the weeks go by, my savings dwindles, though I still have the money Mrs. Caldwell gave me.

Getting a job takes time. Walking around with you on my chest, a scarf to hold you there securely. No one thinks I am equipped to work with a new baby, it seems, though you are quiet, sleeping, when I stop at shop after shop to ask if they're hiring. I look in the classified section of the newspaper and do what Mrs. Caldwell described as *cold calling*.

I've thought of phoning her many times, but I can't bring myself to ask for more than she's already given me. *One more day*, I tell myself. *Another week. If things get really bad, you'll call her*. There are times I think of contacting your father. He'd want to know if we're struggling, but this is my fault, not his. My choice, not his. I took you from him. Can he forgive me? It feels wrong, even, to pray. How can the God I believed in before I left be the same one now? But He is.

God can be *anything*, *anyone*. I know this now. He's in you, in Eli, in what I don't know. In what none of us will ever know, about where we begin, where we end. He's with me, with us, when I call another restaurant from the yellow pages, a tavern, and someone picks up and takes my name. Says I can come in tomorrow to try out for the job. They don't ask for my phone number or address. *Under the table*, they say, *by the hour*, and though I'm not sure what this means, I'm relieved. To have another day to buy our freedom in small increments.

I've put some money aside to pay for a daycare while I'm at the tavern. My first earnings pay for more daycare, and then more. I skimp on food, whatever it takes to scrape by. And it works. It helps that I'm good at my job. After all those Saturdays helping Mother at the market, I know how to please people.

Each time a customer walks in, I smile. I ask how many in their party. Tell them how long the wait is if there is one. I memorize the tables and seat people in the right sections, alternating so all the servers get tips.

The owner of the tavern is an older man. Older than Dr. Caldwell. He tells me I'm a good worker. Tells me to keep smiling, to bring extra bottles of ketchup and maple syrup without anyone asking.

Mornings, I peel potatoes for the garlic mash. I make the gravy, our family recipe that everyone likes. I don't tell anyone I'm Amish. That I *was* Amish. I blend in, like I'm just another girl with a recipe for gravy. I need to make the hours count until I have you in my arms again. I pick you up at daycare and kiss your cheeks. When you are two months old, you smile at me.

I've started a real book for you. More than spare pages from my legal pad. I have a folder stuffed with sonograms and other things from the hospital, including the first photo of myself—at least, the first one I've ever seen—holding you in my arms. I'm wearing a blue hospital gown, and you're swaddled in a white blanket striped with two thin lines, one pink and one blue.

I borrow books from the library, as many as I can carry in a canvas bag. When you're four months old, I know certain ones by heart. Enough to recite them, half-awake, while you nurse in the night. These first months, you make soft murmurs when you sleep. Sometimes you raise your hand in the air like a tree trunk, like you have something to say, and I wonder what it is.

When I can't sleep because I'm worried about money, I write things down. I pull out my legal pad and light a candle, as I would back at Mother and Father's. Against the soft flicker, I record the things that are happening now.

*The sheets are crisp white cotton. Go to the Dollar General for more socks.*

At the hospital, I filled out a form for a breast pump a nurse recommended. She asked me if I was working, and I said not yet, but soon. I rent the machine monthly, like I rent our room, at a cost I can afford, from the services I get from the city. It is the only way I can go to work, to make enough to sustain us.

On breaks at the tavern, I go to the employees' bathroom to pump, then store the bottles in the walk-in fridge. I wake and pump every couple of hours during the night, to fill more bottles to send with you to daycare, in a little bag that keeps them cool.

When you're three months, I've saved enough on top of the extra money Mrs. Caldwell gave me to rent a small apartment in East Poplar. Eveline Mitchell, Mrs. Caldwell's friend, warns me that while the price is good, it isn't a safe part of the city. I tell her I'll take my chances. By now, after what I've been through—what I know I can survive—little scares me. I've heard of this expression: *thick skin*. That to have thick skin is to be unaffected by little things.

We're quiet in the old apartment building. You don't cry much, and when you do, you're easy to soothe. We keep to ourselves. Below us, an older couple keeps the TV on all the time. Another couple lives above us, a pair of musicians. I can hear them playing instruments in the evenings. Woodwinds, I think, from what I learned from Mrs. Caldwell, and sometimes a piano plays Billy Joel, the song about a piano man I've heard on the radio at the tavern.

On the weekends, I take you to the fancy playground on Oxford Street. At first, we just watch the other children play. Kicking themselves high and higher on the swings. Squealing down the slide. You watch them eagerly, babbling into the crisp air. *Soon*, I tell you. *Soon you'll play with them*.

Sometimes when we're there, I hear other mothers comparing their children's lives. After-school activities, daycares, teacher names. They recommend brands for things. Clothing and types of strollers. They talk about the makeup and skin creams they use. Where they go for exercise. It seems they have everything, but still, they complain of their troubles. *I am so stressed*, they say, like this makes them miserable, and I don't understand. I'm stressed. I'm worried, but I am free.

What would Mrs. Caldwell say if she saw me now? That I'm doing well on my own? Even as I can't afford, and likely never will, certain

English luxuries? I don't miss them because I grew up without them. I grew up with candlelight and kerosene oil. With few toys, but with my imagination and my sister and the cornfields. Though I left, sometimes I prefer it the simple way. There's less to keep track of, less to fear, even in this English world where there are things to buy your fear away.

I want you to know that home can be whatever you want it to be, something you can make as you go. When you're older, you can paint your room any color. The walls here are yellow, so yellow—more than a border trim on a blanket, or the cover of your baby book like I first imagined. When you're old enough to know why yellow was forbidden, I'll tell you everything about the life I left behind. Everything you might want to know about your father. *Isaac Ames*. If you want to find him, I'll help you. If you ask me the kind of person he is, I'll tell you he's good, he loves you, and that I miss him. I'll tell you how I see him in you each day that passes. In the fine curve of your cheeks, in your soft eyes and full lips. If you ask me why we can't go back to see him, I'll tell you it's because your mother has been shunned.

I am shunned, and yet we can have yellow here, now, in this room. We can have all of the yellows. *Some soft like moonlight, or the hazy glow of a cold morning. Some bright and full, nearly blinding us like the sun as we step outside in summer. And even this kind of yellow is not to be feared.*

When you're four months old, in July, you're getting your first tooth. Riding in your stroller calms you, and teethers from the cooler. The plants and flowers in bloom at the park distract you. I tell you the names of the ones I know—cosmos and black-eyed Susans, and zinnias like in Mrs. Caldwell's garden—and you babble after me. I sing the same lullaby Mother and Aunt Rosalie used to sing to us in the dark when we were weaning, because no woman can sing alone. *Schloof, Bobbeli, schloof*, I sing softly in the park, and though it is strange, it makes me happy to hear my own voice. *Sleep, baby, sleep*—though you never sleep when we are walking. There is too much to notice.

In the park, you show me what is *now*, what is *alive*. You show me the world in pieces, and also how the pieces fit together the longer we look. The longer we let ourselves see.

In August, I've saved enough to rent a plot at a community garden near the park. I set the stroller in the shade so you can watch me plant things, or drowse because you're most comfortable outside. By October, when you are six months, the butter lettuce is a rich, bright green, the tomatoes tender and sweet. I tear the vegetables in little pieces for you to try like a rabbit. You like tomatoes, but the lettuce you throw on the ground, and this makes me laugh.

I take you with me to the garden whenever I have time. Sometimes I work without shoes. You cry for me to take you out of the stroller, so I let you practice sitting up in the soft dirt while I weed around the vegetables. Fearful as I am of you eating dirt or other things you shouldn't, I let you play. *This is your story now. Not mine.*

# RUTH WALSH

## FALL 2019

Finally, it is morning. Ruth can tell because the noise increases. Engines starting, music blasting, beeps and honks and voices. Even people entering and exiting the stairwell, though no one comes to the top where she is hiding. She reaches for her map, unfolds the little rectangle, smoothing out the wrinkles. It takes a minute to register that this is real—her place on the map, in this parking garage, where she can't remember actually sleeping. When she rises, her ankles tremble as they had before—on her walk from the station. And her hands, too, as she folds her clothes into her bag. The cash is still gone. Of course it is. She's thirsty, but there is no stream to drink from, no clean water like there is back home.

She descends the stairs, like Alice going down, down, and she tells herself it's okay, this isn't the first time she has gone against the wishes of her community. She reminds herself that she's asked for forgiveness, from both God and Joanna, whom she would be so glad to see, should God look kindly upon her and reconcile them somehow, in the city where her daughter now lives.

Inside the stairwell, the October light is brighter, somehow, than at home. Through a window at the landing, the sun refracts off the dirty glass, catching airborne dust. Ruth shields her face with her hand, now that she is without her bonnet, the one she took off on the train as if it alone revealed her for who she was. But everyone knew—the man at the station store, the man at the corner grocery—that she was an Amish woman in plain dress.

At least she has Mrs. Caldwell's sandals, she thinks as her steps echo until she reaches the bottom floor. She hears more shuffling, more beeping, more voices, more jangling keys. There is someone in the glass room now, a man with a small badge pinned to his jacket. Will he ask her where she's coming from? Arrest her, because he's a security guard, or the police? No, she decides. She doesn't see a holster at his belt, or a black stick—*a baton*, yes, that was the name for it—along with handcuffs and a spray to stop offenders. Abraham said sometimes there was no rhyme or reason. To always be aware of what such people were capable of, even if they were supposed to defend us. They had tried to stop the milkman thirteen years ago, but it had been too late.

No, this man is not the police, and he doesn't sense her staring at him while he works, taking payment from people, answering their questions. But on the way out, she passes someone who does notice her. He's dressed the same as the other man, but this one stops and looks at her like she's a ghost. He doesn't say anything, and she keeps walking to the street, into the sunlight.

At least it's a warm day. At least she won't be cold. God reminds her of this when she passes a woman who, unlike Ruth, had chosen to sleep in the open, on the sidewalk, surrounded by garbage bags. She is holding a paper bag, which she drinks from. There is dirt on her nose and under her eyes.

"God bless!" the woman exclaims when she sees Ruth, but Ruth doesn't think she means the blessing. This woman's dress is tattered, and she is shoeless—sandal-less—her toes gnarled and greasy.

"God bless," Ruth replies, watching as the woman drinks again. Why hadn't she packed a thermos? A piece of fruit? Not even enough for her, much less to offer this other woman in need. She has only a few clothes and her two aching feet to rely on as she crosses the street when the light blinks *WALK WALK WALK*.

She feels a presence behind her—was the woman following her?—but when she reaches the other side and turns around, the woman is still there, among her bags. Ruth resumes her journey to the office of

Eveline Mitchell, eyes straight ahead, then down to protect them from the sun. When she passes a sewage grate, she sees it: the sign she has been waiting for. A quarter glinting over the filth.

She hurries to secure it in her apron pocket. Keeps walking, this time with her eyes roving, looking for another sign. Eventually she finds a nickel, then four pennies. It's hard to pry some from the ground, requiring a certain balance she presently lacks. Reaching for a fifth penny, she falls to her knees. They throb, as do her hands and feet, but no one seems to have seen her. No one seems to care. Quietly, she collects herself and continues to the next block. Here, she gathers another quarter, a few more nickels, some dimes—enough to buy something to drink? She isn't far from the corner grocery. She knows her way back.

Inside, the man is still there, sneering behind the glass.

"No Holiday Inn?"

She sets the small change she's collected on the counter. "Can I exchange these for quarters?" she asks.

The man looks perplexed. As if this money isn't real. He sneers again, replacing the nickels, dimes, and pennies with five quarters.

"Short on your room bill?" he says.

Abraham once told her that the English relied on sarcasm in doing business. Of course, Ruth encountered it a few times at market. But something about this man makes Ruth wonder if sarcasm isn't just an excuse to be mean.

She could use this money to buy a bottle of water in the store, but she won't give him what she's worked so hard to procure. When she's on the street again, she looks for another sign. God will tell her where her money will be best spent.

And then they appear, like a vision, the glimmering gold arches. She has passed the sign on Oregon Pike, on the way to market in the van. They had one in Lancaster, too: *McDonald's*. Inside, the air cools her off. She smells salt, and grease, and there's a line of customers waiting to order. She needs to use the bathroom—this, too, becomes suddenly clear to her, how she has suppressed the need for so many hours, traveling without water. There has to be a public restroom, like the one at market. She looks for it like she knows where she is, like she belongs, but when she sees the sign for the women's room—this cutout of a woman in a triangle dress—the door won't open. There's a box with numbers on the outside. They didn't have this at the market.

"On your receipt," someone says, and Ruth turns around. A woman waiting behind her waves a bit of paper, this ticket Ruth doesn't have. There is a kindness in the woman's eyes.

"Like this," she says, reaching forward and pushing numbers while she names them.

"1–8–8–9," she says, and the door latch audibly releases. "I'll wait."

Ruth reasons it's like using the phone to call for help in an emergency, or to do necessary English business. It isn't a sin.

"You are so kind to help," she says.

The bathroom is clean, and when she sits, she sees graffiti on the walls, same as the night she met at Abraham—though this graffiti is worse. FUCK, it reads. HELL. Proof of Satan. Ruth hurries to finish, to flush, and washes her hands forcefully over the sink. When she looks up, she sees with shock her own face in the mirror. Of course they had mirrors in English bathrooms. She'd forgotten.

She knows she's seeing herself, and yet it's Emma's face she finds looking back—a version of Emma—here, in this desperate place. It is a different kind of bearing witness now. Not of Satan, but of Truth. Her daughter saying, *Mother, look at me. See me.* And Ruth does see her daughter, acutely now, sees all the times she turned away, refusing to recognize Emma's suffering. Wanting to dismiss it, her daughter's experience with darkness, just as she had her own?

Ruth pushes through the door into the bright hallway. It isn't too late, she decides. To recognize Emma's pain. It must have been great for Emma to leave her community, to have her baby alone. Ruth knows she will never understand, but she tries to imagine now, as she waits in line behind men with construction hats, what it had been like for Emma to order her first meal in the city.

"Welcome to McDonald's. Can I help you?" asks a teenager in a black visor.

"I'll have a hamburger," Ruth says, because she knows McDonald's serves this. A classic hamburger with ketchup. But the teenager says the lunch menu isn't available yet. Ruth doesn't know what time it is; she doesn't want to know, not yet. "Can I get anything for this much?" she asks, placing the change on the counter.

The teenager looks surprised, not just that an Amish woman is here, in this restaurant, but that she must do the math on Ruth's behalf. She does. "A sausage burrito," she says. Then: "Anything to drink? Orange juice? Water?"

"Water," Ruth says. "Thank you."

The girl is Emma's age but has long bangs half-covering her eyes. Her hands move quickly over this screen Ruth can't see, then another screen lights up above her, with Ruth's order number.

"Do you want any salsa?"

Ruth nods, because why not? It was food.

"How many?" she asks, holding a wad of small packets in her hands.

"That's plenty, thank you."

Her order arrives minutes later, after her number is called and she presents her ticket, her receipt. Ruth has never eaten a burrito before, though she'd seen such things amid the grocery items at the McPherson home. She had helped place the rolled sandwiches in the freezer.

The burrito is covered in yellow paper, and seated at a table by the window, Ruth unwraps this gift from God, even if the color is wrong. God is in the steam rising, in the warm oil and cheese when she takes a bite. It's enough to relieve her stomach of its aching. She adds the salsa, red like ketchup, except spicier. She'll save the other packets in case she needs them on the way home.

No one seems to notice her, an Amish woman with English food, going through the motions of eating as her daughter might have done, to fill her belly and survive another day. Why hadn't Ruth tried to send money sooner? What if Emma was in a homeless shelter? She'd heard about them from Lettie Ames—that they were like prisons, but for people who hadn't done anything wrong. Lettie had described how people waited in line for soup, for cots when they had nowhere else to sleep. And the city paid for it. The same way it had paid for foster care for Isaac. Perhaps, Ruth thinks, Isaac understands far more than she what it's been like for Emma in this city. Her daughter must depend on strangers now, as he'd had to do, though for him it had been out of necessity, not by choice.

Ruth is so hungry, and yet she can barely eat because of the sudden shame she feels. It was one thing to let your child go, to accept she could never come back, and another to realize what her choice to leave meant in this great, confusing place. She thinks again of the woman on the bench, the one with dirty feet and matted hair. Even after Ruth saw her, she'd tried to forget her, to deny that she could be like this woman, and yet she was. She, who had picked coins off the street for this meal.

Ruth rises from her booth, wondering what God would say as she approaches the drink machine and presses the little tab for *water*. Would he say it was permitted, an extension of the code she'd needed for the bathroom? Where was the limit? At what point did it become corrupt, unfounded and sinful in His eyes?

Ruth waits for someone to spot her, accuse her of wrongdoing. No one does, not even an attendant at the register, who might have been watching this whole time.

She starts with a sip, a furtive one, but before she knows it, she is drinking all the water at once. Already she's thinking what it would mean to refill her cup, but she doesn't. She stops herself. At some point, there has to be a limit. This is what God wants her to know. And she doesn't have much time—not if she's to be home before dark. Though what will she do for the train ride back, without any money? How much time will it take to collect enough change to pay for that?

She can't think this far ahead—to do so was to risk giving up, give in to despair. Better to focus on the next task, which was to find a bus to save her from walking any further on painful feet. On the sidewalk, she looks for a bus stop with a map. It doesn't take long to find one, to match her purchased map with the street names listed on the route, along Walnut Street, where she is. She doesn't know how many blocks until 45, but she'll travel until she sees offices and start counting from there. When the bus pulls up, she hands the driver her last quarter.

The driver laughs. "Need more than that," he says. He stares at her plain dress, wrinkled from her night among the cars.

"How do I get a ticket?"

There are people waiting behind her, impatient for her to pay. Her hand is quivering again, still extending her quarter.

The driver shakes his head. "Get in," he says, and she does, quickly, so the people behind her can too. Another miracle, Ruth decides. She is certain that for her to make it this far with so little, it has to be God's plan. She makes her way toward an open seat next to a man wearing a baseball cap and English sportswear. People who liked sports were friendly, weren't they?

But the man appears annoyed when he sees her coming. He doesn't seem to want to make space for her and her bag. When she sees the other passengers, the newest ones like her, holding onto the looped handles, she joins them, clinging tight to the plastic.

She looks out the window, to the yellow line of taxi cabs before a big hotel. There are more fast-food restaurants and corner grocery stores. A young woman in a short pink skirt is walking her dog. At a stop sign, the woman meets Ruth's gaze through the window—or at least that's what Ruth thinks—and her eyes widen. Like Ruth is the scandalous one, not she in her immodest skirt.

Ruth looks away, down at her sandals.

"Are you from *Amish* country?" A man's voice says behind her.

The *A* is long, the *M* harsher than she expects. She says nothing, pretends not to hear.

"I know someone Amish," the voice continues.

Ruth turns to face him, this bearded man in red shorts and sneakers. A gold chain around his neck, dangling over his white t-shirt. "She left her farm and drives an Uber now."

*Uber*. Ruth can't imagine what it could mean.

"Someone else I know of in Lancaster. That where you're from, right?"

She nods, fearful her silence might appear unfriendly, or rude. She doesn't want to make him angry.

"Whole family left to sell chicken houses. Now they're rich people. Drive a Mercedes. Own some billion-dollar international business. Crazy," the man says, looking around to see if others are listening.

"Crazy?" Ruth asks.

"My bad," the man says, eyes crinkling with silent amusement. "Can't believe it, I mean."

Ruth nods again. "Oh," she says. *Crazy that I am here, too, talking to you in this city.*

"Is it true that once you leave, you can't come back?" the man asks.

She wants to pretend she hasn't heard. It helps that her stop is next, at least she thinks so. If she's wrong, she can't get back on without more money, but it's better than talking to this man.

"God, I couldn't do it," the man adds. "Never see my family again. Might as well be dead."

These words knife into Ruth. She wants to argue, *No, No, the person doesn't die. We might pretend they are dead, but they are always alive in us. My daughter is alive!*

To prove it to herself, she asks the man, "Do you know where Eveline Mitchell's office is?"

The man laughs. "I don't think I know a single person named Eveline. Some Mitchells, maybe."

"I know the address," she says. "I'm looking for 45 Walnut Street."

"Have a cross street?" he says. "Landmarks? Anything?"

"A real-estate office," she says. "Eveline is a realtor."

"Gotcha," the man says, pulling out his phone. "Let me look her up. Eveline Mitchell, realtor," he mutters, repeatedly poking at his device.

"Found her," he announces just seconds later. He shows her his screen, uses his thumb and index finger to make the map larger. "See the dot?" he says. "The red one?"

She nods. The circle is red and bright, like the one in the painting in the doctor's office.

"That's where you're headed," the man says. "South 34th is your cross street. By Drexel," he says. "It should be another two stops, my best guess."

His stop is next; and he moves to get off. "If you get lost," he says, "just mention the cross street to someone, and they'll know." The man smiles.

"Thank you," Ruth says. "God bless." She feels the words more this time. This gratitude to God as much as to this stranger who has been kind.

For the next two stops, she repeats the words to herself, *South 34th Street. Drexel.* And then the driver announces it: "Next stop, 34th Street."

When she gets off, there's a huge image facing her on the enclosure where people wait for the bus—of a smiling mother holding a laughing child. It reads: GIVE YOU AND YOUR CHILD A HEAD START. Ruth continues to study the poster, the information about services for children, for families, *from birth to age* 5. There's no mention of insurance, which she doesn't—will never—have. Dr. Caldwell had explained the idea behind the strange word. Like *assurance*, to be assured of a future. But only God could know such a thing. And of course her people didn't subscribe to English plans like these. But Emma . . . Emma could, if she'd had to?

Under the image is a small caption: *Enroll today in one of our convenient locations*. It's as if God has ordained this, too, for Ruth to see—really see what Emma needs now to survive. Strangely, it gives her hope, that He has planted these signs along her journey, as if to say: *keep going, and you will find her. Keep going, and you will see for yourself.*

Ruth has taken it all for granted, hasn't she? That Dr. Caldwell gave their family a discount on his services, educating them about genetic disease and referring them to English *specialists*. Just as he'd done for Emma. He'd had Ruth SIGN HERE for the tests Emma would need to ensure the baby was healthy, and he'd sent her the bills for the costs they were responsible for. She and Emma never spoke of it, because Ruth didn't want to know about the tests. She'd been afraid to ask. If something were wrong, she'd reasoned, surely Emma would tell her?

And now . . . how was Emma paying her bills, paying for her life with the baby? Sara Caldwell must have helped, Ruth decides. This time, the idea fills her, not with resentment, but relief.

*Early child and development services*, the sign reads. Would Ruth's own life have been different if she'd had these resources, these opportunities, especially for Eli?

Joanna likely depended on them too. If she was still alive. No longer *shooting up* on the streets. Ruth had heard this horrible phrase once.

It took many forms, this violence the English inflicted on themselves, not just on others.

At the corner, Ruth sees another sign—for Drexel, a city college. Joanna had wanted to go to *community college* for her *degree*, she'd said. So she could work a job that paid more than hourly wages. *I don't just want to get married and have kids*, she'd insisted.

When Ruth was Emma's age, knowing of Joanna's unhappiness, she told herself to take pity on her friend. Unlike Ruth, Joanna had been unlucky in not finding her husband during Rumspringa.

*I don't just want to get married and have kids*. Ruth hears these words again. And then: *I might as well be dead*, Joanna had said. And then she had been. To their community, anyway.

In the months after Joanna left, Ruth had prayed to God to absolve her of this knowledge, lest she be cursed like Joanna was. She'd been fearful that He might take Abraham away and leave her as unlucky as her friend. But this thinking, too, now seems wrong. There is no telling, Ruth decides, who is lucky and who is not in God's eyes. As she walks past a scattering of pigeons, past more bus stops with other signs, sunlight strikes the road, a bright beam hitting the dirty pavement so she can see it: In the sun, she is bearing witness her daughter's strength and courage. Her resilience, despite everything that has happened. And then, as if fated, she sees the number—45—for Eveline's office.

Somehow, she has made it. She can feel her body again. The blisters on her heels, the sweat along her brow. When she looks at her hands, her fingernails have dirt under them. What will Eveline think when she sees Ruth? Will she turn her away?

Inside, the building is taller than she imagines, an attendant guarding the front. He asks what floor she needs.

"I don't know," Ruth says. "Eveline Mitchell's office."

"Sixth floor," the man says, pointing down the hall to the elevator.

She has never been in one before, not even at the station after Mrs. Caldwell dropped her off. She'd taken the stairs, running to catch her train.

The train doors had stood open, like these do. When Ruth enters the metal box, she scans a panel of numbers and presses the button labeled 6, only to see another woman, an English woman, rushing toward her as the doors close.

"Can you hold it?" the woman calls, but Ruth doesn't know what to press. Still, the woman manages to squeeze in, shaking her head at Ruth like she's done something wrong.

"I'm sorry," Ruth says.

"Don't worry about it," the woman says, pressing 9. As they go up, she feels the same eyes on her, this same mixture of curiosity and judgment—what could she be doing here? This Amish woman in a rumpled dress.

When they reach the sixth floor, Ruth rushes out, scanning the hall for the door she needs. For Eveline's name on a little plaque. When she sees it, she turns the handle. Immediately, a woman greets her on the other side.

"Can I help you?"

Her short blonde hair is styled and sprayed, her eyes shadowed blue. Ruth can smell her English perfume.

"Sara Caldwell," Ruth says. "She told me you know where my daughter is."

The woman's eyes go large. "Oh. Yes, of course. Sara called about that." There's a pause before Eveline asks Ruth to take a seat. "Would you like something to drink? Some coffee?"

"Coffee," Ruth says gratefully. It's something she enjoys at home, and she is still so thirsty. So tired.

As Eveline prepares the coffee from a machine that buzzes and hums, she turns to Ruth. "You've come such a long way."

Eveline, like everyone else she's come across today, scans her dress, her lank hair with its missing bonnet.

"Please tell me where she is," Ruth says, taking the steaming cup.

"I want to help you," Eveline says. "But the truth is, I don't know if Emma's still in the apartment we found for her. She wanted something month to month, and I wasn't sure the neighborhood was a good fit."

"Month to month?" Ruth asks. She's already halfway through her coffee, comforted by its familiarity.

"She pays one month at a time," Eveline explains. "She's a renter. She wanted the flexibility, in case it didn't work out."

Ruth finishes her drink. The heat and caffeine have revived her, and Ruth finds herself impatient for answers, for the next step. "The address?"

"It's not far," Eveline says, writing the number on a slip. "A few miles away."

"A few miles?" Ruth repeats. Her fists tighten around her cup. She can't imagine walking any more, searching for more street names and numbers on her map.

"You can take a taxi," Eveline says. "In fact, I recommend it. The neighborhood isn't super safe."

*It wasn't safe?* What is this woman telling her—that she put Ruth's daughter, knowingly, in the way of harm? All she can think to say is, "I don't have any money. I did, but it was stolen."

"Oh my God," Eveline says. "I'm so sorry. Here, take this." She reaches for her purse, retrieves a twenty dollar bill. "This will cover it, and a little more."

"I can't," Ruth says. She wants to, but even more she wants to prove she isn't helpless.

"Sara is a good friend," Eveline says. "Please, it's the least I can do. Your daughter has been a pleasure to work with, too. She's a gem."

*A gem?* Ruth wonders, a shining stone—something the English value.

Ruth is surprised when Eveline helps her get a cab. They take the elevator down together, pass through the doors to the street. Eveline waves down the first yellow car she sees, more yellow than the arches of McDonald's—the irony of this color, this continued sign—and opens the door for Ruth.

"Brown and North 5th," she tells the driver, then waves at Ruth as the taxi speeds away. Another whirl of storefronts and gas stations, stoplights and buses and other cars, and they are there, in the neighborhood where Emma lives now. East Poplar. The buildings aren't shiny like they are downtown. The apartments look like giant houses, in red brick. Some standalone houses have simple wood siding, the paint peeling, the front porches in need of sweeping. But there's a playground, and Emma's building is clean. On a little box by the door with labeled buttons, she reads until she finds 3, Emma's apartment number. Ruth isn't sure what to do. Press the button, like on the elevator? What if Emma doesn't answer?

Then another sign appears—a man with a musical case on his back pushes through the door on his way out and holds it open for her.

"Thank you," she says. God wants this for her, for Emma too. Ruth is sure of it.

On the first floor, the apartments only go up to number 2. Ruth doesn't see an elevator, but there is a door to the stairway. Musty cement steps like they had in the parking garage. Her shoes echo again. Mrs. Caldwell's sandals. When she's on the next floor, she sees Emma's number—the door to her apartment.

Ruth almost thinks it can't be real, that she is finally here. That she has come this far. She raises her fist, closes her eyes, and knocks. When no one comes after a minute or so, she knocks again, this time more forcefully.

# SARA CALDWELL

## FALL 2019

This morning, two days after Sara dropped Ruth at the train station, Peter finds the rotted cobbler in the trash. "What's this?" he asks.

"Oh," she says. "That." It takes her a second to remember why she didn't dispose of the pie more discreetly by taking it to the can outside. "I got it at the farmer's market," she says. "I meant to freeze it for the holidays, but then I forgot."

Peter nods, though she senses he knows she's lying. How could he trust her now? They've never spoken about it, but she knows he blames her for Emma leaving. Even if it was Emma's decision, ultimately, she had paved the way, hadn't she?

Now Ruth was gone—or at least she had been for the past twenty-four hours. Sara was certain word was spreading by now. Would he blame Sara for this too? And what if he found out about her helping with Emma's medical appointments, filling out paperwork for the Maternity Care Coalition and the low-cost city clinic? She'd set up Emma's transfer of care at twenty weeks without anyone knowing, showing Emma the way, so she'd be safe and cared for when she went into labor. And then, of course, there was the money Sara had given Emma for rent. Far as Sara could tell, Peter had no inkling of this. Why would he?

When Sara had started holding garden shows, they agreed that she should have a separate account for managing these expenses. And Peter had no business asking to see the receipts, because the garden is Sara's domain and always would be. The garden represents her sacrifice—in moving here so Peter could start his clinic. In giving up her career for his.

If it became known Ruth was missing, however, Peter might demand explanations. He might ask about her account, about her involvement, in ways she'd be unable to deny. Could he blame her for wanting to help one woman, when he'd devoted himself so completely to helping the larger community?

And what was a marriage without forgiveness, anyway? Without faith in the unknown?

It's October, the month of the shooting—the anniversary month—when Amish families planted more trees. Every year, they planted another for each of the girls, to fill the old plot with new life. It seems right to go there—spiritually right—to Sara somehow. As if the answer to her marriage lies in the young trees.

On her way, Sara passes the Zucker Farm, where Emma said her father works, where Isaac now makes his living too. As she slows along the dirt road that leads to the driveway, she recognizes the spot in the grass where she and Peter had stopped once, early in their marriage. They wanted to get *the lay of the land*, as Peter had put it—and they had—learning the name for the Zucker farm, famous for its hand-crafted walnut bookcases and kitchen tables and wagons for hauling children around.

That day, just outside of the car after they'd parked, Sara heard the sound of something like wind above them. When she'd looked up, a large brown bird landed on the branch of an elm tree a few feet away.

*A barn owl*, she said, and Peter glanced up and saw it too.

*It's beautiful*, he said, pausing over the bird, which was utterly still, its narrow eyes staring back at them.

*You know they're mates for life*. Peter squeezed her hand.

*I didn't*, she said. *But where's his companion?*

Peter had laughed, as she had, as they watched the single bird, its golden eyes bright in the sun. Everything had seemed possible that first summer after they moved. They'd loved each other. Still loved each other, didn't they?

Before Sara takes 896 to Nickel Mines, she can't help but drive to the site of the home Abraham and Isaac had been building for the young couple to move into in the spring. She doesn't know if they finished it after Emma left—why would they? But when she reaches the small house, it looks completed. The sideboards newly painted white. She's surprised to see Isaac there. Isaac splitting wood like it's just another day providing for his family.

How much older he looks than the boy she first saw with Emma, when she passed them in her car on their courting walk. His beard is long, much longer since the wedding, as he works under the heat of the autumn sun. Sara drives closer, too close, because he looks up and stops, holds the head of his ax and his hand and studies her. Does he know her Volvo? Why is she risking this—even now—being seen?

Her windows are tinted as they've always been, but she feels he sees her behind the glass. She's reversing out onto Snake Hill Road, back in the direction of 896—her original plan—when she sees Isaac turn like he's going to take some action, perhaps tell someone else that he's seen her? Tell Abraham that she has something to do with Ruth going missing? It's what everyone must think. She accelerates quickly, passes the Walsh farm still more quickly. Then, without thinking, she swerves. She turns around too fast, her tires kicking up dust. It's as if she wants to draw notice, but when she circles back around to the farm, slowing intentionally before the driveway, the house is completely silent and still.

She searches for some sign of Abraham rushing around in a panic. Or the silhouette of Eli in his wheelchair by the kitchen window. She sees nothing but the Walshes' empty porch. The same baskets of red geraniums hanging above, the same wicker chairs where she'd watched Ruth and Emma pitting cherries by lantern light last summer. Nothing moves beyond the open windows, not even the curtains.

Sara looks in the other direction, to a field across the way, wondering what might live beyond it, in the woods by the creek. This land continues on like it won't end, but it does. At some point the borders converge. And then she sees a woman walking through the field. She's carrying a basket covered with a cloth. Sara watches as she sets the basket by the front door of the Walsh house. Then, almost without pause, she turns around and makes her way back across the field.

A gift to mark the anniversary; was this what she was doing? Would she head to the schoolhouse next—where they were planting the trees—for the same picnic they had every year? Or is she providing for Eli and Abraham in Ruth's absence? The community certainly looked out for one another.

When the woman disappears into the trees, Sara turns back onto Snake Hill, winding on and on into the distance. She rolls down her window, imagines she can hear Isaac's ax splitting wood. As she passes another farm, young children follow their mother into a barn. Little boys in black suspenders holding tobacco spears, little girls in pale-green dresses carrying sheaves of grain. The mother wears lilac, her bonnet strings long. When everyone is inside the barn, the doors remain open.

Sara has read about this. How during threshing season, the Amish leave their barn doors open so the chaff can blow away once the grain has been separated—dispersing into the wind.

# RUTH WALSH

## FALL 2019

Ruth is still knocking forcefully when the door opens. And there is Emma. Emma . . . but not Emma. Her hair is short, by her chin, her eyes somehow a deeper brown than Ruth remembers. She's wearing a green t-shirt and a pair of denim shorts, cut-off and frayed. Her son is perched on her hip. Ruth's grandson. He's six months old already. She is almost stunned by the sight of him, his flushed cheeks, his eyes bright and happy. Healthy.

Emma draws her hand to her mouth. "Mother," she says.

"Emma." Ruth's eyes turn glassy. There's pain where before there had been only anger. In what Emma had done to her family. To Isaac and his family, too.

"You left us—" is all Ruth can think to say. She is weak, looking for something to grip. She clutches the doorframe to keep her balance.

"Oh—please, Mother." Emma reaches for her. "Will you come inside? Let me get you some water."

In the haze of Emma gripping her arm, in the haze of her thirst, Ruth still can't believe it; her grandson is well.

"Leo," Emma tells Ruth as she guides her to a chair in the small kitchen. "This is Leo." She fills a glass of water and hands it to Ruth.

On the table is a small bowl with loose change and safety pins. Another bowl with apples and bananas.

"Are you hungry?" Emma says. "You must be."

She talks to Ruth like she never left, as if they're just home from services and Ruth needs to rest her legs. But this is Emma's apartment—her kitchen table—her window with a spider plant along the sill, drinking in the sun.

This plant, Ruth thinks, these shelves filled with books—these are all things Emma managed to buy on her own?

Leo's hair is a soft tuft of blond, curling in little waves below his ears, just as Beth's had when she was a baby. His eyes are blue as Abraham's, as Beth's were too. How much he resembles her in his coloring. What of his temperament?

Emma hands him a bright green sippy cup, and he drinks with both hands gripping it.

"He's happy," Ruth hears herself say. *He is here*, she thinks. *He is happy here*.

"He is," Emma says. "He keeps me busy. Don't you?" she says, addressing Leo. Once more, Ruth forgets where they are, almost does, maybe because she wants to? Wants to forget and simply be with her daughter.

"That's your grandmama," Emma says.

Ruth nods, agrees. This is her grandchild.

"Ba ba," Leo babbles. Then he sticks out his tongue, and they both laugh. "Grandma. Not ba ba," Emma says, kissing his head.

"I'm glad he's well," Ruth says. "That you're both well."

"We are," Emma says.

Ruth waits for her to say something else. Something real, about what it means for her mother to come all this way, but she doesn't. So Ruth does. She says, "I almost thought I'd never find you."

"How did you?" Emma says, not looking at her straight on.

"Mrs. Caldwell," she says. "Who else?"

Emma nods.

"She was kind to give me the name of your realtor."

"Does Father know? Or Isaac?"

Ruth shakes her head. "No. I couldn't tell them. But I had to see you. I had to meet Leo." She smiles then, and Emma does too.

"I'm glad you came," she says.

"Can I hold him?" Ruth asks.

"Yes, of course. Well, you can try. He can be clingy."

When Ruth reaches to take Leo, he's calm.

"I think he knows you," Emma says.

It feels so good to hold him. It feels like he does, in fact, know her. Knows that she raised his mother, and two other children. She gazes into Leo's eyes for a long while, holding still, putting him at ease. When she finally looks up, Emma is crying.

"It's all right," Ruth says. "I'm here." She wants to comfort Emma, too, but she must wait. Listen.

"I thought I'd never see you again."

"I know," Ruth says, "but I needed to find you. I needed to know you were okay." She is the one crying now, even as she tries not to. She wipes away a tear, warm along her cheek.

"I'm sorry," Emma says, reaching over to grip Ruth's hand. And then she gets up. She hugs Ruth's shoulders, kisses Leo's head again. "I miss you," she says, "and Eli and Father."

"I saved your writing." Ruth didn't intend to say this, yet she is glad she has. "I found it in the jam cellar. I keep it in the kitchen, in an old butter dish, folded up."

Emma looks stunned. "You did?"

Ruth nods. "I'm the one who is sorry. I never listened to you."

Emma looks at her, but says nothing.

"I can't forgive myself." She stops to gather herself before continuing. "You were alone in this. I should have come sooner." She can't finish because she is weeping now.

Emma takes Leo from her lap, hugs him to her as she sits beside Ruth.

"It isn't your fault, Mother," Emma says. "Of course it isn't."

"The truth is," Ruth says, "I could never be as brave as you are. In building all this. Your own house, here, in this city?"

"It's hardly a house," Emma says, laughing even as she is still crying. "Look at the size."

"But it is something," Ruth says. "And I know it's what you want."

When she covers her face with her hands, Emma reaches for her again, embraces her, like she is the child now, and Emma the mother.

Leo starts to fuss.

"It's okay, Leo," Emma says. "I'm right here." When he won't stop, she says, "It's just your grandmama. See?"

Ruth wipes her face. She smiles, then reaches for Leo's foot and tugs it. He smiles back, and she is so glad for this moment. This is still her family, no matter the distance, the hurt, or the passage of time.

Only the present matters, and in the present Emma is navigating the English world on her own. She tells Ruth that she's found work, and while she's there, Leo is in a place, a daycare, that charges on a *sliding scale*. Emma explains, "It's where they let me pay as much as I can." She says she qualifies for state services, too, to help with grocery and doctor bills for Leo. When Ruth asks if there is still testing to be done, Emma says yes. That they ruled out genetic disease, but she continues to take him to a clinic on a *no-cost basis*. This other term Ruth has never heard before, but she understands. Just as she understands the term Emma uses for her city garden, the *community plot*, without Emma needing to explain.

Emma tells her about the walks she and Leo take to the park and playground. To museums to learn about art and science. To the library to read books together about animals, with shapes and colors Leo likes to touch. Ruth imagines reading to her grandson, too, the joy it would bring.

It feels impulsive, but Ruth says it anyway: that if Emma wishes it, she'll find a way for Isaac to come, without anyone knowing. As she says it, she knows she means it, and that it's right to help Isaac meet his son.

"It's too dangerous, isn't it?" Emma says.

"It's a risk," Ruth says. "But worth it to try, don't you think?"

Emma looks worried for a moment, but agrees she wants to try—if Isaac is willing—and Ruth finds herself relaxing. Emma will never know what it has taken her to come this far, but the unspoken things between them give Ruth hope, where before they brought only pain.

They leave it like this: Emma promising to send word through Mrs. Caldwell if she moves or is struggling. Ruth says she will do the same—have Mrs. Caldwell write with news about Isaac, if he is coming with her next time. Through the window the sky has deepened to dusk. Ruth knows she must catch the train. She tells Emma about the missing money, what must have happened at the train station. Their roles are reversed again when Emma goes to her bedroom for the amount Ruth needs to get home.

"It's for emergencies," Emma says. "I keep for days just like this. Please take it."

Ruth doesn't want to, but she has no other choice. "I'll pay you back," she says quickly.

"You don't have to," Emma says, but they both know it doesn't matter whether Ruth does or doesn't. What matters is they will see each other again

Without another word, Emma calls her a cab. Time collapses again, quickens. Some minutes, like these, would always pass faster than others.

When Ruth is on the train again, staring through the window, everything is different. Not just that it is dark by now, but the world is less unfamiliar, less strange. The smell of the leather seats, the tray she can unclip for resting her hands. The oval window she looks out while the landscape turns a darker blue. Leo's eyes are in this blue, and in the wallpaper before she peeled it away, but it's not too late to repaper again.

"I forgive," Ruth whispers, just loud enough for herself to hear.

# EMMA WALSH

## FALL 2019

By now, I've written it again, and again. The sound of the bell, clanging heavily under Teacher Martha's grip. The words she'd written on the chalkboard for us. *All visitors welcome*. We had visitors before the man that morning. Visitors of our own. The teacher's sister-in-law, Jenny. Her niece, Lilian. The ones who escaped through the back door after he came for us. The ones who survived, like me.

I still wake from the nightmare; I wake fearful I'm still in the schoolhouse. But then I rise, and I find you in your crib, sleeping soundly. *There*, I say. *Here. We're safe now.*

I write the story again, and again, until the words start to mean different things. Such as how *clevis pin* is another name for fastener, how words themselves are fasteners, holding the pieces of my story together, straddling the betweenness of what was then and what is now.

When Mother came to visit us the other day, I almost didn't recognize her without her bonnet and cape. Her hair in the open, glinting silver. As she held you, I thought, *You are beautiful. Both of you*. For a few moments it felt like I had never left. But I have. Time spins forward, passes on. The way you can never swim in the same river water twice: The current is always moving.

It's similar to leaving a place on a train. As you watch through the window, you can see the land you left, where you were standing before, but as the train speeds away, it turns blurry. Almost like it isn't real. Like a dream, or the memory of a dream.

The more I write, the more time feels like this. The more time ripples and recedes. I watch each memory pass—think of what could have been, how it might have changed what is now—but then I stop. What's now is the only thing, *me* here with *you*. How I used to feel with Eli, reading to him by the fire. That it was enough simply to be. The flames crackling, the whisper of words, the Scripture while he dozed.

When Mother came, I felt this between us. The gift of being alive, of surviving, despite everything.

Remembering Eli reminds me of the fields. Of the crops growing again, despite many harvests, many seasons—some good, some poor.

The seasons are our clocks. This is clearest in the corn—in the stalks that rise tall and ripen in July, when the ears are ready to be picked and cleaned. One day, I'll show this to you: how to pull back each sheaf of corn until the silken hair scatters. I'll let you feel the pearls inside, sweetened by the heat of the sun.

Our people plow the fields through September. They collect what's left of the harvest to live on. Perhaps someday we'll watch the fields burn copper-gold in the early autumn light. Perhaps one day, I'll show you this version of time, which can only be witnessed. No words can signify its passage. Only what *is*.

*It is. It is. It is.*

# ACKNOWLEDGMENTS

My deepest thanks to all those who made this work possible over the years. First, to my editor at Acre Books, Nicola Mason, a fearless visionary and incredible editor, line by line. Thank you to the whole team at Acre: Sarah Haak, Lisa Ampleman, Barbara Neely, Hussain Ahmed, and Sam Simas. To my brilliant publicist, Terena Bell. To Adrian Shirk, for your faith in this project since the beginning. The community we have found and built in Driftless has changed my life.

To all those who have read drafts and offered feedback over the years: Marya Spence, Hafizah Geter, Alexandra Levenberg, Adam Golub, David Ryan, Jessica Denzer, Arturo Vidich, Lidia Yuknavitch, Richard Cohen, Melissa Febos, Lily Meyer, Cara Blue Adams, Cam Terwilliger, Sanjay Agnihotri, Yaron Kaver, Carolyn Silveira, Amanda Parrish Morgan, Hailey Parry, Harris Lahti, Ashley Mayne, Rachel Aydt, and Sean Williamson. Thank you, Sarah Crofts, for your collaboration on the cover art, *Cornfield #4*, conceived during our magical residency at Woodstock the summer before everything changed.

I am indebted to so many other readers and friends over the years, between drafts, between having a child and leaving the city. Stephanie Koven, you have held me accountable in more ways than one around the very challenging balance of writing, mothering, agenting, and—most importantly—living. Thank you to Jim Hanas, Kristina Andersson Bicher, Matthew Lansberg, Kris Wilcox, Caitlin Winner, Tina Kapousis, Judy Davidson, Tavi Meraud, Amy Kvilhaug, Andrea Burdett, Johanna Van Straaten, and Max Schreck for your faith and friendship, your conversation and community. Thank you to Amy Thomas, Christine Kalafus, Amy Eareckson, Benjamin Ding, Tess Bird, Jen Stock, Joanna Radin, and Caitlin Cossman, for helping me build a writing community in coastal Connecticut. Thank you to my college-running teammates who helped me convert miles into pages: Katie McKinstry, Katie Dewitt, Ashley Campbell, Claire Hamilton, Cara Kiernan-Fallon, Karen Porter, and Julia Emanuel.

Thank you to Hanna Sosin for helping me reimagine this novel into a fresh context. Hanna, your faith in the unknown allows me to find my way to my desk, in search of more light, each morning. Thank you to Francoise McAree for offering constant inspiration beyond the limits of language. Thank you to AD Lauren-Abunassar for seeing *Butter Road* through to the end, supporting every aspect of my publishing process these past months. Thank you to everyone in my writing group—*LINTS!*, started at the Vermont Studio Center in February of 2025—for showing up each week to fit some fragments of ourselves into a larger whole.

Thank you to my parents: to my mother, Carolyn, for supplying me with books before I could walk, believing in me always. To my stepfather, Dave, no longer with us, but who speaks to me in wind chimes and the shape of low-flying hawks, reminding me to keep going no matter what. Thank you to my sister, Sam, for being my first reader and champion since grade school. To my aunt Marci and uncle Tom for providing a writing haven in Ohio at the peak of the pandemic. To my uncle Steve for being the first writer in the family to inspire me, and to my aunt Andrea for reading my work and sharing it with others. Thank you to my godmother, Reggie Knoll, in Cincinnati, for supporting me in every way. Thank you to my grandparents, Dave and Mary Pine. We lost grandpa this past year, but he is with me as *Butter Road* enters the world in stages. Grandma, I am grateful for the many walks we took through the covered bridges when I was a child, which shaped my observations of nature and affinity for language.

Thank you to Kim and Brian Gilbert, my parents away from home, and to Cay and Derek Gilbert, for their love, support, and care.

Thank you to my good friends in Madison, Connecticut, where I continue to make a home and expand my understanding of family in the present tense. Thank you to Carolyn Fredericks for your shared love of books, coffee, and writing. Every writing session with you spiritually willed this work to completion.

Last, there aren't words for my husband—Jared—my partner-in-crime, my cheerleader and supporter in everything I do. Every page is made possible by your love: the pulse that gets me up to tie my shoes and sharpen my tools. Thank you to Leland, our son, for filling our house with joy, passion, and curiosity in all things. This book is for you.